THE SEA IS SILENT

Also by Cameron Kent

*When the Ravens Die*
*The Road to Devotion*

# The
# Sea
## Is Silent

## CAMERON KENT

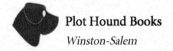

Plot Hound Books
*Winston-Salem*

Plot Hound Books
c/o Press 53, LLC
PO Box 30314
Winston-Salem, NC 27130


First Edition

Cover design by Kevin Morgan Watson

Cover art, "Man Walking Toward Sea," Copyright © 2012
by Sergei Gontsarenko, licensed through iStockPhoto

Plot Hound Books is an imprint of
Press 53, Winston-Salem, North Carolina


Library of Congress Control Number 2017954776

Printed on acid-free paper
ISBN 978-1-941209-61-5 (paperback)
ISBN 978-1-941209-67-7 (hardcover)

The Sea is Silent, the sea is discreet,
Deep it lies at thy very feet.
The sea is still and deep,
A single step, and all is o'er,
A plunge, a bubble, and no more.

—Henry Wadsworth Longfellow
*Christus, The Golden Legend, Pt. V*

# Part One

# Chapter One

The story that Harold Motsinger dropped in my lap is the kind of tale every journalist dreams of writing, especially one desperately trying to rediscover his passion. The pitch: "Downtrodden residents of a trailer park sickened by tainted groundwater because uncaring Big Oil had refused to clean up its mess." It had all the elements. A victim, a villain, and a tangled web of manipulation and deceit that I was about to unsnarl. Because of the mighty pen of Seth MacClellan, the little guy would triumph over the giant petroleum monolith. It was the kind of headline that sells papers. It's the story that makes everyone else shake your hand and slap your back as you walk through the office on the morning it hits the newsstands. The kind of journalism that elevates you from reporter to columnist and eventually novelist. They make movies out of stories like this. More than anything, my diligent reporting would unleash earthshaking words that would capture a Pulitzer.

I first dipped my toe into the investigation when Harold showed up in the lobby of the *The Atlanta Herald*, unannounced, yet persistent that he meet with me. In ten years of working at newspapers, I'd come to realize that some of your best stories are born from ordinary people simply calling or writing you with a problem they can't solve, so I was eager to trot down to the lobby and hear him out. Listening was what I did best. It was my greatest strength as a reporter. I could always get people to talk to me, to reveal information and share their secrets, mostly because I simply *listened*. I tried to find common ground with my interview subjects, and make some sort of personal connection that would ease their fears about talking to a reporter and get them to open up. Most of the people who sat in front of me as I took careful notes had been victimized in some way, usually by a huge and powerful corporate entity. They needed to get the sense that I cared about them, that I was making *their* problem *my* problem. That's because I *did* care. It's why I became a journalist. I wanted to give those powerless people a voice, and let the world know about injustice in its many forms. And right now I cared deeply about what Harold Motsinger was telling me.

Harold was in his early forties, but still sporting the same mullet haircut from his teens. He had a long scar across the side of his temple, which I would come to learn was from a metal plate that was inserted after a motorcycle accident. He was uneducated, unemployed, and now unrelenting in his pursuit of the matter at hand.

As we sat down in a small conference room to hear his story, Harold pulled out a stack of Xeroxed documents from a manila envelope and spread them on the table in front of me. To an investigative reporter, official documents are the equivalent of fresh fingerprints to a homicide detective. They provide irrefutable proof of a crime. I mentally salivated at the treasure trove of notarized paperwork that lay before me. As I perused the documents and listened to Harold's rambling discourse about the poisoned drinking water at his trailer park, his story began to take shape. I could already envision the headline in one-inch type: *Poor People Dying of Cancer— Big Oil to Blame.* My byline would go directly underneath.

"Have you told any other reporters about this?" I asked Harold.

"Well, I did send a letter to a guy named Kell-something at the *Journal-Constitution.*"

"Gordon Kelleher?"

"Yeah! That's the guy. But I never heard back."

Gordon Kelleher was my counterpart at *The Atlanta Journal-Constitution.* More like my nemesis. He was an intrepid investigative journalist who already had the wall space for his Pulitzer filled. I wasn't about to let him get wind of another prizewinner.

"If he calls you back, don't answer. This is you and me on this one, okay?"

"Okay," nodded Harold, having no idea of the undercurrent of the fierce competition among reporters at competing papers, all vying for reader attention. And awards. Major awards. Pulitzer Prizes.

My phone booth of an office at *The Atlanta Herald* was covered wall to ceiling with plaques, certificates, and golden statuettes. Atlanta Press Club, Associated Press, Scripps Howard, and virtually every other news organization that wanted to host a black-tie dinner and hand out trophies. All testaments to journalistic excellence, and I'd won almost every one they offered. Almost. In the middle of all those awards and commendations hanging on the walls was an empty space the size of a college diploma. It was reserved for the Pulitzer Prize, the Holy Grail of investigative journalism. It was like a Super Bowl ring. All the great ones had at least one, and whenever you were in their presence, they made it abundantly clear that you were not yet in their sacred fraternity. I craved that award. The conspicuous gap on the office wall that I'd intentionally left blank had always been my driving force. It provided the constant and haunting reminder to make me work harder and dig deeper. To devote myself fully to my mission of unearthing the truth, especially when so many others were trying to cover it up. That elusive award was my inspiration and my muse. And now, more than anything, I wanted to make Grace proud of me. Harold Motsinger's tainted tap water was going to take me there.

Like a hunter who'd just gotten word that a trophy buck had been spotted deep in the forest, I sprang into action. With a pen for my weapon, I jumped in my car and followed my new guide to the hunting grounds.

Harold Motsinger lived in a mobile home park in Molena, Georgia, about fifty miles southwest of Metro Atlanta. The park had clearly seen better days, and was now devoid of activity. The only other vehicle on the premises was a shiny new silver pickup truck in front of a rundown trailer at the end of the driveway. The lone visible trace of upkeep was what appeared to be a new sign hanging over the rutted entryway: *Welcome to Sunny Acres*. There has never been a more inappropriate name.

The eight single-wide trailers were lined up next to an abandoned gas station, formerly owned by Ludwig Oil. What had once been the thriving hub of commerce in Molena providing gasoline, sundries, and a gathering place for yarns and lies, was long since gone. The cinderblock walls were strangled by kudzu vines. The once translucent glass panels on the garage bay doors were now opaque, darkened by oily vapors, exhaust, and time. Besides a few wistful memories among the old-timers, the abandoned service station had left only one thing behind. . . two underground gasoline storage tanks, that nobody realized had been leaking petroleum into the local groundwater for years.

Here was Harold's concern; the residents of the trailer park, all living on well water for decades, were now suffering from a range of illnesses, including cancer. Harold's stack of documents included their medical histories, each one a lawsuit in the making. Kidney damage, anemia, bone and joint pain; all hallmarks of lead poisoning. The kind of lead that comes from gasoline. Most incriminating, though, were the samples from an independent lab of their tap water, revealing dangerously high levels of benzene in the plumes of groundwater that feed into their wells. Benzene, a known carcinogen, was further evidenced in the residents' medical histories, pocked with cases of various cancers. As visual proof, Harold showed me the rainbow of colors in the streams around the trailer park caused by petroleum products seeping up from the ground.

"Can I talk to some of the people who live here?" I asked Harold.

"Sure can," he replied, already walking.

We knocked on the door of a rundown trailer at the rear of the park. The old man who immediately appeared at the door wouldn't let us come inside. He quickly shut the door behind him and instead held court in the rooted dirt outside the trailer. The elderly man identified himself as Johnny Spainhour. With a voice that sounded as though he were trying to cough up wet gravel, Spainhour told me he'd run the service station for the last twenty years it was in business. Looking cautiously around him, as if there were prying ears hidden among the surrounding oak trees, he whispered his allegations.

"Ludwig Oil knew full well them tanks was leakin', but they didn't do nothin' about it. Every time I mentioned it to 'em, they told me to hush up, or they'd find another person to run the station. It was a big cover-up, pure and simple, and now we're all sufferin' on account of them bein' so greedy. Don't nobody care about no trailer trash, even when their drinkin' water can catch on fire if you put a match to it."

I nodded my head. He was right. Poor people have absolutely no recourse. They can't hire lawyers, they can't call in favors from elected officials. They have no voice. Except mine. If I could shed light on this travesty, they could get restitution. Medical care. Perhaps even move away from the dismal confines of Sunny Acres to a decent home. I wielded the power of the pen, and I was about to unleash it on Ludwig Oil.

"I can promise you, Mr. Spainhour. . . I care."

As the two men walked me back to my car, I reached in the back seat and pulled out my old Nikon. I preferred taking my own shots rather than depending on a staff photographer, something I'd done since my days on my high school paper. "I just need a few pictures." I snapped various photos of the trailer park, the old service station, and the Sunny Acres sign that seemed to mock the entire toxic environment. I attempted to capture the rainbow of colors on the oily waters of the stream Harold had showed me a short time ago, but the tint wasn't quite as strong as it had been earlier, and the image didn't translate to the camera very well. Not to worry. I had enough photos to complement my words.

Almost as an afterthought, I snapped a quick candid shot of Harold and Johnny leaning against my car. It seemed to unnerve them that I'd done it without asking permission first, but I didn't want the picture to look staged or posed. They exchanged a momentary look of concern, but then let it pass. I immediately regretted not having been more polite. I put the camera away, shook their hands, and assured them that their lives were about to change. As was mine.

# Chapter Two

**M**acClellan! In my office! *Now!*"

Those were words nobody wanted to hear. It meant I was in trouble. What's worse, I had no idea what it was for this time. I leaned back in my desk chair and took a deep breath, steeling myself for the unpleasantness to come.

Every head in the office swiveled as their eyes followed me on my way across the newsroom into Bynum Sherry's office. Dead man walking.

"You wanted to see me?" I asked casually, as if I imagined he were going to ask me if I wanted to squeeze in a quick nine holes after work.

"Good guess," Sherry barked as he sat down and rummaged through the raft of papers on his desk that was in dire need of an in/out box. As City Editors go in the newspaper business, you couldn't ask for a better one than Bynum Sherry. Or a tougher one. He chain-smoked, ate most of his meals from vending machines, and never backed down when he knew he was right. And he was *always* right. Even the owner of *The Atlanta Herald* feared him, so imagine what I was feeling when he finally peered at me over the glasses on the tip of his nose.

"Where are you on the trailer park piece you've been promising?"

"Well, sir. . . about that—"

"Oh, for cripes sake, Mac, what now? You've been on this story for two weeks now. Does the word 'deadline' mean nothing to you?"

"I think if we hold this piece for one more week, and let me get just a little bit more, it'll have a much bigger impact."

"Another week?"

"Why not? Nobody else knows about it."

Sherry shook his head in exhausted frustration. "You people are *killin'* me." He sighed heavily and plopped down in his well-worn leather office chair. He pushed his glasses on top of his forehead and stared at the ceiling. "Whatcha got so far?"

I told him about my trip to Sunny Acres, and the tales of illness I'd collected from Harold Motsinger and Johnny Spainhour. I was still looking for more victims who would go on the record.

"When do we get to the part that might sell some papers?" asked Sherry.

I shifted forward to the edge of my seat, hoping to instill a sense of urgency. Sherry didn't budge, but I continued with enthusiasm. "I'm getting more testing done on the water, and then I'm confronting Ludwig with the results. And then I finish the piece. I'm almost there."

Sherry leaned back and stared as the ceiling, exhaling slowly and loudly through bulging cheeks as he mulled it over for a solid minute. "Okay. You got your week. But not an hour longer."

I jumped up from my chair. "Thank you! Thank you, thank you, thank you!" I blurted out like a kid who'd just been given permission from his dad to borrow the family car.

For the next few days, I worked feverishly on the Sunny Acres project. Partly because I was relishing the thrill of the hunt, and partly because the deadline for the Pulitzer was looming.

Back in work mode, I called every name and number contained in the documents Harold Motsinger had provided me to verify their veracity. It all checked out. Just to bolster my case, I had him bring me additional water samples from the trailer park and had them tested. Again, the levels of lead and benzene were off the charts. In fact, worse than before.

I had intentionally avoided pushing too hard through all my phone calls out of fear that Ludwig Oil would get wind of my investigation and shut it down. Over my many years of turning over corporate rocks, trying to separate truth from lies, I'd learned that big money has a way of shutting down the information pipeline with swiftness and finality. Their reach was far and wide, and I was determined to foil any roadblocks they put in my way. Finally, when I had the piece nearly finished, I called the legal department at Ludwig Oil to get their comment. After all, it was only fair to hear the other side of the story, even when you were trying to take them down. I expected a stone wall, and I got it. I was put on hold for an interminable length of time while I waited for a reaction to the benzene bomb I'd just dropped on them. I could only imagine the frantic legal scramble now taking place on the other end of the line. Finally, a response.

"We have no idea what you're talking about," crackled the voice of an abrasive corporate attorney. "Our records show we've never had any holdings in Molena, Georgia." I knew this wasn't true because I was holding a copy of Ludwig's deed for the land in my hand. It wasn't the first time I'd been lied to by someone trying to cast shadows over the truth, and it wouldn't be the last.

"So you unequivocally deny any involvement with leaking gasoline storage tanks in Molena and the resultant medical problems that ensued?"

"That's correct. We have nothing more to say. And if you run this story, you'll be talking to more lawyers than just me. Is that clear?" The next sound I heard was a phone being slammed back into place.

"Thanks for your time," I said out loud, long after the line had gone dead. Anytime a corporate lawyer makes a sweeping threat like that, you know you're onto something. I smiled, leaned back in my chair, and stared longingly at the blank space on my wall of fame. Grace would have been so proud of me.

I could tell that Bynum Sherry didn't love the story nearly as much as I did. He had a way of drumming his fingers on his desk when editing your copy that made you feel like your words weren't worthy of receiving printers' ink.

"I don't know, Mac. You got a lot here, but it seems like we could go a little deeper. Did you talk to anybody else who lives at the trailer park?"

"Harold found me two more people, both with the same basic story. Bad water, worse cancer. The rest have either moved away and didn't leave a forwarding address, or they're dead from various illnesses. But my guess is once we break this, more folks will come out of the woodwork and make for some great follow stories."

"Hummm," was all Sherry could muster. I could sense his hesitation. I'd seen it before. It was his job to hold the horses, but it was mine to whip them into a lather. So I pushed. I fought for my story, but for all the wrong reasons. For one, I was getting increasingly worried that Gordon Kelleher was finally sorting through his voluminous mail over at the *Journal-Constitution* and then there'd be two dogs in the hunt. Of greater concern, truthfully, was that the deadline for submission for the Pulitzer was in two days and this would just slip in under the deadline if I could get it in print. I knew that Harold Motsinger was my golden ticket to the winner's circle and I wasn't going to let another year slip by without joining in the chase. Bynum Sherry also knew I was the best investigative reporter he'd ever had. I'd never let him down. "You're sure?" he asked, reading over my copy one more time. "Every word?"

"Absolutely. Airtight."

"Okay. Start the presses."

The story ran in the morning edition. Front page. A banner headline, 72-point type, above the fold. Twelve inches on the front page with a photo, then continuing with a hundred and twenty more inches on the jump page with two more pictures. It sold papers and wagged tongues. It was immediately picked up by the Associated Press and Reuters and disseminated to newsrooms across the world. It went viral on the internet. The local TV news stations picked up on it and sped their live vans out to Sunny Acres to recap what they'd read in the morning paper, trying to make it their own. As I'd hoped, I received the handshakes and backslaps and all the other praises and plaudits that come with breaking a major story. And above all, I'd made the deadline for the Pulitzer. That blank space on the wall was about to be filled. There was only one problem with Harold Motsinger's tale of poisoned water; none of it was true.

# Chapter Three

The entire legal team of Ludwig Oil was seated in front of me in the *Herald's* conference room. I'd only ever been in this room for going away parties. Somebody was going away this time as well, but there was no cake. The power that seethed out of their suits was nuclear. I sat sullenly next to Bynum Sherry and Lloyd Wilson, the Managing Editor. Seated next to him was an unnamed young woman, apparently our corporate attorney, who was clearly overmatched. If we were Atlanta, they were Sherman. I could only stare into the faux woodgrain of the conference table, my mind completely numb, as the Ludwig legal army pilloried my work on the Sunny Acres piece. If I heard the phrase "forged document" once, I heard it three dozen times. All I could do was shake my head as it sank closer to the table. Their carefully organized litany of my journalistic transgressions and shortcomings was sickening. I couldn't believe this was happening. My stellar ten year career of raking through the muck of corporate corruption, political greed, and government waste was all crashing down as the suits on the other side of the table continued their caustic recitation. I wanted to die. Just keel over and die from a massive aortic event and it would all be over.

When the smoke of the Ludwig cannonade finally cleared, it would mean retractions, lawsuits, and immediate firings. Understandably, me. Regrettably and tragically, Bynum Sherry as well. Two months shy of retirement from his legendary career of pecking at a typewriter and I'd sent him out under a fog of shame.

As we walked out of the conference room, Sherry shook my hand and gave me a silent nod. I could barely look him in the eye.

To his unending credit, he publicly shouldered half the blame for the disaster that had befallen us. We both knew better. The byline to this tragedy belonged exclusively to me.

With two security guards lording over me, apparently worried I might snap under the intense stress of spectacular personal failure, I cleaned out my office. Tattered accordion files from hundreds of stories, two bulging Rolodexes, and my dozens of awards from all the pieces I'd managed to get right, all hauled away. The next occupant of my office would have plenty of blank wall space to hang their Pulitzer. Ten years of meritorious labor, all for the greater good, now unceremoniously stuffed into two cardboard boxes and a shopping bag in less than an hour. The last thing I put in the box was a framed photo of Grace and me, taken at sunset after a Bordeaux-filled cruise down the Seine. My favorite picture that brought me both pleasure and pain.

As I trudged through the workspaces, box and bag in hand, it was pitifully quiet. All activity had been suspended as I made my ignominious exit. I was well-liked and respected by all my co-workers, but nobody knew quite what to do or say. I kept my gaze downward, the shame burning off of me. On the few occasions I dared to look up, I could see tears glistening in a few of their eyes. They knew I'd breached the sacred rules of journalism, but they also realized it had been unintentional. I think they were all more stunned than angry. I sensed pity. I sensed sorrow. I sensed forgiveness. I also knew there was only one person in that room who could never forgive me for my mistake. Me.

I collapsed on the couch in my apartment, reeling from the swift and terrible events of the last few hours. I felt a massive dead weight pressing against my chest, threatening to crush me under the unrelenting laws of gravity. It wasn't sadness or worry, not even anger. It was shame. More than embarrassment, more than humiliation. Pure, undiluted shame. The kind of old world shame that brands you with a scarlet letter and banishes you from the village. I'd seen that shame before, on the faces of the men and women I'd exposed in my reporting. Usually sitting in a courtroom, flanked by lawyers, looking down at the table where defendants sit as the judge reads the charges against them. They wondered how their lives had gone so wrong, and how they could ever face the people who'd mistakenly placed their trust in them. I now knew exactly how they felt.

That burden of shame meant I had to leave Atlanta. I couldn't find work here, and even if I could, there was no way I could withstand the whispers that would surely follow me around. And though I couldn't stand to see my own reflection right now, the damage I'd inflicted on my reputation wasn't even the worst of it. Eating at my soul was how I'd pulled Bynum Sherry into my own ship's collision with an invisible iceberg. On top of that, I'd tarnished the newspaper's reputation, and that of journalists everywhere. The credibility of modern print was already reeling from reporters who'd deliberately divorced themselves from ethics and refashioned facts to sell papers and win awards. Although unintentionally and without malice, I'd taken yet another chunk out of the wall that protects the Fourth Estate.

The only thing I could think to do next was go for a run. A long run, giving me time to ponder where it had all gone wrong. My mind wandered back to a beach in South Carolina, where my Grace had first entered my life.

# Chapter Four

## Two Years Earlier

It was close to ninety degrees on Folly Beach, due east of Charleston, South Carolina. My calves were burning from running along the hardened sand just at the edge of the surf, putting in my miles for an upcoming marathon. The sun was just bowing out in the western sky, but the moon hadn't fully awakened in the east. A small flock of willets lighted along the water line, searching for a few mollusks to end their day. The only other people I saw were a handful of locals flying kites in the steady evening breeze, looking skyward at the dancing tails of ribbon, and oblivious to anything or anyone around them. And then I saw her. She was standing in the white sand in front of an easel, studying the blending light of dusk as it warmed the waving sea oats in the foreground and a pale yellow beach house tucked behind the dunes. I veered behind her and stopped to take a long look at the genesis of her seascape on the fresh linen canvas. Even in infancy, it was already a work of art. I was heaving for breath when she finally turned around. Her floppy straw hat covered most of her blonde hair. The first notion that struck me when I saw her is that she lived in an approachable light.

Fittingly, my first words to Grace were an apology. "Sorry! Couldn't help but notice. It's. . . well, it's beautiful. Simply beautiful." I pointed to the fresh oil paint on the canvas to clarify my point.

Grace smiled and turned back to her work. "Isn't it an *amazing* time to be out here?" she responded in a voice that sounded to me like the smell of honeysuckle. Whatever she said next, I don't remember. The moment I saw that full-faced smile, showcasing those aquamarine eyes, I didn't hear another word. We all have our preconceived ideal as to what perfect beauty is, and here was my ideal, standing in front of me, wearing a cornflower blue sundress, holding a palette in one hand and a paintbrush in the other. Visual perfection. I also noticed the absence of a ring on either hand.

"It *is* amazing," I managed to choke out, thinking that it had just gotten much more so.

She didn't seem to mind that I watched as she mixed colors and gently guided them into place on the canvas. I had always been fluent in the language of small talk, so I eased into a respectful dialogue as she continued to create. Alone on the sand, we shared the basic conversation of strangers; *where are you from? what are you doing here? how long are you staying?* Nothing of import. It's usually the kind of facile conversation that ends after a few minutes and several awkward pauses when the noninvasive questions run out. However, sometimes those chance meetings provide the launching point of what may turn into a lasting friendship. Perhaps more.

She offered that she was living and working in Charleston, but that painting was her passion and sunsets on the beach were her chapel. I revealed much less, saying only that I was from Atlanta, and in the area for a few days on business. Finally I quit talking and simply watched. I don't know how long I stood there, but by now the sun was dropping below the horizon and the moon had amplified its presence. Satisfied with her progress, Grace nodded in approval and began to pack up her paints.

"That's all for today."

"Do you have plans for dinner?" I suddenly blurted out, emboldened by the fear that I might not have another chance to cross her path if I didn't act quickly.

"I always have plans to eat dinner," she responded coyly, as that smile rippled across her delicate cheekbones. "Why do you want to know?"

She knew exactly why I wanted to know, but was going to make me say it anyway. I told the truth. "I just want to continue the conversation."

She paused, thought for a moment with narrowed eyes, then cocked her head and looked at me with circumspection. "I don't know anything about you."

"Nor I you. Which is why further discussion is warranted."

She almost laughed. Not quite, but almost. "I suppose that would be okay. You look harmless enough."

"You're an excellent judge of character."

"Or maybe I just want a free meal. You know, starving artist."

"I'm fine with that."

"What's your name?" she asked.

"Seth MacClellan. My friends call me Mac."

"Then I suppose I'll call you Seth. Tell me, Seth, you like shrimp and grits?" she asked as she folded her easel.

"Probably."

"There's a little cantina called the Acme, on the Isle of Palms. They have the best. I'll see you there at nine o'clock."

"I'll be there!"

"I would hope so. It was your idea."

Grace picked up her paints and easel and started to trek across the warm sand.

"Wait!" I called after her. "I don't know *your* name!"

"Which is why further discussion is warranted," she chirped, her words floating to me on the breeze. Even with her back to me, I could sense she was smiling, enjoying my boyish nervousness.

For reasons still unclear to me, I suddenly looked down and noticed a seashell where Grace had been standing just moments before. I picked it up and blew off the grains of sand clinging to its bleached white casing. It was no bigger than my thumbnail, and vaguely heart-shaped. The two halves of the shell were joined at the bottom by a tenuous thread of tissue, barely clinging together. I tucked it into the pocket of my running shorts, a souvenir of a special few minutes in my life. I stood in place as I watched Grace move easily through the heavy sand of the barrier dunes and back into reality.

I turned and sprinted back to my car, worried for the first time in years about what I might wear to dinner.

Just over an hour later, I was sitting across from Grace at the Acme Lowcountry Cantina, trying to talk, trying to eat, but mostly just staring.

"So what is it that you do, Mr. Seth MacClellan?"

"I'm a reporter for *The Atlanta Herald*. Investigative journalism.

White collar crime, mostly. Your basic high dollar swindlers and Wall Street con artists."

"Oh," she said plainly, paying more attention to her food than to me. I could tell she was not overly impressed with my chosen profession. "So what brings you to Charleston?"

"I'm working on a story about a Ponzi scheme. I had to track down a hedge fund manager who handled the bulk of the transactions, trying to find out what he knew and when he knew it. Nothing too exciting."

"No, doesn't sound like it." She took a bite of grits without looking up. "Are you good at it?"

"Some people think so. I'm not so sure."

"So what do you *really* want to do when you grow up?"

"You're assuming that I don't love my job, and that I want to grow up."

"Tell me I'm wrong."

I laughed. It was the first indication that Grace would come to know me better than anyone else. Better than I knew myself at times. "The job pays the bills and finances my hobbies. It's okay for now."

"What about the future? What's life look like to you in ten years?"

"Wow. I thought it was *my* job to ask the tough questions."

"Right now it's your job to answer them. What gets your blood flowing?"

"I don't know. I guess I should have a better response." I picked up a shrimp by the tail and bit into its spicy, orange flesh. It was my way of changing the subject. "So what do *you* do?"

"I'm an architect. Some new design, but mostly historic preservation."

"Charleston's a great city for that."

"The best. It's like a giant canvas surrounded by a beautiful frame of water."

"Well put. And is your job also your passion? Or is it painting?"

"My passion is life. Those are just facets."

"Life?"

"Yes. Living life. Creating, exploring, expanding. Making every day count. I love life. It's pretty simple."

"Wow. Again, wow. I don't think I know anyone quite like you."

"That's where you're wrong."

"I'm not kidding. I honestly don't know anyone like you."

"I'm not saying that. I'm saying, you don't *know* me."

"True. I don't. Not yet. Maybe that's going to be *my* passion."

Those aquamarine eyes twinkled as she dipped her spoon and gathered in another bite of warm grits.

I dug into my front pocket and retrieved the tiny clamshell I'd found on the beach a few hours before. I separated the two halves and placed one in her hand.

"What's this?" she asked.

"A souvenir."

"Of what?"

"Our first meeting. Hopefully not our last."

Grace smiled and pushed the tiny shell around in the palm of her hand. "Thank you."

"May the two halves meet again," I said.

"One never knows," nodded Grace.

Within hours of first saying "hello" to Grace, I would abruptly have to say "goodbye". It was at the airport, the morning after our dinner at the cantina. She was off to Boston for a conference, and at dinner I'd offered to give her a ride on my way out of town. The gesture was more selfish than noble. I hugged her briefly at the curb, realizing it was the first time I'd actually touched her. Our embrace lingered just fractionally longer than mere friends, until we slowly separated.

"Goodbye, Mr. Seth MacClellan," she whispered, her voice beginning to tremble.

"Goodbye, Grace. It was nice to meet you." I knew it was stiff and overly polite, but it was all I could muster without choking up.

Her eyes never left mine as she reached into the pocket of her sweater and pulled out the tiny, white seashell I'd given her the night before and held it up for me to see. I dug into my own pocket and extracted the other half, holding it high and silently nodding. She grabbed the handle of her suitcase, nodded back in understanding as she returned the shell to her pocket, and turned to go. As I watched her walk away, not knowing when or if I'd see her again, I raised two fingers to my lips, kissed them sweetly, and pointed in her direction. She was choking back tears under her sunglasses as she vanished inside the terminal, knowing that within hours, we would both be back in our own worlds and may never cross paths again. I missed her already. I drove slowly away, already sick with the pain of missing. Suddenly, a great clarity washed over me. I accelerated, jerked hard on the steering wheel, raced around the entire circumference of the airport and back into the parking deck. Out the door, over the retaining wall, dashing across the street through moving traffic, up the stairs, pushing through the throng inside the concourse. There she was, just stepping into the security line. "Grace!" I called out over the din. No response. I cupped my hands. "Grace!" I yelled louder. She turned and caught my eye.

I didn't know what to say next. In the most critical juncture of my life, at the crossroads that demanded swift action, I simply couldn't think of what to say next. I wanted to yell *I love you!* I wanted to yell *will you marry me?* I wanted to yell *will you just stop and run away with me?* But nothing came out. She continued through the security line. How fitting. Security. Safety. Moving from one world into the safety of another. She smiled, waved goodbye, then disappeared. I just stood there, sensing that my future was departing. A scene from the movie *Roman Holiday* came to mind, where Audrey Hepburn, the coddled Princess, spent the most irrational but joyous of days with Gregory Peck, the journalist with no direction. As the Princess got out of the car, she told him she would turn the corner at the end of the street and return to her life behind palace gates. She begged him not to follow. A final embrace. She walked away, turned that corner, and out of his life. Out of sight, but never out of mind. Why we let people turn corners without chasing after them, I would never understand.

When she arrived in Boston, her voicemail was jammed with a dozen messages I'd left, each one sounding more emotional and desperate. I wondered if the connection I'd felt was as alive in her as it was in me. Did she ache the same way I did? I wanted to see her again. I wanted to feel her touch and hear her laughter. She called me the moment she landed and confessed that she was feeling all the same things. And so our life together, but apart, began.

From that first shared meal, our time together over the next two years would be like the ever-changing colors of the low-country waters Grace loved to paint. Blue, green, turquoise, azure, sapphire, beryl, cobalt. Sometimes calm, sometimes churning, but never really stormy. For Grace and me, that chance encounter on Folly Beach was more than chemistry. It was the start of a melding of the minds so true and so mad and so deep that only twins could begin to understand. A magnetic uniting of souls so unique, so cosmically aligned, where every syllable the other person uttered made perfect sense, and meaning was derived even from moments when no words were spoken at all. No one, *no one*, could understand our connection, and we never tried to explain it to them. She was my partner in the truest sense of the word, particularly on our frequent travels. She embraced my innate penchant for adventure, enduring anxious episodes like the morning I ran with the bulls in Pamplona, or rafted down the untamed waters of the Amazon basin.

In exchange, I relished our quieter moments in foreign lands. I cherished our memories of strolling down Las Ramblas in Barcelona, hand in hand. Whenever the moment struck us, we would stop at a café to sip sangria or Pernod, soaking in the aromas of the open markets and the colorful parade of pedestrians and street performers at Placa de Catalunya.

We moved so easily in tandem, always wanting to explore the same museums, and hungry for the same food at the same time. We'd spread out a picnic lunch wherever we could find room for a blanket and a bottle of Bordeaux. We kissed abundantly, we laughed generously, but mostly, we just talked. Meaningful conversation had always been what we did best.

In Paris, we fell in love more deeply than ever. There is nothing more romantic than a long, deep kiss under the Eiffel Tower on a moonlit summer night. Nothing. Quiet walks in teeming parks, drinks in lively street cafés in St. Germain, dinners at cozy restaurants punctuated by laughter and longing. It was a dreamworld and we moved gently through it.

We loved to simply wander, exploring the avenues and alleyways off the beaten path. We ventured anywhere we thought might be interesting. Grace with her charcoal pencils, sketching the rhythms of life, and me with my notebook, jotting notes and plot points for the novels I would write someday. Our passports were well-worn and our scrapbooks overflowing with precious memories.

Much to her chagrin, I had the uncontrollable habit of staring at Grace across the table. Without realizing it, I would go several minutes without saying a word, so totally swept up in the sight of the woman I considered to be the most beautiful creature on God's great earth. I was mesmerized. I couldn't help but lock my eyes onto hers, trying to catch a glimpse of her soul and spirit. I loved to study her, watching her bite her lower lip as she pondered her next brush stroke or decided what entertaining spice to put into our evening meal. Despite her occasional protestations, I made no genuine attempt to stop.

Grace had her own habit of staring, but thankfully not at me. She loved to lean over anything high up and soak in the unobstructed view. *Vistas* she called them. Railings and rooftops, bridges and balconies, these were the perches from which she beckoned the horizon to come to her. She never spoke as she fixed her gaze and I never interrupted the silence to ask her what she might be imagining. I only knew that the process seemed to bring her a deep down peace, and that in turn, made me happy.

The only negative to our globetrotting were the long goodbyes at airports. Grace and I shared a secret language, words and acronyms that carried meaning only for us. "A&F" for "Always and Forever," or "WBT" for "We Belong Together." But of all the words in our private lexicon, "goodbye" was not among them.

Each time we parted, even though we both knew we'd see each other again soon, the separation was always wrenching. We never seemed to be able to do it on the first try. It always involved a spontaneous turning around in a crowded concourse and racing back to each other for a final kiss farewell. And then it was over. A painful exit from our supernal days together in paradise and reentry into our own individual worlds. Back to work. Back to paying bills. Back to saving our pennies for the next big adventure.

The distance between us was bridged by frequent visits, along with fifty calls and texts every day, but our strongest bond came from our letters. It was the communication of choice for two old souls living in a modern word of instant messaging.

Through paper and pen we poured out our hopes, our desires, our worries. We devoted pages and pages to express everything we loved about the other. She was a gifted writer, better than me if truth be told. My letters were organized like essays, usually drafted on a computer, often employing metaphors. Try as I might, I could never fully express the depth of my devotion and admiration. Grace had the amazing ability to precisely capture her emotions and translate them to paper, as only an artist could. Her letters were free-flowing and profound, exuding raw emotion. Grace's considerable artistic talents transferred onto the written page to create a visual memory of our adventures. To flip open the creased pages of her letters was to take a trip back in time, where two smiling faces soaked in the world and made it their own. Her stationery often held the faint scent of her perfume, making the moment that much more ingrained in my senses.

I kept everything she ever wrote. At first I stored all of these precious mementos in an antique wooden box, but as my collection burgeoned, I moved them into an old suitcase with a faded tweed covering. Every letter, every postcard, every note, I saved them all. And then, after two years of halcyon days filled with indelible memories, the letters suddenly stopped coming.

I had postponed a trip to Ireland with Grace, needing every spare minute to flesh out an investigative piece about an investment banker who had been buying up licenses for cell phone transmission using a little-known government provision that gives minorities a huge discount on the cost of cellular licenses. He'd been purchasing them through his maid, his gardener, and anyone else he could find, setting himself up nicely for an auction between major cell providers in two weeks. He stood to pocket about a hundred million dollars. Brilliant. Also highly illegal. I had found some people who would talk on the record, exposing what he'd done. I needed a few days to put it all together, and then I was off to Ireland to join Grace.

She was attending a symposium on medieval architecture, castles and cathedrals I presumed, and I was more than eager to tag along. Just not now.

"I just need a few days. I'll fly over on Sunday night," I explained over the phone. "I'll meet you in Dublin Monday morning and we'll go from there. Okay?"

The brief moment of silence on the other end of the phone betrayed her disappointment that I was choosing work over her, but she let me off the hook. "Okay. I'll see you Monday."

"Thank you. I promise I'll make it up to you."

"Just write something great."

"I will. I promise."

"I love you, Mr. Seth MacClellan."

"I love *you*, Miss Grace Chastain."

We both made a kissing sound, then hung up. I shook off an awful sinking feeling of missing her. Even after two years, that feeling that half of you is missing never seemed to wane.

The next three days flew by as I worked feverishly on the story. I made my deadline and after our lawyers vetted it, it ran on the front page of the Sunday edition. Headline news, with a Seth MacClellan byline on top. I could already hear my name being called—*and the Pulitzer Prize goes to*—

I would get on a plane in a few hours and be with Grace in Ireland by morning. I called her to let her know my flight was on schedule, but it went straight to voicemail. I left a brief text, hoping that might have a better chance of getting through. No response.

I finished packing for my trip abroad, beginning with the tiny black box harboring an engagement ring. I opened it for the thousandth time, admiring the brilliance of the Marquise cut diamond. In a few days, after a bended knee and undoubtedly a few tears, the ring would be on Grace's finger, never to be removed. I snapped the box shut and placed it securely in my carry-on bag. I was already rehearsing my speech in my head. I couldn't wait to ask her.

I was jarred out of my wistful trance when my phone rang. My heart leapt, as it did every time Grace called me. I snatched up the phone with boyish enthusiasm.

"Hello!"

"Seth?"

I immediately recognized the voice on the other end. It was Grace's father, Lawrence Chastain, who had the unmistakable refined Southern drawl you would likely associate with old money. "Mr. Chastain? What is it?"

"Seth, I'm afraid I have some terrible news."

I don't exactly recall what he said next. Only snippets of sound made their way into my reeling consciousness as her father recounted the events that had recently transpired in Ireland. *Rental car. Rain. Fog. Wrong side of the road. Head on. No survivors.* It was too much to take in. I don't even remember saying goodbye or thanking him for letting me know.

I sat on the floor and sobbed for hours, trying to exorcise the cold, hard pain that had stabbed me. Grace was gone.

The next week was an exercise in somnambulism. As if drugged by grief, I flew to Ireland, and together with Grace's parents, brought her lifeless body back to Charleston. I didn't dare look at her face, not wanting that to be my final visual memory of her.

We buried her in a ceremony attended by hundreds, all of whom loved Grace in their own way. I wanted to speak, but simply couldn't form any sentences longer than "thank you for coming."

I embraced her parents on the porch of their stately home on East Bay Street, promising to be in touch, but already suspecting I wouldn't. Coming back here would churn up too much pain, and I didn't see how I could ever bear it.

As the sun collapsed from a long day's work over the lowcountry, I drove out to Folly Beach, to the same spot where I'd first met the radiant artist in the cornflower blue sundress. I sat down on the warm sand and wrote Grace a final letter. It would be the truest writing I'd ever done, but still wholly inadequate. Through all of our correspondence, I had never been able to conjure up the right words to express how much I loved her, but I would attempt it one final time.

> My darling Grace,
> To recap all of the blessings you've brought into my life would take more pages than I can write. I will only say that every minute together has been a privilege, and I know in my soul that I have loved you purely and deeply, and for all the right reasons. The love I have carried for you these past two years won't diminish, even with the passage of time or the fading light that passes through the prism of perspective. It can't possibly. I know I'm going to

experience the greatest pain of my life in the coming
months, and as I write this, I have no idea how I
will surmount it. At this moment, there is nothing
more wrenching than the thought of living without
you. The pathway through the maze of my
imagination has always ended with you and our
future together. You have been the first thing I
thought about when I woke up, who I thought about
all day, and how I rocked myself to sleep. Thank
you for loving me. I hold out hope that someday,
we will be together again.

A&F... Always and forever,
Seth

I sealed the envelope and kissed the back of it, then walked to the
water's edge and gently placed it in the swirling white foam of the
outgoing tide. I pulled the tiny shell out of my pocket and let it run
through my fingers, staring across the infinite waves of the Atlantic. I
still couldn't bear the thought of it. Not talking every single day, not
waking up in the middle of the night and finding a message that the
other was also having a sleepless night, not planning our next adventure,
not receiving pictures, not loving and laughing whenever we could
possibly steal the time, not holding her, not seeing that beautiful smile
that could make flowers bloom. I saw a thousand snapshots of her in
the scrapbook in my mind. I couldn't imagine the abyss I was about to
enter. All my vivid daydreams of moving to Charleston to be with her,
writing books and fixing up old houses together. . . the laughter of
children and grandchildren. . . vanished on some winding narrow road
in County Wicklow. *If only I'd been there. If only I would have been the one
driving. She'd still be alive. If only. If only. If only.* The haunting words pounded
through my head like the unrelenting waves crashing in front of me. I
couldn't make them go away.

Heaving, unable to catch my breath, my tears mingled with the
mist of the churning sea as I stood alone along the shore. The pain
washing over me was crippling, and I knew that no matter how much
time passed, I would never get over her. It wasn't just a torch I carried

for Grace. . . it was a bonfire in the middle of what had been a vast, empty cave. I had been warmed by its heat and inspired by its light. Now the flame was extinguished, gray smoke rising, taking my soul with it. Never again would I experience the joy of sitting across the table and staring into the face of the girl with the aquamarine eyes.

I returned my precious shell to safekeeping in my pocket, and walked away into the bleeding sun of the Western sky.

With the newspaper's blessing, I took a month off, only vaguely recalling anything I did as I simply existed from sundown to sundown. Mostly I just ran. Usually at night, sometimes as much as twenty miles. No map, no watch, no agenda. Just racing against the shadows of the wind to ward off the depression that lurked next to every memory of Grace Chastain. Pain and exhaustion became my bedmates as I searched for any sign of her in my dreams. My six foot frame was getting leaner, bordering on unhealthy, but running kept me sane at a time when my subconscious was begging to ease into the quicksand of misery.

When I finally returned to work, I was greeted for days with sympathetic stares and well-intentioned queries of *are you okay?* I assured everyone that I was, but I knew I wasn't. I slowly realized that the only way I would be able to move forward would be to pour myself back into my work. I was going to make her proud, whatever it took.

# Chapter Five

My brain cleared somewhat as I ran through the heart of the night to nowhere in particular. I found my investigative mind was starting to come back online. How did this happen? How was I swept up in this nexus that destroyed my reputation and wounded so many around me? I'd somehow fallen victim to the alluring cocktail of blind ambition and false information. Through my haze of disbelief, I reached a simple conclusion; I'd been set up. But by whom? And *why*? I could think of only one person who had the answers. My pace quickened as I rolled home.

The next morning, I returned to Sunny Acres, and as I fully expected, it was devoid of any activity. I peered through the window of the trailer that had belonged to Johnny Spainhour, only to find it completely empty except for a few empty beer bottles. In hindsight, realizing that I'd never actually gone inside the trailer during our initial meeting, I started to wonder if he'd ever lived there at all. Probably not.

I walked back to the stream where I'd first seen the colorful oily sheen on the surface of the water. It was now as clear as a Rocky Mountain river.

The only thing I knew to be true about the man who'd presented himself as Harold Motsinger was that he rode motorcycles. The jagged scar on his forehead and a Harley-Davidson belt buckle he wore were clues enough that this was a man who enjoyed the wind in his face from the open road. With the picture I'd snapped of him at the trailer park in hand, and nothing but free time on my hands, I went in search of the architect of my demise.

It gave me time to mentally retrace my steps and piece together the perfect storm of deadlines, ambition, and blatant fabrication. The lawyers for Ludwig Oil had made it excruciatingly clear that the documents Harold had provided were all forgeries. The water samples, lab results, medical records and contact numbers, had all been the product of some evil imagination. Excellent workmanship, the attorneys had conceded, but fakes nonetheless. The fact that they were all on crisp and uniform paper, like counterfeit money hot off the press, should have been my first red flag. In hindsight, I also realized that the samples of tap water Harold provided for my further independent testing were brought to me in Mason jars. I didn't actually see the water come out of the faucet. No wonder the benzene levels were elevated. Someone had obviously added it later. I now also recalled that it struck me funny that Johnny Spainhour, complaining of tumors and mounting medical costs, was driving a shiny new pickup truck. It either got past me in haste, or I chose to ignore it out of blind ambition. It had all been painstakingly orchestrated to tell a story that never really happened, and I'd gobbled it up like a ravenous wolf. It was a bitter irony that here I was, thinking I was helping these downtrodden people get a better life, and they ended up ruining mine.

After ten hours of systematically traipsing through motorcycle shops and biker bars, I finally found him. He was at a table inside a rough roadside bar called the *Free Wheeler* off highway 41 in Kennesaw. The cracking of pool balls was one of the few sounds you could hear above the blaring jukebox. As I turned heads with my conspicuous entry, I seemed to recall at least a half-dozen stories we'd run about stabbings in this establishment. Harold's table was filled with bikers and their women, and littered with empty longneck beer bottles. He was motioning to the barmaid for another round for everyone. I could only imagine where he'd gotten the money.

"Harold?" I blasted above the din of the jukebox.

His head whipped around with that startled "hand-in-the-cookie jar" expression.

"Harold?" cackled one of the biker chicks derisively. "Who's *Harold?*" It brought an explosion of laughter from the weathered and leathered gathering, now edging closer to me in a menacing circle. The word "stabbing" raced through my brain once again. The only two people not laughing were Harold and I.

"I think we need to talk," I said with as much bravado as I could muster. I'm certain I reeked of fear, but that was offset by the notion that at this low ebb in my life, I really didn't care what happened to me. Nobody wearing a skull and crossbones bandanna could do anything worse to me than what the Armani suits of Ludwig Oil had already done.

Harold, or whatever his name was, clicked the roof of his mouth with his tongue as he sized up the situation. He was no longer the wilting flower I'd known from Sunny Acres, begging for my help to fight the injustices of corporate America. He was very much in control, operating from strength. I sensed that at his signal, everyone in the bar would bring their tattooed arms raining down on me. Nonetheless, I stood my ground, waiting for his next move. With a quick flick of his neck, he motioned me outside. He snagged two fresh longnecks between his gnarled fingers and led me out a back door.

Moments later we were seated next to each other on a picnic table out back of the *Free Wheeler*. We both stared straight ahead, fellow actors in a sordid tale.

"Figured you might show up," he offered first.

I nodded, and drew in a deep breath to calm myself. "I suppose I know *why* you did it," I started. "Money?"

He nodded. Even grinned a little. Clearly it had been a sizable payday. "Ain't that why everybody does everything?"

I flashed back to the blank space on the wall of my former office. "I suppose greed can be a powerful motivator."

"I wouldn't exactly call it greed." Harold tipped back his beer and took a long drink, preparing himself for the confession to follow. "Remember that fella you met that day at the trailer park? The old guy?"

"The one with the new pickup? Yeah, I remember. What about him?"

"That's my daddy. He's sick. Real sick. Lung cancer."

"Not from benzene, I'm guessing." We both managed a snorting laugh.

"Nah. More like sixty years of Marlboros. Anyway, he needs medicine. He needs treatment. It's expensive. I sure can't afford it. He's my father. You do what you gotta do."

I nodded, actually understanding his motives. My own father died when I was in elementary school. My mother followed him eleven years later, languishing in some crumbling hospital with hallways permeated by the stench of human urine because we didn't have the money for anything better. I knew all about the toils and snares of unaffordable healthcare.

"Okay," I said. "I guess I get the *why*. My bigger question is *who*? With all due respect, Harold, or whatever your name is, I don't see you as the mastermind type."

He laughed again, kicking the dirt with his oily boot. "Nah. I reckon I was what you might call a pawn in this game."

"So who's the King?"

"I honestly don't know his name. Truth be told, I never spoke to the guy behind it. I only dealt with a dude who seemed to me to be an assistant of some sort."

"How'd you get involved?"

"He just showed up at my house one day. Told me he'd heard about my daddy and our predicament. Said he had a way out. All I had to do was contact you, give you a buncha papers, show you 'round the old trailer park, and collect my money. Simple as that. I had some serious bills to pay, so I didn't think it through much more than that."

I shook my head and sucked on my beer. "I'm an idiot."

"Ah, don't beat yourself up too bad. You gotta admit, I was pretty convincing."

"I'll say. All those people I called? All the contacts in the documents you gave me? Who were they?"

"Some kinfolk, some friends. Most of 'em are inside this bar right now."

"And I'm assuming *you* put the oil in the stream you showed me?"

"Daddy did it before we got there. Coupla drops of 10W-30 and it looked like the whole place was sittin' on poison."

"Man," I murmured, as I thought back to that first visit to Sunny Acres. No wonder the rainbow of colors on the water's surface had dissipated when I went back later to snap a few pictures. I was beginning to realize I was more gullible than I'd ever imagined possible.

"So how's your dad doing?" I asked, my humanity temporarily trumping my anger.

"He's a lot better. Thanks for askin'." There was a long pause as we both went over the events of the last month. "Look, Mr. MacClellan. . . for what it's worth, I'm real sorry for what I done to you. I ain't proud of it, but truth be told, it ain't the worst thing I've ever done, and I'd do it again if it come down to it. Bottom line, money buys you better medicine in America. Simple as that."

I exhaled loudly, unable to disagree with his logic. Lifesaving cancer treatment for a dying father was the only good that would come out of this entire debacle. Well, that, and his new truck. I turned and faced Harold, man to man. "I need to find out who set me up. Point me in the right direction."

He shook his head. "Can't do it. *Won't* do it."

"Why not?"

"Because he told me if you ever came snoopin' around, tryin' to connect the dots, I was to kill ya. And if I didn't, he aimed to kill *me*. I took him at his word."

"But can you at least tell me why someone would go to such great lengths to ruin me?"

"I don't know. He never said. Best I can figure is that maybe you was pokin' around into somethin' that was about to cause somebody rich and powerful a whole lot of trouble if it showed up in the newspaper. That's my guess, but I don't really know. You're the reporter. You figure it out."

I took a long sip from the longneck, wiping the foam off my mouth with the back of my hand. "So," I casually muttered to Harold, "are you going to kill me?"

"Not if I can't find you. And I don't aim to come huntin' for ya. From what all I know about ya, it seems like you're a decent man, and I figure I've done you enough harm. So the sooner you walk away from this, the sooner you can stop lookin' over your shoulder."

Harold polished off his beer and slapped me hard on the thigh as he stood up and ambled away.

# Chapter Six

I was going to disappear, but not because of the chilling threats from Harold Motsinger. I had to leave Atlanta. My debacle was all over the news, to the point where I had to sequester myself from television, newspapers, and the internet, just to avoid hearing my name and seeing my picture. I was sure Gordon Kelleher at the *Journal-Constitution* was enjoying every moment of watching me drown in an unforgiving sea of printers' ink.

Several trips to the dumpster turned out to be liberating. Bank boxes full of notes, documents, and newspaper clippings were heaved into the square cavern of rusting metal. The last thing to go was a box filled with my awards. The panes of glass shattered with the same broken tone I felt inside my soul. None of it mattered anymore.

I had never before realized how easy it is for someone to just disappear, assuming the authorities aren't looking for you. With no immediate relatives to worry about, it was relatively effortless for me to fall off the grid. For the next four hours, I erased Seth MacClellan's besmirched name from the rolls. I canceled subscriptions, closed accounts, and left no forwarding address. Cashed out. As I wallowed in my tailspin, I wanted to be unreachable. Unfindable. Untouchable. *Tabula rasa*. Clean slate. The only fingerprint from my old identity I kept was my phone number, and I really didn't know why.

My apartment was now empty, sound bouncing off its bare walls. The sum of my life's efforts were now jammed into the back of a rented trailer hitched to my car.

I placed the tweed suitcase with Grace's letters in the passenger seat, briefly considering securing them with the seatbelt. How I loved those halcyon days with Grace. How I missed them. How I wanted them back, even as I understood with searing sadness that they were gone forever. Grace. Disgrace. Intertwined. I leaned over the steering wheel and purged what few tears I had remaining, wanting to just let go of life. *What am I going to do?* was all I could think. Numb from pain, I finally turned the ignition and backed out, leaving my world in Atlanta and everyone in it behind. I had no idea where I was going next.

It was newpaper editor Horace Greeley who popularized the saying, "Go West, young man." Go explore. Conquer new horizons. Seek out your manifest destiny. I headed east.

As I sat on the hood of my car at sunset and stared at the marsh birds flitting across Murrells Inlet, South Carolina, it felt like this was as close to the end of the earth as I could get on four wheels. How I missed not having Grace beside me to soak in the vista.

The sudden separation was at times too painful for me to ponder. Only occasionally did I allow myself to conjure up the future I had envisioned for the two of us. I used to imagine us sitting in a cottage or a cabin on a lake in New Hampshire, or South Carolina, or Canada. Wherever. Our days would be spent kayaking, exploring, laughing. Our nights reserved for reading and listening to music in the warmth of roaring fires, soft flannel, and earthy Merlot. I would be on one end of the sofa, she on the other, our legs intertwined. I would peer over the top of the pages of my novel and she would instinctively already be looking back at me. I would lean over, kiss her as I had a million times before, then we would both settle back into another chapter. Then off to bed, where sleep would always be postponed. Those were our dreams. Distant, distant dreams.

The sudden buzzing of my phone interrupted my misery. I didn't recognize the number. For some unknown reason, even as I sat crestfallen, I still accepted the stranger's call. " 'Lo?" I said in a clipped tone.

"Seth? Seth MacClellan?" came a vaguely familiar voice on the other end.

"Who wants to know?"

"Seth! It's Paul! Paul Munce!"

There was a moment of awkward silence as the Rolodex in my brain flipped to the name Munce. I'd known him in college, working on the newspaper staff together. I didn't know him very well, and what I did know, I didn't particularly like. His attitude towards me always blended an arrogance that came with being two years older than I and a jealousy of being six inches shorter. I did recall that he was a very capable editor who made our copy better, even if meant wading through the muck of his schoolboy condescension. I remember that same smarmy disposition when our paths occasionally crossed after graduation. He worked as Managing Editor for a small daily in Virginia, and couldn't resist tossing subtle spears at my lowly position as a 'simple reporter.' I never mentioned that my readership outnumbered his something on the order of 20,000 to one. I figured he already knew. "Paul Munce. Wow. There's a blast from the past. Wait, how did you get this number?"

"Seth, even though I'm in management, I'm still a reporter at heart. Any reporter worth his chops knows that. Come on."

There it was. Another dig. "So why are you calling me?" I asked with annoyance.

"Well, we all read what happened to you. Tough break. But I have a proposition. You interested?"

I drew a deep breath. "I'm listening."

"As you may or may not know, I'm the Managing Editor of *The Bay Breeze* in Virginia Beach."

"Again," I said with some mild irritation, "why are you calling me?"

"I figure you need a job. I'm always looking for talent, and as I recall, you were pretty good."

I let those words tumble through my mind. A guy in middle-management from a penny-ante rag telling an award-winning journalist from a major metropolitan paper that he was *pretty good*. And he'd even used the past tense to say it. I bristled. I had a wall covered with awards that reeked of *pretty good*. And then I stopped. I *used* to have a wall covered with awards. Now they were sitting in a dumpster. Perhaps past tense was applicable.

"What kind of job?" I asked, none too happy about it.

"I need a fishing reporter."

"A what?"

"Fishing reporter."

"What is that, exactly?"

"You just go down to the local piers and marinas and see what they're catching, and what kind of bait they're using to do it. Believe it or not, a lot of people buy the paper just for that one section. Probably a little beneath what you're used to, but who knows, maybe it'll lead to something better. At least it gets you back in the game."

*Probably* beneath me? *Probably?* The veiled insult was almost enough to make me hang up. But I didn't. *Get me back in the game* was the phrase that grabbed me and held on. "When do you need to know?"

"Pretty soon. Right away if you can. I fired my other guy last week and the readers are already clamoring for a replacement."

"Can I sleep on it?"

"Sure. You know where to find me."

"I'll be in touch."

I hung up and spread myself across the roof of my car, staring at the changing clouds.

Sleep had been elusive in the tumult of the preceding days, and it fully escaped me on this night. I tossed and turned on the thin mattress of the seaside motel and weighed my options. It was like trying to link together the pieces of a solid black jigsaw puzzle; I had all the pieces, but I couldn't begin to figure out how they all fit together. I loathed the notion of going to work for Paul Munce, but my reporter's salary at the *Herald* hadn't provided much of a nest egg, and the money would soon run out. The bottom line was that he had a job and I needed one. At least this would provide a little income until I could sort out my shuffled life. *Get back in the game* again echoed through my brain.

It was just after midnight when I picked up the phone and dialed. "Paul?" I said into the illuminated display. "It's Seth."

# Chapter Seven

With a tattered road map spread out in the seat next to me, I had driven to a place I'd never heard of before. Sandbridge Beach, a narrow strip of barrier island about ten miles south of Virginia Beach. It was four miles long and a quarter mile wide, with the ocean on one side and the brackish waters of the Back Bay on the other. Hundreds of beach houses both large and small lined the two main drags and connecting streets. The only commercial entities were a small grocery store, a few modest restaurants, and a couple of beach stores that sold everything from bait to bathing suits.

I'll always remember that very first time I set foot on Sandbridge. The start of the tourist season was still a few months away, so except for the year-rounders, it was virtually empty. Under a dome of blue sky, I sat on the cool sand and dug into the sandwich I'd bought at the Seaside Market. Blowing sand plinked off my sunglasses, covering my rye bread with a fine grit that crunched in my teeth with each bite. I didn't care. It was the first sense of calm I'd felt in days. I sat back on one elbow and soaked it in. Pelicans dive bombing the water to swallow up a meal, a few surfers searching for a ride, sparkling mist flying off the tops of waves. A solitary loon sailed by, riding the current. Fifty yards south, scores of seagulls stood motionless, facing the wind, grouped by their markings and size.

I thought of Grace and her easel, and how well they'd blend in to this scene. She could capture every droplet of water, every grain of sand, even a puff of sea breeze with a stroke of her brush. Her painting provided a voice for her soul. It's what she was born to do.

Above me, the F/A 18 Super Hornets from Naval Air Station Oceana left behind miles of contrails, crisscrossing the sky like threads, weaving the cirrus clouds together. Like lightning, you could always see the strike-fighter jets long before you could hear their thunder. It was a majestic sight and sound of fury I would soon come to love. It was reassuring to know they were on *our* side. This was the theatre of my new home. I could sense I was going to like it here. It was a good place to work, the perfect place to run, and above all, the ideal place to disappear.

Later that afternoon, I met Paul Munce at his office on Princess Anne Road, near the Virginia Beach municipal complex. I'd forgotten how short he was. I quickly remembered what a little jerk he could be. As a journalist, Paul Munce couldn't carry Bynum Sherry's notebook.

"Well, well, well," Munce greeted me as I tapped on his office door. "Seth MacClellan, the great man of arts and letters, slumming it with the rest of us." He took a bite of a carrot and stood up to shake my hand across the desk. "Sit down, sit down," he half-offered, half-ordered. I heard the words *I don't need this!* bang against my skull as I had the sudden urge to back out of the door and wash my hands of the situation. Unfortunately, I *did* need this, so I obediently sat down.

"So how's it goin', Seth?" asked Munce, his dingy teeth orange with carrot. He knew perfectly well how it was going.

"I've had better days."

"No doubt. But you're back on track now. Back in the game. Once you get those reporter juices flowing again, you'll be good as new."

Even though the words were spilling out of Munce's smarmy mouth, they actually provided a modicum of comfort. However mundane, this job would at least get me writing again, and take my mind off all my troubles. "Thanks for the opportunity, Paul. Your offer came at a very good time."

"Well, I must say, it was a happy coincidence. You needed a job, I needed to fill a spot. It worked out well for both of us." Munce handed me a security card for access to the building. "You'll need this key card if you ever need to get into the office after hours. Can't imagine you will, but just in case."

I tucked the thick card in my wallet. "So what exactly is it that I do?"

Munce snapped off another bite of carrot and reached into his desk drawer. He gave me a manila folder stuffed with old clippings from *The Bay Breeze*. "We'll call your column *The Fish Finder*. This is all you have to do. . . find out what kind of fish they're catching, when they catch it, and how they caught it. Simple as that. I need twenty-two inches of copy, Monday, Wednesday, Friday, then forty on Sunday, with art."

"Who provides the art?"

Munce reached under his desk and pulled out a dented Canon camera with no case and handed it to me. "*You* do." He leaned back in his swivel chair and broke into a condescending grin. "Go get 'em, boy."

I flipped through the manila folder and nodded. Humbled, but challenged. Somewhere under the pile of broken glass that was my spirit, the light of optimism glinted. There was still that sliver of hope that perhaps I could be made whole again. This was rock bottom, and there was no place to go but up. Or so I thought.

# Chapter Eight

Paul Munce had set me up with a small but neatly furnished condominium at *Seaside at Sandbridge* on Sandpiper Road, about halfway into the island. It took me all of ninety minutes to unpack my few belongings and set up house. Spartan, but entirely adequate.

My new job at *The Bay Breeze* provided me with two important things; flexible hours and anonymity. I changed my byline to Mac Rellman. I would be the only one who knew it was code for "Mackerel Man," but I didn't care. Seth MacClellan was gone, and I didn't want anyone to find him.

Munce had been right. This was definitely a step down from what I had been doing at the *Herald,* but I convinced myself that at least it was in the same general arena. As if Monet painting houses for a living still qualified him as an artist. In truth, getting started provided a greater challenge than I'd imagined because there was a huge learning curve involved. I'd fished a fair amount as a young boy, but this was a lot more complicated than simply tossing a Zebco with a nightcrawler into a stocked lake and waiting for whatever lurked beneath the surface to make the bobber dance.

For example, as I read through some of the past fishing articles that had run in *The Bay Breeze,* I realized I had no idea there was something called "braided line," much less that there were two kinds of it, Spectra and Dyneema. As I delved deeper, I learned that some braids are wax coated and some have a thin sheath coating around them offering abrasion resistance, improved knot strength and increased color retention. And for people who bottom fish, there is apparently no other choice. *Who knew?* Freespool, backlash, and

Albright knots were all terms I would have to rapidly integrate into my meager piscine vocabulary.

All of the maritime minutiae contained in the old clippings seemed incredibly dull and unimportant to me, but I would come to understand that these details mattered greatly to dedicated anglers. Bait and tackle were the subject of intense debate while they stood on piers and shores and waited for action. It could only help my credibility as a reporter that I now knew that braided line is ideal for anyone who needs zero stretch, extra line capacity on their reel *and* the ultimate in sensitivity *and* was also excellent for sharking due to its hook setting power. I had a lot to learn. Fortunately, the first thing I would learn was that the island held plenty of teachers, eager to help.

It was just after seven o'clock, my frozen dinner still settling in my stomach, when I drove the mile and a half south to the Little Island Pier. I couldn't look at the ocean without thinking of Grace. I missed her so much it was nauseating. I had to press on. Writing would be my only salvation.

As I locked the car door and jammed my reporter pad into my back pocket, I had no idea what I was about to get into. I would soon discover the pilings and planks of this pier would change my life in ways I could never have imagined.

Little Island Pier had several names. Most people called it simply Sandbridge Pier, but the regulars called it "the LIP." It stretched about a hundred and twenty yards into the Atlantic, and like so many things at the shore, the wooden structure was a blend of the worn and the new. It was the embodiment of the endless beach battle to replace what's been battered by the incessant wind, seawater, and salt air. A plaque and photo just past the entry gate proudly boasted that this was home of the Virginia state record King mackerel, 522 and a half pounds, caught in 1999. It was also home to a cast of characters that I would grow to love.

Where you stood on the pier dictated what you were trying to catch. Flounder rigs near the shore, squid rigs for spot and croaker in the middle, maybe some blues if they were running.

At the far end, the regulars held their rods with the tips pointed straight down at the water, jerking the pole back and forth to zigzag their cigarette shaped Got-Cha plugs through the swells in an effort to attract a Spanish mackerel. It was on this first night that I met three of the regulars of the Little Island Pier. Though I didn't know it at the time, this trio would always occupy the same spot; south side, near the end. Lyman Gregg, Billy Boudreau, and Dominic Rubio. Each sat quietly in well-worn lawn chairs, their saltwater rods resting in hand hewn notches carved into the railing. I ambled up without speaking, leaning over the railing and staring out at the water. There were a half-dozen other men at various stations around the pier. Everyone glanced my way. Nobody greeted me. I eventually found out why. The regulars constantly bickered over the best bait and tackle, but they all agreed on one thing. . . they hated tourists. Tourists meant crowded quarters and tangled lines. They were the only people on the island who didn't welcome the lifeblood of the tourist dollar.

It was Lyman Gregg, an older African American, who first acknowledged my existence in their sacred realm. Perhaps he noticed that I didn't have a pole, making me a little less threatening to their dominion. With graying hair and weathered skin, Lyman had the look and a voice reminiscent of a bayou bluesman. Unless there was lightning in the air, Lyman Gregg would always be holding down a seat on the Little Island Pier.

"You new?" he asked, sizing me up. His throaty voice wasn't exactly threatening, but not all that friendly either.

"I knew? I knew *what?*" I answered, taken off guard. *What did I know? And how did he know I knew it?*

"I mean to say, are you new to the pier? First time?"

"Oh! I'm with ya now. Yeah. New. Brand new. First time. Nice place."

"Tourist?" said Lyman with a hint of disdain.

"No. Just moved here. First night. Thought I'd check it out."

"What brings you to Sandbridge?" asked Lyman, *zinging* his line out into the darkness.

"Actually, I'm the new fishing reporter for *The Bay Breeze*." I moved closer to Lyman and extended my handshake. "My name's Mac."

I'd hardly gotten my name out of my mouth when suddenly all nine men on the pier abandoned their rods and closed ranks around me. Broad smiles broke out on every face. A fishing reporter meant attention. Names in the paper, pictures with trophy catches, clippings for their scrapbooks. I was to be the official recorder of their niche history and they were thrilled I had arrived. What a difference. In all my days at the *Herald*, people had *hated* to see me show up. An investigative reporter was like Typhoid Mary with a ballpoint pen, to be avoided at all costs. On Little Island Pier I was immediately hailed as the conquering hero. I was instantly welcomed.

As they introduced themselves, it would be the first and last time I'd ever hear their full names. Everyone on the pier was on a one name basis. Not necessarily their first name, and not necessarily their real name. Just something quick and easy to remember. Dominic Rubio was simply "Rubes." Newcomers like me were called universal nicknames like Chief, Sport, and Buddy until the appropriate moniker could be permanently attached. This was normally Rubio's job, with input from Billy Boudreau.

Some people had nicknames they thought meant one thing, but actually held an unkinder meaning. Cat was a dermatologist from Lynnhaven who tried his best to blend in with the blue collar crowd on the LIP. He should have naturally been nicknamed Doc, but with his L.L. Bean clothes and expensive Shimano reels they called him Cat, short for catalog. He assumed it was short for catfish, and he was fine with that.

Billy Boudreau was better known as Topper. He was always working some angle to save money, or at least make you think he'd gotten the deal of the century. Topper was the kind of guy who would try to get a refund on a tattoo. He always had a giant nail clipper on a red lanyard looped around his neck, and wore lots of souvenir tee-shirts, usually red, white, and blue, and mostly from Tennessee. Topper was never without a hat, and always sported a giant brass fishhook on the bill. John Deere hats, NASCAR hats, the free kind of hats they give away at feed mills and hardware stores, a different lid every night. Topper naturally assumed his nickname was because of his vast collection of hats, but in truth, it had a hidden meaning and he was the only one who didn't know. They called him Topper because if you had a story, Billy Boudreau could top it with a better one. If you caught a Cobia on a twenty-pound test line, Topper had caught a sand shark on just fifteen. If you found a barely used spinning reel at a yard sale for ten dollars, Topper had found a new one at the flea market for only eight. If you'd patched a leak on an old canoe, Topper had built an ark.

Sometimes Rubes would bait him with outlandish tales of conquest, just to see if Topper could come up with a better one. He always did. Most of his stories started with the phrase "that doesn't hold a candle to the time—" and then he was off and running from there. I don't really think Topper was a liar as much as his recollections of past events were simply uninhibited by facts. Sometimes his memory was so good he could recall things that never actually happened. Thankfully it didn't stop him, because "Topper Time," as I would come to call it, was highly entertaining, even when you knew it was mostly invention.

In future days, the boys on the pier would try to stick me with the nickname of Scoop, but it never took. I was just Mac, which seemed to fit all the requirements of the pier. . . quick and easy to remember.

Lyman Gregg was the only exception to the nickname game. They just called him Lyman. It was either out of respect for the ex-Navy man, or there just didn't seem to be any other name that suited him. With eyes that were cheerful and undefeated, I always thought they should have called him Santiago in a nod to Hemingway's *The Old Man and the Sea,* but I certainly never suggested it out loud.

As the anglers all returned to their unattended poles, it dawned on me that they all seemed to live in the moment. Where they were going or where they'd been was never as important as what they were doing at that very moment. The next cast and the next catch were all that mattered. How I envied them. I now lived most of my life in the past. Whereas they lived in the sunshine of hope and success, I lived in the twilight of regret and despair.

I took a few notes, said my goodbyes, and headed back to the car. As I walked in and out of the light from the streetlamps affixed to the side of the pier, I actually felt at home. This is exactly where I wanted to live my life. In the shadows. Suddenly, driven by unexpected impulse, I took my phone out of my pocket and hurled it as far as I could into the dark waters of the Atlantic. A plunge, a bubble, and no more. My last connection to my former life, dead.

I came back to the condo and went for a run, just an easy three-miler to get my legs going again. It had been awhile since I'd laced them up. I loved that I was the lone inhabitant of the midnight streets. I breathed in the salt air and let it soothe me. Free therapy. Running always reminded me of Grace. How she'd always rubbed my weary legs after long training runs, how she'd waited for me at marathon finish lines, how she'd inspired me to run further and faster. She had no idea what an inspiration she'd been in that realm. I'd always wanted to make her proud of me, which in turn pushed me to train harder and lower my race times. I fully understood that how fast I ran a 5-K on Saturday morning didn't matter one whit in the grand scheme of world events, but just knowing I'd done my best with her cheering me on seemed to matter greatly at the time. As I crawled in bed for the first night of my new life, I launched a new ritual that would provide a synchronous comfort and torture. I would reach into the tweed suitcase under my bed and randomly pull out one of Grace's magnificent old letters, seeking solace in the words of her brightly drawn cursive that brought back a high tide of special memories.

> My Darling Seth,
> I am thankful every day, every minute, that you are in my life, and making my life part of yours. I've never felt so loved, so warm in someone else's eyes. Though we're miles apart, I know we will be together someday. We will share coffee on a wraparound porch, Guinness in Ireland, a beach umbrella somewhere. Anywhere. Mostly we will hold each other, closely, as we laugh our way along life's path. I love you so. Please stay by my side. . . we have a sunset to enjoy.
>
> All my love,
> Grace

I tucked the letter back into its original envelope and returned it to the suitcase. This would become my nightly self-flagellation. Read her words, stare at her picture, then search for the peace of sleep that never came. Her letters brought me a brief, tranquilizing joy in my quarantine of misery, but also reminded me of everything I'd lost, never to be regained. All of our dreams spelled out in letter perfect form, and none of them coming true. All of it my fault.

# Chapter Nine

I slept late, and rolled right out of bed into my running clothes. I was grateful to be able to finally shed my windbreaker and let my skin drink in the sunshine. I have never liked winter, so I was grateful that springtime was cautiously arriving at the coast in fits and starts. Winter is the season of brown and gray. It is the season of death, heartless and chilled. Shorter days, longer nights, when living things go into hibernation. Trees are bare, fields are windswept, creeks run shallow and cold. It has always been the season of my discontent.

I am a child of spring and summer, of blues and greens. Crimson sunrises, lavender sunsets, yellow moons. Rainbows and steam rising from meadows after a hard rain. The music of crickets, waterfalls, and nightingales through open windows. The first firefly makes my heart jump. The smell of mown grass invigorates me. Lying on my back and scanning the infinite blackness for shooting stars is my idea of heaven. Honeysuckle is my elixir. The green arms of daffodils pushing through thawing earth are reaching out to touch me. New life, new adventures, new hopes and dreams. They all arrive in spring and stay alive through summer.

This winter had been harder than most. Long periods of silence, where the sweet symphony of Grace's voice and laughter didn't find their way to my ears. There had been forced slumber, when the natural inclination was to be awake and alive. I had a dry, thirsty soul. I was sleepwalking with the solstice, mindlessly moving through space and time, searching for my summer. There was doubt. There was fear. More than anything, there was despair. How I missed her. My only hope was the knowledge that winter is always followed by spring, and summer patiently awaits its turn.

"I throwed an eight and a bait all day and nothin'!" Topper declared loudly, holding court at the end of the pier as he recapped his recent adventures down to Ocracoke on the Outer Banks of North Carolina. "So then I switched over to pin rigs and we slayed some blues. I mean to tell ya, flat *slayed* 'em. Three coolers full. Couldn't throw it out there fast enough. You shoulda been there, boys."

I saddled up to Lyman, who was sitting on the top of an old cooler that had certainly given him his money's worth. It was only my second night on the pier, but I already felt a kindred spirit. "What's he mean, *eight and a bait*?" I asked him quietly.

"Just like it sounds. . . an eight-ounce weight with bait on the other end. Most of us stick with one or two-ounce weights, which is a gracious plenty to cast a hundred yards of line. You'll come to find that Topper is prone to overdoin' it on most things. Facts bein' one of 'em."

I scribbled some quick notes in my pad and exhaled loudly. "I've got a lot to learn."

"Whatcha need to know?" asked Lyman, slowly reeling in his line.

"That's part of the problem. I don't even know what I don't know. All I know is that I gotta write four pieces a week. Any suggestions?"

"I know them other guys always like to talk about rods. That always makes for a good story. Always somethin' new out there, bigger and better than yesterday."

I immediately glanced at the rod in Lyman's steady hand, one of three he brought with him every night. It was the essence of generic. Graphite black with no markings, no adornment. Just a plain rod with a reel on one end and hook on the other. It reminded me of Willie Nelson's guitar. Lyman stood up and leaned his pole in a notch on the pier railing. I got the sense that he knew I was examining it, and this was his subtle way of giving me a closer look. He dug his hand into a small paper box and peeled off a chunk of half-frozen squid, a viscous clear liquid dripping off of it. He set the white flesh on the railing and without really looking, reached into his tackle box and retrieved a sharp fillet knife. With great precision, he first cut the white flesh down the middle, then into triangular strips. I was mesmerized, like a medical student standing on a mezzanine watching a skilled heart surgeon in action. He attached the strips loosely through the two hooks on his rig to mimic a squid tail, then satisfied with his workmanship, pulled his trusty old rod behind his head, whipped it forward, and hurled his line into the night sea and sat back down.

"Fish don't know or care if your rod cost five dollars or five hundred dollars," offered Lyman, reading my mind. "It's all about the bait and the wait. Give 'em what they want on that particular day, and be patient enough to let 'em take it."

I realized that Cat, the dermatologist from Lynnhaven, was noticeably quiet on the subject. I suppose it had something to do with the fact that he was wielding something called a Daiwa Saltiga Surf Spin 6000, list price about nine hundred dollars, and he'd caught fewer fish than any of the regulars. Lyman was right. It's more the musician than the violin.

Within seconds Lyman proved his theory. A quick snap of his wrist toward his right shoulder and it was fish on. Twenty seconds later he had a good sized croaker flopping in the air as he reeled in his line to the top of the pier. He deftly unhooked his catch and gently tossed it in the cooler alongside two dozen others that had met a similar fate. No fanfare, no whooping, no posing for pictures. Lyman Gregg was a man who seemed to fish with a purpose. He rebaited his hook and the line was ocean bound once again.

"What motivates you to fish every day?"

"Not every day. Take Sundays off."

"Okay, *almost* every day. . . why?"

He shrugged and allowed a wistful smile to touch his lips. "Just gives me somethin' to do. Somethin' to look forward to. A man's gotta have somethin' to look forward to."

"How many you catch a night?" I asked.

"As many as God thinks I should. All depends on the conditions. And I don't have no control over that part." I was beginning to realize that I was going to learn more from Lyman than just fishing.

I spent the next hour mingling with the boys on the pier and quizzing them about their rods and reels. I immediately learned their personal preferences on this subject were not only a great source of pride, but also bitter disagreement.

"An Elec-Tra-Mate don't hold a candle to a Calstar!" proclaimed Topper with robust disgust.

"You're crazy," shot back Rubes. "My Abu Garcia puts all your junk to shame." Rubes received a healthy round of razzing for his bold pronouncement. Criticizing another man's tackle was akin to casting aspersions about his wife.

About the only thing they agreed on, besides their dislike of tourists, was that you could equate any situation in life to angling. JLF they called it. . . just like fishing. If you were buying a car, going grocery shopping, or picking out a new hat, it was all just like fishing.

"Chasing women," said Rubes to the group, "if one bait doesn't work, try another."

"JLF!" they all responded in unison.

Later that night I ran five brisk miles down Sandfiddler Road, a long stretch of sand-covered asphalt as straight as arrowwood. I could close my eyes for blocks and run without worry. It felt good to push myself again and get my legs and lungs back after several weeks of laying off. The rising perspiration was therapeutic. With my flexible hours at the paper, I was quickly becoming a creature of the night, and these midnight outings were my reward for my labors. Long runs had always cleared my head and allowed me to organize the bric-a-brac of files that were tossed in a pile in the cortex of my brain. It had also been the time when I flipped through the pages of my mental scrapbook and reflected on my perfect days with Grace. Now I was running to forget.

Back home in my quiet condo, the only light in the room was emanating from the screen of my laptop. I penned a very thoughtful essay on the latest on tackle technology, comparing and contrasting the virtues of Star Rods, Lamiglas, Penn, Fenwick, Okuma, Tica, and Jarvis Gregg. The bard himself could not have written more eloquently about the new Shakespeare Ugly-Stiks. I honestly had no clue what I was talking about, but it certainly *sounded* as though I did, and that was all that mattered.

I proofread it, making certain that foreign phrases like *lure rating* and *aluminum oxide ring inserts* were being used in their proper context. *The Fish Finder* was a far cry from my days of chasing Wall Street knaves and plunderers, a painful reminder of how far I'd fallen in such a short time, but if this was going to be my job, then I intended to do it well. I labored over details, making absolutely sure that every word was valid. To make even the smallest mistake in this arena meant a precipitous loss of credibility in the fishing community. After an hour of staring at the strange collection of words on the screen, I finally decided that Mac Rellman's first byline was fit to print.

I knew it was better writing than the pedestrian prose of my immediate predecessor, but I also feared it might be overwritten for my target audience. There was only one way to figure out how it would be received. I hit SEND.

I crawled under the covers without setting the alarm. The only item on my "to do" list tomorrow was buy a new phone. As was my new habit, I dug into the tweed suitcase under the bed and fished out another of Grace's letters.

> My darling Seth,
> Thank you for loving me just as I am. No one has ever looked at me the way you do. I love the man who cups my face so tenderly with every visit. We have so many more memories to make. . . so many more pages to add to our scrapbook. . . let's explore a little more of "us."
>
> Always and forever,
> Grace

I turned off the light and tried to sleep.

# Chapter Ten

Any insecurities I had about being a capable fishing reporter were dispelled the very next evening as I made my nightly sojourn onto Little Island Pier. The boys loved *Fish Finder*, and immediately started firing story ideas at me faster than I could scratch them down on my notepad.

"You need to write somethin' about the *so-and-so* lure," was the recurring refrain. The acceptance into their selective fraternity brought me a happiness I hadn't felt in months.

I sat down next to Lyman as he slowly reeled in his line.

"How they bitin'?" I asked, the universal icebreaker on any pier in America.

"They're a little finicky tonight. I think the warm water's got 'em upset."

"Did you get a chance to read my article?"

"Yep."

"What did you think?"

"Not bad. You may have a future out here, Mac Rellman." Lyman glanced at me and smiled. "Mackerel Man. Clever."

It was then that I first realized that Lyman Gregg was a lot smarter and wiser than most men I'd ever met. I know it was a small thing, but he was the only one to notice the weak pun in my byline.

"Yeah. Kinda corny," I said, now slightly embarrassed that someone had figured it out.

"It's workin' for ya. I'm gonna assume that's not your real name?"

"Uh, no."

"I 'spose the reason why you don't use your real name is your business."

I didn't say anything, letting his words float away on the breeze.

Lyman let the moment pass as he switched out the squid on his hooks for bloodworms. He heaved his line back into the water and rested his rod against the railing. He wiped off the residue from the bloodworms on his pant leg, then reached into a threadbare duffel bag and pulled out a thick notebook binder. It was overstuffed with pages by at least fifty percent. Lyman flipped to the back and carefully jotted a few notes, like a monk inscribing divine words in a Bible. He gingerly placed the notebook back in the duffel bag and attended to the slack line on his pole.

"What's that?" I asked.

"Oh, just notes."

"Notes on what?"

"Little bit a everything."

I could see I was going to have to pry it out of him. Fortunately I was trained to do it. "Could you be a little more specific?"

"You're gonna keep askin' until I tell you, aren't you?"

"I suppose so. Can't help it. It's kinda what I do."

Without taking his eyes off his line, Lyman reached back into the duffel bag and pulled out the notebook. He handed it to me. "See for yourself."

I flipped through the warped pages and realized I was holding a fisherman's fortune of maritime information. Going back at least a decade, Lyman had recorded the fishing conditions of every single night he'd spent on the pier. Wind speeds, ocean currents, temperatures, baits used, fish caught, tides, sunsets, phases of the moon. . . everything you could imagine down to the last detail. As I sifted through these modern day Sea Scrolls it became crystal clear why Lyman's cooler was always fuller than everyone else's. It had nothing to do with luck. It was a highly scientific approach to angling, more meteorological than mystical. Of all the expensive equipment on the pier, he had the most valuable tool of all.

"This is amazing," I gushed as I tried to decipher all the notations. "Why don't the other guys use this?"

"They never asked."

I shook my head in amazement as I continued to read. Lyman Gregg definitely fished with a purpose. I still didn't know what it was.

Lyman violently whipped his pole back across his right shoulder and started cranking his reel, his wrist briskly rotating like a chef whisking a thin batter. The tip of his pole bent more than usual and when he stood up to complete the task, I realized there was more than a croaker on the end of the line. As the fish breached the water and Lyman pulled it through the dim light of the pier to the top of the railing, I saw him break into a toothy grin. It was the first time I'd seen anything other than workmanlike stoicism crease his face. Dangling off the hook was a zebra-striped creature the size of a serving platter. It looked like an angelfish you'd see in an aquarium at the dentist's office, only twenty times bigger.

"What is *that*?" I asked, moving closer to get a better look.

"This here's what they call a spadefish. Don't see too many of these." Lyman held his catch up in the light, examining its blunt snout and distinct markings.

By this time, Rubes, Topper, and several others had spotted Lyman's treasure and raced over to take a look.

"Nice fish!" gushed Rubes. "What were you usin'?"

"Bloodworm. Hit it on the first cast." Unlike many of the others on the LIP, Lyman was always willing to share information.

"I can 'member gittin' into a mess of spades down at Hatteras two years ago," chimed in Topper. "We had so many I ran outta bait. I caught the last two on a piece of bubblegum."

*Sure you did* was the unspoken collective thought swirling through the crowd.

"Really?" said Rubes. "What kinda bubblegum?"

"Big League Chew," fired back Topper so quickly and confidently that you suddenly believed he might actually be telling the truth. "Comes in a pouch. Shredded. But you can only chew it enough to soften it up. Any more'n that and it takes all the flavor out."

"I'll have to try that," said Rubes, winking at me behind Topper's back. Despite their incredulity, something told me that the other guys were going to secretly add a pouch of Big League Chew to their tackle boxes. You never know.

With the hubbub over Lyman's catch having run its course, the other fisherman meandered back to their usual perches. I noticed more than one was now changing over to bloodworms.

Lyman carefully unhooked his prized spadefish and placed it on top of the ice in his cooler. "Now *that's* gonna be some good eatin' right there."

"How do you cook a spadefish?" I asked, not that I was ever going to do it.

"I like to soak 'em overnight in some lemon juice, some seafood marinade, little bit a ginger spice, then bread 'em up next day with cornmeal and rosemary leaves and toss 'em in a hot skillet with olive oil. Boy, howdy. Don't get no better'n that." Lyman's mouth was visibly watering. He affixed another bloodworm to his hook and sent it flying. "Hey, Mac. . . why don't you write about how to fix 'em? Lotta people can catch fish, but ain't got the first notion as to how to make 'em taste good."

"You mean recipes?"

"Why not? Never been done. Might get ya some women readers. And from what little I know about you, it probably wouldn't hurt you to attract a few women. Think of it as bait." Lyman cranked his line taut as he broke into a wry smile, smoothing out the wrinkles on his forehead.

"I do all right," I said, a little defensively.

"I'm sure you do."

"I do!"

"Never hear you talk about a gal."

"Well I never hear you either."

There was a long pause. "Hmmph," was all he could muster.

I looked out across the water, deciding how much to reveal. "I had a girl. Didn't work out the way I hoped."

Lyman nodded. "If there's one thing that life has taught me, it's that not even the medicine of time can fully repair the lingering wounds of a tender human heart." He left it there, not explaining, and not probing me for any more. His gentle patience translated to all realms. We sat in silence as Lyman continued his quest for another spadefish and my mind wandered back to days of Grace.

Recipes became a regular feature in my Sunday piece. It meant about seven more inches I didn't have to research because Lyman spoon fed them to me. Best of all, they were a hit with our female readership. Women who were tired of trying to make a decent dinner from the catch-of-the-day their husbands dragged home in Igloo coolers suddenly had a new resource. Mac Rellman was their new best friend.

# Chapter Eleven

As the early tourist season slowly unfolded in mid-April, I discovered there is a certain rhythm to life at the beach. This unique world moves in a pattern that's as regular as the waves and their unceasing pursuit of the shoreline. As the temperatures warmed up, the activity on Sandbridge Beach increased tenfold and the rhythms were accentuated.

On Saturday afternoons, the tourists arrived for their three o'clock check-ins to the hundreds of rental properties. License plates from all over the Eastern Seaboard made the right turn onto Sandpiper Road and off to a week of seaside bliss. Remedies for sunburn pain were out of stock by Sunday night. By Monday, the garbage cans already reeked of discarded crab shells from Pungo Seafood. Wednesday was bingo night at the fire station. Friday night, the salt air was overwhelmed by the aroma of charcoal grills as family reunions savored one last cookout together. Saturday morning was a flurry of activity in the driveways of the rental houses with the stuffing of hastily packed suitcases into car trunks, strapping down fishing rods and beach chairs on roof racks, and tearstained hugs goodbye to friends and relatives. A year's worth of saving for vacation was spent, and all that remained of the week was the long car ride with sandy floorboards. Time to go home.

At precisely ten o'clock on Saturday morning, an army of maids arrived with vacuum cleaners and fresh linens, racing against the rhythm in preparation for the next round of new arrivals.

Even the regulars of the beach community, the "year-rounders," were creatures of habit and routine. I would see them all on the days I chose to run along the packed sand at the edge of the water.

Mornings brought dog walkers, surf fishers, bike riders, joggers, shell collectors, and old men with metal detectors, searching for recently buried treasure. The oceanfront decks were dotted with people practicing Tai Chi, yoga, and Pilates, or just enjoying fresh coffee and the morning paper.

On most mornings, I would see a man I only knew as Melvin. I wasn't sure if that was his first name or last, but it was written in faded magic marker on the side of a canvas tote bag he always had with him. Melvin sat cross-legged on a tattered blanket and played chess with himself, stroking the thin gray whiskers at the tip of his chin as he studied the worn wooden pieces on the board. He wore the same tired visor every day, often wore dark socks with sandals, and wore his reading glasses over his sunglasses instead of the other way around. I imagined Melvin had been some sort of professor or scientist who had somehow lost his way, or just decided to drop out of the mainstream and turn his thoughts and energy inward. I clearly remember our one and only conversation.

"Who's winning?" I jokingly asked him one day, pausing from my run to sip some water.

"I'm not sure," he replied in all seriousness, without even glancing up to see who had intruded upon his quietude. "There's still very much to be decided."

I changed my tone, realizing that ironic humor was not Melvin's strong suit. "How do you decide who wins?"

"The purpose of this exercise is not to win. The purpose is to train your mind to recognize all possibilities and be prepared to react to them. To not accept one's fate as pure destiny. So if your wife is thinking about leaving you, or your superiors feel it necessary to dismiss you from your job, you can see it coming, and make the necessary moves to prevent such calamities. And when I use the word 'superior,' that is only on paper." I tried to decipher the subtext of Melvin's proclamation, and if he were referring to any specific events in his own life. It seemed so. "It is only the fool who doesn't anticipate what his opponent will do. Not just his, or *her*, next move, but their next six or seven." He moved his white bishop from c1 to g5 and knocked over a black pawn with more force than was necessary. A hint of gleeful satisfaction washed over him as he cast the fallen pawn to the side. He made a notation in a spiral notebook and spun the board around to devise his plan of attack against such a worthy opponent. He seemed to be done talking.

"Well, good luck," was all I could think to say, feeling both pity and admiration for him. Melvin offered no response, verbally or otherwise, once again totally absorbed in the sixty-four squares of strategic battlefield on the board in front of him. Melvin was like so many other people who made their home along the sands. They shared an undercurrent of dysfunction that had washed them out of inland life. Here you were accepted. At the beach, nobody much cared where you'd been, only where you were going that night. You could invent a new life, better than the one you left behind, and not necessarily built on a foundation of truth. The sea was silent. It made no judgments. The ocean excused your foibles and embraced your fables. Eccentricity was not only tolerated, it was celebrated. The foamy waters and shifting sands of Sandbridge beckoned the Melvins of the world and provided them safe harbor. No wonder I liked it here.

As I resumed my run down the beach, I theorized where Melvin's journey had taken him, and what pain he might have endured that brought him to this point. I briefly pondered our similarities. I wondered if he were happy living life essentially alone. I wondered if I could do the same.

By late afternoon, when the winds and waves had kicked up, the surfers arrived with their waxes and wetsuits. A young woman in her early twenties danced untamed in the heavy sand outside her house, presumably to strengthen her ballet muscles. The only music was the tune playing in her head. She never seemed to care that people stopped and stared at her graceful leaps and twirls with either delight or derision.

A mere fifty yards off the shoreline, dolphins, usually in groups of four, would breach and disappear as they searched for an evening meal.

Every night at sundown, a year-rounder known to all as Gus would swell his bagpipes with eighty-year-old breath and let loose with some variation of *Scotland the Brave*. Depending on the wind, you could hear the piper's drone for miles and it always provided a soothing end to the day for my MacClellan blood.

As I learned from Lyman Gregg, even the fish maintained a rhythm. Blues and Spanish mackerel liked a south wind with clean water. Puppy drum feed off the sand fleas in dirty water. Cobia preferred warm water. Drum needed sixty-seven degrees. Most fish bite within four hours around the changing tide, but as soon as the wind shifts, it's all over. Time to go home.

My own rhythm over the last five weeks had become so routine, it bordered on a rut. I woke up most mornings around ten and put in a few lazy miles on the beach. As I loped along on these quiet retreats from civilization, I developed a fondness for the clever names people on Sandbridge gave to their houses like *Leg A' Sea*, *Sea-Air-Ahh*, and *Crabby Pelican*. Like the other year-rounders, this was how we landmarked the island. "Go down to *Bimini Breeze* and make a left." I came home, showered, then ate a bowl of cereal over the morning paper and swallowed two mugs of black coffee.

Lunch was always a peanut butter sandwich consumed slowly on the couch while always pondering the same question that consumed me. *Who set me up to fail, and why?* I was no closer to an answer, and starting to think I'd never get one.

After a meager dinner, usually some form of pasta, I would trek down to the pier to see what I could dig up. Around midnight I would file my report for *The Fish Finder*, then torture myself with another love letter from Grace.

Sometimes I would alter my pattern and read my own words to her. I was never as naturally creative as Grace, so I wrote many of my long letters to her on my laptop before copying them over in longhand and mailing them off. Now I owned a hard drive full of old sentiment. I clicked on a file labeled "color."

> My Darling Grace,
> How do you tell someone that you love them far beyond the meaning that word holds for most people? How can words alone possibly capture the excitement I feel when I'm about to see you, or the anguish that fills me every time we have to go our separate ways? The assembled talents of Byron, Keats, and Shelley could not adequately describe

what I feel for you. I hope you feel respected, needed, desired, admired, adored, beautiful, safe, and warm. I hope you feel excitement as well as contentment. I hope you know that you're cared about, thought about, worried about, and dreamt about. I hope that you know that I love you without hesitation, without limits, without conditions. You're the greatest gift I've ever received, and I will protect and treasure that gift forever. Come with me to a world where tears only flow from laughter and joy, and where voices are only raised to sing above the radio.

All my love,
Seth

I shut down my electronic memory book. Deep sleep remained elusive.

# Chapter Twelve

I stood at the end of the pier and fixed my eyes on the full moon in the eastern sky. Its light spread like a carpet across the water, beckoning me to step onto it and follow. The water below churned like my stomach. It had been almost two months since I'd first set foot on this island. I enjoyed a little bit of celebrity in my new world through *The Fish Finder*. I had a sense of belonging in a world where I didn't know anybody's real name. Yet I still felt lost. Empty. Lacking purpose. I wondered how much longer I could survive just writing about Sting Silver lures and coastlock snap swivels.

I soon learned the most enjoyable aspect of my new occupation was taking pictures of people holding fish. For the first time in my professional life, people were happy to see me pointing a camera at them. The proud smiles I could create just by pulling out my digital Canon were immediate and lasting. My shots were rather basic, but it was the best I could do using a flash against a night sky. Not that it mattered. I soon discovered my amateur photography work was being clipped out of the newspaper and put into picture frames and scrapbooks all over the island. It was literally a snapshot of that special moment in time when they'd landed "the big one" and they didn't have to use outstretched hands to prove to the folks at home that they were telling the truth about their fish tale.

I focused my attention on the men clinging with hope to their assorted tackle. "Anything tonight?" I asked, pulling out my notepad. A dozen heads shook "no" in unison.

"But keep your camera handy," said Topper. "I feel a state record is swimming my way. And I'll give you the exclusive interview."

"Thanks, Top," I replied. "Because we all know the competition for exclusivity out here is fierce."

My comment brought a few smiles, but not the usual round of cackling. There seemed to be a gnawing uneasiness in the air that I couldn't explain.

Rubes took it upon himself to get Topper going and ease some of the tension. "Hey, Topper, tell us again about that time you caught a barracuda with a car key."

Topper nodded as he took the bait, happy to oblige. "It was down at Debordieu, South Carolina, and it was actually a house key. We were 'bout five miles out, water as smooth as an ice rink." He rested his pole against the railing so he could get his hands involved in the telling of the story. As Topper held court, nobody really believed what they were hearing, but they all certainly listened.

I ambled back to the middle of the pier where Lyman was slowly reeling in. I leaned over the railing next to him and watched the swell of the waves. For no particular reason my thoughts wandered back to an evening in Paris when Grace bought two dozen flowers from a poor little girl, then started randomly handing them out to passersby as we strolled through St. Germain. It was a simple gesture that made everyone happy, especially me.

"You okay over there?" asked Lyman.

I tore away from the misery of my history and nodded. "Sorry, just lost in thought for a moment."

"You seem to do that quite a bit."

"Yeah. It's my hobby. You know, JLF."

Lyman chuckled and cast his line in the moonlit surf. I changed the subject. "Doesn't seem like anybody's catchin' anything tonight." I gestured to the end of the pier where faces and coolers sat empty. "They all seem a little restless over there. Uneasy. Like someone died."

"Dunno," was all Lyman offered. I sensed that he did.

"Makes my job a lot harder, ya know, when you people fail to cooperate."

Lyman smiled. "Patience."

Patience and optimism. Something Lyman had in abundant quantities. Maybe that's what brought him out here night after night to try his luck. Or maybe he was as lonely as I was. I had learned from Rubes that Lyman was a widower. No wonder he never talked about a woman in his life. I'd spent months on the pier before I noticed that Lyman had carved his wife's initials in the weathered boards of the railing. SPG. Sarah Peyton Gregg.

I stood up and tucked my notepad into the back pocket of my jeans. "Good luck, boys," I said, the same way I signed off every night. I slowly walked off the pier back to the parking lot. Without anything to write about, I already knew my five mile run later that night would turn into eight, followed by hours of aimless pacing, ceiling staring, and fitful sleep.

As my moccasins sank into the deep sand at the end of the pier, I wondered about Grace. Was she at peace? I hoped so. I dug into my pocket and pulled out my precious half of our seashell. I held it in my fingertips, examining it by the bright light of the moon. The shell was linen white with ridges smoothed by years of being tossed about in Atlantic waves. Singularly unremarkable, yet entirely symbolic. It took me back to the day I'd first met Grace on Folly Beach. It was the one piece of God's majesty that reminded me that shifting sands reveal miracles, and one never knows what may wash up after a storm. And it was a reminder that each shell on the beach is in fact only half of what used to be a pair. In the vastness of the ocean, there is only one perfect match. . . there is only one other shell that completes it and makes it whole. Every time I looked at that seashell, I knew that without Grace, I would never again feel complete. As I twirled the shell through my fingertips, I looked up. The moon was brighter than I'd seen it in months. For years we'd had a pact to look at the moon every night. It was our connection across time and space. I drew in the deepest breath I could find. The taste of salt air was the one thing that saved me, night after lonely night. It was the elixir that refreshed me, restored part of my wounded soul, and made me believe that tomorrow might somehow be different than today. The ocean's night air held more than moisture. It held hope. Hope that whenever there is water beside you and a moon above you, anything is possible.

Several hours later I eased into bed and read myself to sleep.

My darling Seth,
I have spoken to the moon several times this weekend, shining so round and bright. It's the link that joins us. . . as if God narrows the distance between us. I'm counting on that day when all of nature is perfectly aligned and my silvery moon beams down on us, hand in hand. When life edges in with the harsh realities of the miles between us, I prefer to stare at the moon and say, "I'll think about it tomorrow."

We Belong Together,
Grace

As I drifted off, I noticed a trace of moonlight easing through the windowpane. Goodnight, Grace.

# Chapter Thirteen

As I arrived at the LIP the next night, the moon was hidden. A wall of fog crept towards me as I looked northward toward Virginia Beach, the distant lights from the boardwalk slowly disappearing in the mist. By the time I reached the end of the pier, a light rain had started to fall.

Rubes, Topper, and Lyman were the only ones who'd ventured out on a night like this. Nobody was talking other than a few mutterings about the lack of action.

"What's making news?" I asked brightly. I didn't anticipate the furtive glances Rubes and Topper shot at each other.

Like the bristles on the back of a hunting dog, my investigative reporter senses suddenly bloomed to life. I spread my legs wider and jammed my hands into my front pockets. "Something's going on out here, and it's got you all knotted up. You might as well tell me, because I'm gonna find out sooner or later."

Rubes and Topper both looked at Lyman for guidance. "Might as well tell him," nodded Lyman.

Rubes and Topper leaned their poles against the railing and moved in closer, as if there were anyone within a half a mile of the pier who could possibly overhear whatever secrets they were about to disclose. Lyman continued to fish.

Topper began. "Word is, there's somethin' weird that's got into the water." He looked at Rubes for verification of his bold declaration. "There's some kinda jellyfish that's stingin' people and makin' 'em real sick."

"Jellyfish?" I repeated, pulling out my notepad and trying my best to protect it against the drizzle. I actually felt my pulse beat a little faster. Was this really newsworthy, or just more hyperbole from Topper? "Where'd you hear this?" I asked in my best investigative reporter voice.

"Didn't hear it," said Rubes. "Saw it."

"What exactly did you see?"

The three of them exchanged nervous glances, silently drawing straws to decide who would answer. Rubes finally spoke up. "Yesterday afternoon, about four o'clock, we see this guy come runnin' out of the water, and then collapse on the beach, right over there." He pointed south towards False Cape. "The guy was screaming bloody murder that he'd been stung by somethin'. There was a woman with him and she comes runnin' down the beach and yells up to us to call 911. I walked down there to get a closer look. Coupla minutes later Beach Patrol shows up, and then after awhile, an ambulance pulls up in the parking lot and they cart him off. Looked to me like he was in really bad shape."

Topper chimed in. "A lot of us think it's why the fish ain't bitin'." Lyman shook his head. He wasn't convinced about that part of the story.

"Does anybody else know about this?" I asked the group.

Rubes shrugged his shoulders. "There was only the two of 'em out there, but last night I mentioned it to a coupla guys over in Pungo and they told me they'd heard rumors of a woman gettin' stung by somethin' really bad last week."

"The guy who responded from the Beach Patrol. . . do you know his name?"

"It was a girl. Don't know her name, but I know she hangs out at the Baja most nights."

I pointed in the general direction of the Back Bay. "This Baja? The one right across the street?"

"Yep," nodded Rubes. "She's in there everytime I've ever been there."

"How will I spot her?"

"It's easy," said Rubes. "Just look around and see all the women that are smiling and havin' a good time, and then you'll know, that ain't her."

I closed my notepad and tucked it into my back pocket. I tried to maintain a casual demeanor, but inside, my heart was racing. This had the potential to be a story with actual news value. "Well thanks for letting me know. I'll look into it."

As I turned and walked down the wet planks of the pier, Lyman came up behind me. I'd never seen him move that fast.

"Hey, Mac," he called out in a loud whisper.

I stopped under the shrouded light of the lamppost. "Yeah?"

Lyman glanced over his shoulder before speaking. "You might want to look up the word Irukandji." He made the quiet declaration in the same nervous hushed tone I'd heard from a hundred anonymous sources I'd talked to over the years with the *Herald*.

I snatched my notepad out of my back pocket and scribbled the phonetic pronunciation. "Ear-uh-CON-gee?" I repeated.

"That's right. Irukandji." Lyman nodded.

"What is it?"

"Look it up." Lyman walked backwards for two steps, then turned around and headed back toward the end of the pier.

Ten minutes later I'd driven the quarter-mile back to the Baja. It was one of only two restaurants on the island, and a regular hangout for locals. It provided fine seafood dining in the front, and a lively bar in the back.

A local blues band blasted out covers of Stevie Ray Vaughan and Creedence Clearwater Revival as I eased into the throng, unnoticed. It was primarily the surfing crowd. Lots of sun-bleached hair and pooka shell necklaces. It was more crowded inside than usual as the nightly dodgeball game out back had been suspended because of the rain. The leather couches were overflowing with arms and legs and there was a waiting line for the pool table.

A Hobie longboard hung over the colorful array of top shelf liquors behind the bar. I squeezed my way in between two people and held up my index finger, trying to catch the lone bartender's attention. He was the classic surfer type with a wild shock of blond hair and matching macramé choker and bracelets. He moved with the finesse and economy of motion of a matador, filling drink orders with amazing speed as thirsty patrons kept yelling "Trey! Trey!" over the din of the drummer.

"Whatcha need?" Trey called to me over the cacophony as he whipped together fruity rum drinks for two girls who simply waved at him.

"Guinness," I yelled.

"Half-pint or full? You look like a full guy!" he yelled back, already filling a pint glass with the thick brown stout. Perfectly poured, he set it in front of me.

I handed him a five. "We're good."

"Thanks, man!" Trey slapped the bill into the cash register, pulled out a dollar tip, tossed it in a jar and rang a ship's dinner bell mounted on the bar. He was already filling another drink order before the ringing had evaporated.

I scanned the bar, trying to figure out who might be the mystery lifeguard I was trying to find. It didn't take long to spot a likely candidate. She was at the end of the bar, seated in between two couples, and clearly alone. Short, feathered brown hair, no makeup or jewelry, and a navy blue tank top that showcased the broad shoulders and muscled arms of a swimmer. The most striking feature of a very attractive face were her emerald green eyes, but I could barely see them because they were transfixed on the whiskey sour in front of her. It had to be her. With my instincts as an investigative reporter kicking in, I watched her closely. It's amazing what you can learn about somebody without ever asking a question. Just observe their actions and interactions with those around them and their dossier begins to write itself. There was no chance she'd catch me staring at her because her eyes never lifted from the glass in front of her. I noticed as she finished the last swallow of her cocktail, Trey immediately put a fresh one in front of her. No money changed hands and I wondered what their connection might be. Romantic? Perhaps. But then why hadn't she smiled, or even spoken to him, for nearly a half an hour? The third time this happened in a span of fifteen minutes, I also realized that Trey was actually shorting her drinks. He was packing her glass with ice and cutting the bartender's standard four count for an ounce and a half of liquor down to just two on his free pours. Odd. Usually if a bartender has romantic intentions toward a woman he does just the opposite. Peculiar.

After watching her emerald eyes become glassier after what had been at least five cocktails, it dawned on me. There are fewer things sadder than an alcoholic. Even worse if she's young and pretty. As someone who runs fifteen miles at a clip in a futile effort to forget his past, I had seen that faraway look before.

A stool opened up next to her and I seized the opportunity. I grabbed my pint glass and quickly moved through the crowd and sat next to her. She didn't acknowledge the presence of her new neighbor.

"Hi," I said brightly. "My name's Mac."

She slowly cocked her head to one side to see who was intruding in her space. She flicked her chin upwards a half an inch, the most imperceptible and unwelcoming of greetings possible. She returned her gaze to the fascinating ice in her vanishing cocktail.

"You alone?" I asked.

"Clearly," came a terse reply. "And I'd like to keep it that way." She took another sip and angled her shoulder away from me.

I was used to people not answering my questions. Undaunted, I continued. "Do you work for the Beach Patrol?"

She turned her neck to face me. "I'm sorry, I don't do small talk. I don't do bar talk. I don't do whatever it is you want to do. So we have two choices. Either you can stop talking, or I can get up and leave."

My backdoor approach had clearly failed, so I decided to pound on the front entrance. "I'm a reporter for *The Bay Breeze*. Mac Rellman."

"Goodbye." She polished off her drink and brusquely walked away. As I sat there and tried to figure out what just happened, I saw Trey shaking his head with dismay.

I angled my way through the crowd and followed her out the door into the gravel parking lot.

"Go away!" she yelled over her shoulder as she marched into the night.

"Wait! I just want to talk to you!" I had to run to catch up. "Can I just ask a coupla questions?"

"What's your angle? Anniversary story? Sorry, pal, you're off by a few weeks."

"I don't know what you're talking about. . . anniversary? Anniversary of what?"

"Back off!" she yelled, now breaking into a jog, despite her slightly inebriated state.

I picked up the pace to keep up. "Look, I honestly don't know what you mean. I'm a lowly fishing reporter. . . and I *do* mean lowly. I just want to talk to you about the beach. You *are* with the Beach Patrol, right?"

She picked up the pace. "Listen, pal. I live two miles from here. You're gonna run outta breath before I do, so you might as well save it."

I smiled and let out a wry chuckle. "I don't think so."

She gave me an *oh yeah?* kind of glance and accelerated even more. About a 7:30-mile pace. Very impressive, I thought, especially considering the amount of whiskey coursing through her veins. I stayed with her, stride for stride, barely breathing hard. I sensed that irritated her more than just my mere presence. She shifted to another gear and was now running about a 6:50. I stayed on her shoulder, unrelenting. We ran in silence down Sandpiper Road for over a mile. This was no longer a conversation. It was a competition, like spontaneous drag racing, and she was determined that I would finish second. I was determined to disappoint her. After one final burst of speed in an unsuccessful attempt to put me in the ground, she abruptly quit. She bent over, hands on knees, heaving for breath. I was worried she might start retching from the alcohol, but she held it in.

"Good run," I said between inhalations, the same thing I'd said to many a worthy competitor at finish lines over the years. She waved one hand in my direction and nodded in agreement. She probably still loathed me, but at least I'd earned a little respect and perhaps gained a foothold on the wall that surrounded her castle.

"A guy named Rubes told me you might help me."

"Rubes?" she asked, still gulping air. "Rubes who? I don't know anybody named Rubes."

"He's just a guy I see every night on the pier. Like I said, I'm the fishing reporter for *The Bay Breeze*. Mac Rellman? *The Fish Finder?*"

She shook her head. No recognition. She finally stood upright and walked in circles with her hands on her hips, breathing a little more evenly. For the first time, her tone softened. "So what do you want with me? I don't fish."

"I just need to ask you about a call you responded to yesterday afternoon."

"I respond to lots of calls."

"There's a rumor that this guy got some really bad jellyfish stings. They rushed him to the hospital in an ambulance."

"Yeah, I was there. It was down on the other side of False Cape. The guy was screaming in pain and starting to convulse. I couldn't really tell what was wrong with him."

"How'd you treat him?"

"First thing I did was rinse his leg with some saltwater, then dumped some good old-fashioned vinegar on the sting. Didn't seem to help much, so I called for an ambulance, wrote up the report, and that was it. To be honest, I wasn't totally sure what I was dealing with because the victim didn't really have any visible welts like you usually get with a jellyfish."

"Didn't that strike you as strange?"

"Hang around the beach long enough and nothing seems strange anymore."

I pulled my notepad from my back pocket and read the word Lyman had given me an hour before. "Does the word Irukandji mean anything to you?"

She shook her head. "Nope. Why you askin'?"

"Don't know. Yet." I slid my notepad back into my pocket. "Well thanks for talking to me. By the way, what's your name?"

"Jenna. Jenna Czarnecki."

"Zarnecki with a Z?"

"Czarnecki with a C. The C is silent."

"Nice to meet you. Hey, I'm sorry we got off on the wrong foot back there. I didn't mean to—"

"Forget it," she said, waving me off. "The fact that you didn't know my name is explanation enough."

"What were you talking about earlier? Anniversary of what?"

"Again, forget it."

"All right. Fair enough."

"How you gonna get back to the Baja?" asked Jenna.

"No problem. It's just a couple miles back."

"And from what I just witnessed, a coupla miles isn't all that big a deal to you. Of all the losers in the bar, I had to tangle with the one guy who probably has a dozen marathon stickers on his back windshield."

"What can I say? I have no life."

"Next time we race, it's in water. I'll dust you there."

"Oh, was that a race? Because if it was, I guess that means I won."

Jenna smiled for the first time all night. "Whatever. You're still a loser."

I nodded. She had no idea how on the mark she was. "Goodnight, Jenna Czarnecki with a C. Again, thanks for talking to me." She nodded as I turned to run back to the Baja.

"Hey!" she called after me. "If you really want to find out what happened to that guy, why don't you find out who treated him?"

I turned back and raised my index finger in the air as if to say *that's a great idea!* I spun back around and raced away.

Later that night I looked up the word Irukandji. My pulse quickened. No wonder all the guys on the pier looked seasick. Usually I was too sad to sleep, but tonight, I was too excited. All I could think about was one word: redemption.

# Chapter Fourteen

By ten o'clock the next morning I was already showered and shaved and standing inside the Sandbridge Volunteer Rescue headquarters. I was poised to take notes. Find clues. Put together the puzzle of a shadowed mystery. I felt like there was fresh blood racing through my veins.

Firefighters are helpful people by nature, and when they're not out on a call, they're often bored, which may explain why a guy named Eddie was exceedingly generous with his time when I asked about recent calls by the Rescue Squad.

"Let's see," said Eddie, tracing his finger down the columns of the log book. "Yep, here it is. We answered a call down at False Cape. Just after four o'clock. Jellyfish stings. That's gotta be what you're lookin' for." He spun the log book around on the countertop to give me a better view.

"Do you know who took the call?"

Eddie looked at a roster pinned to a corkboard. "That woulda been. . . hmmm. . . looks like Watts and Kwiatkowski were on last night."

"Are they here?"

Eddie checked the roster again. "No, they don't rotate in until Monday. But you can probably find Kwiatkowski workin' over at Margie and Ray's."

"Thanks. Really appreciate it."

I'd only eaten there once before, but I'd already decided that Margie and Ray's was the best seafood place in all of Tidewater, Virginia. Not the finest, but the best. It was primarily frequented by locals or the few lucky tourists who had discovered it. It stood alone along Sandbridge Road, a few miles off the island, and looked like it had been built in stages. As profits came in, walls went up. Half restaurant and bar, half tackle shop, it was the only place I'd ever seen where you could leave with a stomach full of fresh lobster or a bucket full of fresh bait. Barrel drinks and barrel swivels all under one roof.

The gravel parking lot was filled with pickup trucks and sport utility vehicles with oversized tires, rod holders, and gun racks. It was only eleven o'clock in the morning, but plumbers, electricians, and construction workers who'd been on the clock since dawn were already sitting down to lunch.

I wandered in and sat down at the bar they called the Mako Lounge and put my elbows on the tile surface. The young waitress, bleached blonde and a little plump, was immediately in front of me.

"Whatcha need, Hon?"

"Sweet tea."

"Lemon?"

"Sure."

As she poured me a tall glass of the official beverage of the South, I noticed the forty or so one dollar bills taped randomly along the shelves of the liquor bottles. They were autographed by regulars in black magic marker. One was signed by someone named Jenna. That could not possibly be a coincidence.

The waitress slid my iced tea over to me and I handed her two dollars.

"What else, Hon? You need a menu?"

"Actually, I'm looking for a guy named Kwiatkowski. They told me down at the Rescue Squad that I might find him here."

"Who are you?"

"My name's Mac Rellman. I'm the fishing reporter for *The Bay Breeze.*"

She gave me that nod that says both *that's nice* and *I've never heard of you.* "I think Walt's in the back. I'll see if he's busy."

As I sat there, my journalistic instincts kicked in and I tried to absorb as much information about my surroundings in the shortest time possible. Like any good neighborhood watering hole, the Mako was full of regulars. A guy they all called Italian Joey was holding court on the end of the bar, turning down numerous offers from the others for free beers. He appeared to have been some kind of ballplayer in an earlier life. An older woman whose face was creased by years of chain smoking walked through the lounge, touching every man she saw and apparently fishing for compliments about her new hair extensions. Her exit was trailed by the whispered nickname "Runaround Rita." This was life for so many people at the beach. Living out their days in a daily routine that lacked direction and ambition, but filled with the numbing therapy of alcohol and facile conversation. Sometimes I wondered what they knew about happiness that I didn't.

Two minutes later, Walt Kwiatkowski was headed my way, wiping his hands on a dirty white apron before extending his handshake. He was every bit of six foot five and a muscular 250 pounds. Short cropped hair and a day's growth of beard. Exactly the kind of guy you'd want to see stepping out of an ambulance if you were in distress.

"How ya doin? I'm Walt," he said with a friendly smile and an accent that carried a hint of Maryland's Eastern Shore.

"I'm Mac Rellman. I'm with *The Bay Bree*—"

"I know who you are. I read your stuff. It's good. In fact, I stole your stuffed flounder recipe. Big hit here!"

"Thanks, but I can't really take credit."

"You should. I did!" He ushered me over to the table next to the window. "Whaddya need from me? I don't fish. And I'm not givin' away any recipes."

I flipped open my reporter's pad. "I wanted to ask you about a call you went on last evening, down at False Cape. Victim suffering from severe jellyfish stings. Does that ring a bell?"

"Absolutely. He was in bad shape. Convulsions, dizziness, nausea, and excruciating pain. I think it musta been some kinda allergic reaction. Never seen nothin' like it from a jellyfish sting."

"What'd you do?"

"After we loaded him up, I applied some Benadryl cream and then some ice packs. That keeps any stinging cells that haven't fired yet from releasing any more venom. Aside from that, not much more I could do until I got him to a doctor."

"What hospital did you take him to? Sentara General? "

"No. The woman who was with him, I'm assuming it was his wife, insisted we take him to a doctor's office on Princess Anne Road. I think it was a friend of theirs, or maybe their regular doc, I can't remember. . . lot going on at that point. But it was rush hour and this doc was about twenty minutes closer than the hospital, and like I said, my guy was in excruciating pain, so that was fine with me. The doc was outside waiting on us when we rolled up, so I dropped off the patient, signed him out, and that was it. We already had another call comin' in."

"Is that normal procedure? To drop off a patient at a doctor's office and not the emergency room?"

"Well, I wouldn't say it's common, but it does happen. Some people just feel more comfortable seein' a doctor they already know." Kwiatkowski suddenly narrowed his eyes and folded his arms in a defensive stance. "I didn't break any rules, if that's what you're drivin' at."

"No, no, no!" I assured him. He relaxed a little. "Do you remember the doctor's name?"

Kwiatkowski thought for a moment, then shook his head. "No. Sure don't. It all kinda happened in a hurry. And I go on a lot of calls."

"Where on Princess Anne was his office? Do you recall that?"

"Yeah. Right where Princess Anne turns into General Booth Boulevard. There's a 7-11 there. It's Tuscany Drive, and there's some medical offices right there. Seems to me it was the first one you come to."

I quickly wrote it down on my pad. "Thanks. That helps a lot."

"Why do you want to know about all this?"

"I really don't know, to be honest. I just heard about this guy getting stung really badly and wanted to see if there was anything to it."

"Who knows. I treat a hundred jellyfish stings a year, but I've never seen anyone in such terrible pain, not even a little kid. It was more like he'd been snake bit, or hit by a blow dart, not just a jellyfish."

"I appreciate your time, Walt. And next time I'm in, I'll try the stuffed flounder."

"You should. Old family recipe!" He winked and shook my hand, then disappeared back into the kitchen.

It was only a short drive to the intersection of General Booth Boulevard and Tuscany Drive, where Walt Kwiatkowski told me I could find the doctor's office where he'd dropped off his jellyfish victim. The building had a distinctive rhyming address: 105 Tuscany Drive. There was only a small sign outside with the name "Dr. Dirk Hartog," and only two other cars in the parking lot; a silver BMW convertible and an old Honda Civic with faded green paint and red packing tape holding together a broken taillight. I wasn't sure, but my instincts told me I was in the right place.

The sparsely furnished waiting room was empty except for the young receptionist behind a desk. She wore blue jeans, a brown peasant smock, and a tiny diamond stud in the crease of her nose. Her pageboy haircut was unnaturally black, the color of shoe polish, except for a patch of crimson from the nape of her neck up to her right ear. It struck me as odd that she was particularly pale-skinned for a young woman who lived at the beach. They apparently weren't that busy because she was fully engrossed in a Stephen King novel.

"Hello?" The young woman jumped with a start. I assumed her nervousness was brought on by the chilling prose of King's *The Tommyknockers*.

"I'm here to see Dr. Hartog. Is he available?"

"Dr. Hartog? No, I'm sorry. He's with a patient."

"Hmmm," I said, nodding. "A patient, you say?"

"That's right." Her continued nervousness, coupled with the fact that there were only two cars in the parking lot, sparked that primal instinct in me that she was lying. I'd been lied to so many times over the years that I could smell it on someone like perfume. It was never productive to immediately call them on it. Much better to allow them to continue to keep lying to you as you jotted notes and then later separated the gold from the dross. It was my turn to lie to her.

"But I have an appointment with Dr. Hartog. Could you check the book to see if I'm on it?" That seemed to throw her into deeper consternation. With growing hesitancy, she fished around in the drawers to locate an appointment book. No luck.

"I'm sorry, sir, but I'm just temping here. I can't seem to find an appointment book."

That explained everything. She wasn't lying. She was just incompetent. My guess was the doctor was napping on his lunch hour or doing some online stock trading in the back room and told this young girl that he was not to be disturbed. "Could you do me a favor and just buzz him? Tell him a Mr. Irukandji is here for his appointment."

She nodded and picked up the phone. "Dr. Hartog? There's a Mr. Irukandji out here to see you. Says he has an appointment." She nodded into the phone as if someone could see her. "Yes, sir. I'll send him in."

Seconds later I was through the door of the anteroom and walking down a short hallway. A balding man in his early forties emerged from an examining room, wiping off the remnants of lunch. I was wrong about the napping, but close. The wrapper in the trashcan told me he'd just enjoyed a Zero's sub sandwich and had not wanted to be disturbed in the middle of it. I couldn't blame him. He'd been avoiding me, but the name Irukandji had clearly summoned his attention and given me audience.

"Well now," he said, motioning me into his office. He had the inkling of a British accent. I couldn't quite place it, and thought perhaps it was the voice of someone who'd grown up on the Outer Banks of North Carolina, who to this day still carried the vocal flavor of their English ancestors. "Since I know your name isn't Irukandji, what is it? And why on earth would you introduce yourself in such a manner?"

"The fact that it got your attention tells me I'm on the right track."

"Oh? And what track might that be?"

I flipped open my reporter's pad, more to make myself look official than to actually refer to my notes. "Yesterday, an ambulance brought a man here to your office. He'd apparently been stung by some kind of jellyfish. The rumor out there is that it was Irukandji. Are you familiar with that?"

"The incident, or the jellyfish?"

"Both."

"Unfortunately, because of doctor-patient confidentiality, I can't really tell you anything."

"Not even if you treated a victim?"

"Not even that. I'm sorry. I'd like to help you, but blame HIPAA laws."

I couldn't tell if he was being evasive or principled. I pressed on. "Can I at least ask you what you know about the Irukandji?"

He thought for a moment, tilting his head from side to side as he gauged the depth of his response. What followed sounded like a recitation from the pages of Henry Gray's *Anatomy of the Human Body*. "One of the most venomous creatures on earth. After envenomation, the victim suffers from intense pain, welts, cramps, vomiting, profuse sweating, headache, agitation, rapid heart rate, and very high blood pressure. This can lead to cerebrovascular hemorrhage, cardiomyopathy, cardiogenic pulmonary oedema, supraventricular tachycardia, a whole host of problems, including death."

I was more than impressed as I wrote furiously on my notepad, mostly phonetically. I got the feeling that Dr. Hartog had recently reviewed this subject. "So, hypothetically speaking, if you ever saw a patient who'd been stung by an Irukandji, how would you treat him?"

"Hypothetically?"

"Absolutely. Not that you ever have, or ever will. . . but on the off chance you ever do."

"The initial treatment is usually an alpha-blocking agent, then, depending on how the patient responds, some sort of analgesic like pethidine. Morphine has also been shown to be effective."

"You seem to know a lot about this particular subject."

"I'm a doctor. I'm supposed to know a lot about a lot of things."

"I guess that's a good thing."

"My patients seem to think so. I'm also an avid diver, so I probably know more about sea life than most physicians. I could talk for hours about the Ficus filosa seashell if you'd prefer." I smiled and shook my head as Dr. Hartog shifted in his seat and leaned forward. "You've been asking all the questions, so do you mind if I ask a few?"

"Not at all."

"Why the keen interest in the Irukandji? They're indigenous to Australia. You planning a trip there?"

"No. My concern is that the Irukandji has made a trip *here*. And I get the sense that you share the same concern."

Dr. Hartog rubbed the bottom of his chin as he looked up at the ceiling. He was clearly measuring his response. "As you probably know, there are any number of creatures in the sea capable of producing a venomous sting that can cause a serious reaction. I've seen patients go into anaphylactic shock from a common stingray sting. Even die from it."

"What's your point?"

"My point is, I don't see the wisdom in stirring up some kind of health scare unnecessarily. I know it's your job to sell newspapers, but you need to consider the impact on the community. Remember the movie *Jaws*? Do you know how many people still won't go in the ocean just because of that film?"

"But that was fiction."

"The lesson still applies. Even asking questions about something like this can spread ugly rumors."

"Asking questions is my job. And what's the harm in poking around if there's nothing to hide?"

"I'm just asking you to proceed with caution. A beach community is like a fragile ecosystem. You change one thing. . . raise the temperature by even a single degree. . . and there's a cascading effect with consequences you cannot anticipate."

I nodded silently. He raised a good point, but I had to balance that against warning the public if there was indeed a true health danger. Right now, I simply didn't know.

Dr. Hartog suddenly stood up. "Will you excuse me for one moment?"

"Sure."

Before exiting, Hartog purposefully tucked a file that had been sitting on his desk calendar into his top drawer. "I'll be right back."

"Take your time." He breezed past me and left the room. Any investigative journalist worth his salt will tell you that the first thing you always do when you're left alone in a room is scan for information that might help you. I'm not certain of the legality of this kind of snooping, mostly because I never asked, but it was common practice in my line of work. If they were foolish enough to leave important information sitting around, reporters needed to be enterprising enough to seek it out. I had no idea what was inside that file that Hartog had just tucked inside his drawer, but I knew I only had a few moments to find out.

I made sure the hallway was empty, then pushed the office door nearly shut. I scrambled to the desk and flipped open the file. Even I was stunned by what I saw. The word Irukandji was prominently written in several places on several medical forms. At least two patients had been in for Irukandji stings. Dr. Hartog wasn't just knowledgeable on the symptoms and treatments, he was also recently rehearsed. Having no time to absorb everything I was reading, I took out my new cell phone, which was equipped with a better camera than the one I'd pitched in the ocean, and snapped pictures as quickly as I could as I flipped through the documents. Within half a minute I felt like I'd captured all the pertinent information and I quickly tucked the file back into its hiding place. I could hear footsteps in the hallway as I scooted back around to my seat. I worked hard to look nonchalant as Hartog walked back into the office.

"Sorry about that. I had to check on something. My day's about to get a lot busier."

I stood to leave. "I understand. And I appreciate your time."

"Glad to do it. And honestly, I think you're paddling up the wrong creek on this one."

"Yeah, you're probably right. Oh well. Thanks for your time."

I now knew Hartog was flat out lying to me as he looked me straight in the eye and shook my hand as he ushered me out of his office. I just couldn't figure out why.

For no other reason than pure reporter's instinct, I took a good long look at the green Honda in the parking lot as I drove away from Dr. Hartog's office. I made mental notes of the parking sticker for Old Dominion University and the airbrushed license plate with the name *Hayley* on the front. I hoped she would make enough money from her temp job to fix her broken taillight.

Fifteen minutes later, I was sitting outside an office of the Virginia Aquarium & Marine Science Center on General Booth Boulevard.

Every sea creature imaginable was swimming in the 800,000 gallons of habitat here, but I was only interested in one, and how in the world it could have ended up in Sandbridge.

I'd called ahead and made an appointment with Dr. Paula Bethesda. She'd been incredibly friendly on the phone, and just as accommodating when she emerged from her office and greeted me with a firm handshake. Tall, even in low heels, tortoise shell glasses, and brunette hair pulled back in a bun. Her name was stitched in cursive on her white lab coat. She just *looked* smart.

"Mr. Rellman? I'm Dr. Bethesda."

"Thanks for meeting with me on such short notice."

"It's nice to meet you in person. I enjoy your articles."

I was shocked. "*You* read *The Fish Finder*?"

"Oh yes. Enjoy it very much. Especially the recipes." Her eyes twinkled. She was not your typical research scientist. "Come on in. Let's talk." I would need to thank Lyman and his recipes for opening at least two doors for me that day.

We sat down in her small office, made more cramped by shelves loaded with books on marine life and assorted shells and pink coral. She put on glasses that hung on the tip of her nose and opened a large textbook to a page that she'd bookmarked. "You wanted to know about the Irukandji jellyfish, is that right?"

"Yes."

"Irukandji," she read aloud. "A close relative to the box jellyfish. Scientific name Carukia or Carakua barnesi and the recently discovered Malo kingi. Found primarily in the waters of northern Australia around the Great Barrier Reef. Named for the Irukandji people of Cairns, Australia. Very small. . . just two and a half centimeters, about the size of a fingernail if you include the four thin tentacles. Believed to be the most venomous creature in the world. Quite a few deaths reported in the waters off Australia. Let's see. . . what else. . . it says here they thrive in water of eighty-two degrees Fahrenheit."

"What's the average ocean temperature at Virginia Beach?"

"Upper seventies is the average range in the summer. We may peak at eighty-two once in a while in late July."

"Hmmm. Eighty-two. Let me ask you… do you think Irukandji could survive here in colder water?"

Dr. Bethesda pulled off her glasses and dangled the frames nervously in her fingers. "Well, it's true that gelatinous animals adapt easily to changes in environment, but it's a stretch. Why are you asking? Do you think there are some Irukandji off the waters of Sandbridge?"

"That's the rumor."

"That's a wildly dangerous rumor. Anything to back it up?"

"Just reports of a few people who claim they were stung."

"That could be anything. Could be regular jellyfish. . . Scyphozoans we call them. . . or Hydrozoans, like Portuguese man-of-war. Could be sea anemones or fire coral. There are lots of creatures in the ocean that sting, Mr. Rellman."

"I know. But would any of those things cause someone to convulse? Or inflict pain intense enough to require an ambulance?"

She mulled it over for a moment, then answered quietly. "No. Usually a good dose of vinegar takes care of it."

"Yeah. This seems to be more than that. But one thing doesn't make sense to me. This guy who was stung didn't have any welts on his body. Does that strike you as strange?"

"Not really. Fifteen to twenty percent of sting victims don't exhibit any visible signs of the actual stings."

"I guess my biggest question is, how would Irukandji get here? They can't possibly swim all the way from Australia, can they?"

"No, but there have been reports of Irukandji down in Florida brought in by a ship from the Northern Territory of Australia."

"So it's possible?"

"Possible? I suppose. But highly improbable. You have a lot more digging to do on this one before you draw any conclusions. And don't let the Visitors Bureau know you're working on a story about deadly jellyfish. You'll be run out of town on a rail."

"I can imagine. But if there *is* something to it, I feel compelled to warn people. Is this something *you* can investigate? Can you send out a team to look for them?"

"I'm sorry, but we don't have the manpower or the equipment. Even though they tend to travel in swarms, like bees, Irukandji are so small, it would be a near impossible task. It could take months, maybe longer to find them. And that's if they're even there, which frankly, I highly doubt. I'm sorry, but this is way beyond our budget."

I stood to leave and shook her hand. "I understand. Well, thanks for your time."

"You're welcome. And I must say, I admire you for even looking into this, but I certainly hope you're wrong."

"Yeah. Wouldn't be the first time."

As I drove away from the aquarium, I was tingling with excitement, the same chemical shift your body feels when you've just met a new girl or landed a new job. For months I'd only been writing about mackerel and mullet. The closest I'd come to covering any real news was a shark sighting, which is hardly the stuff of literary legend. Finally I had fresh information coming into a brain that was starved for stimulation. I felt alive again, and for the time being, the crippling pain that had me limping through life was assuaged. I had not only touched rock bottom, I had been camped out there for months. Now I was packing up, and moving upward.

I also knew that if I told Paul Munce what I was up to, he'd turn it over to a news reporter and I'd be back covering shad and shrimp. I wasn't about to let that happen. This was my story, and my ticket out of journalistic purgatory.

Back in my condo, I immediately pulled up the pictures I'd snapped on my phone in Dr. Hartog's office. As I zoomed in on the details, I realized it was a vault of useful information. What leapt off the page was the laundry list of medicines Hartog had prescribed. . . pethidine, morphine, promethazine, fentanyl, magnesium, phentolamine, sublingual trinitrate spray. . . most of them unfamiliar names until I did a quick internet search. Everything he'd written in the patient's file was listed on a host of websites as preferred treatment for Irukandji stings. I *knew* he'd been lying to me, and it was much more than just maintaining his patient's privacy. Now I just needed to find out why. I certainly couldn't go back and ask the good doctor directly, especially since I'd ascertained this information through means that were less than honest. But as I continued to scroll through the file, I realized who I *could* ask. . . the victim. There was his name and address, written neatly on the insurance claim. Thank goodness Dr. Hartog was one of the few physicians in America with legible handwriting. I hoped his patient was still alive.

I was so infused with excitement I decided to go for a long run before my nightly trip down to the pier just to jettison the excess energy blasting through my body. I stepped out of the condo and checked the wind. Distance runners are as much in tune to the wind as sailors because which way the breeze is blowing often determines the route you'll take. You generally want the breeze at your back towards the end of a long run when you're fatigued, so you start off running into the headwind when you're still fresh. Occasionally, if you're training for a race, you'll opt to finish into the wind so you really have to battle hard at the end. Tonight the prevailing wind was coming from the south, skirting up the coast from the Currituck Sound in North Carolina. I headed that direction, into the Back Bay National Wildlife Refuge.

The Back Bay was the uninhabited section of Sandbridge, a place where you usually only found a few stray hikers and birdwatchers. Before its current incarnation as a wildlife and waterfowl refuge, these nine thousand acres of dunes and marshes had been home to dozens of hunt clubs. For over a century, the shallow waters of the Back Bay had been a magnet for wealthy sportsmen, drawn to skies teeming with tens of thousands of snow geese, ducks, and tundra swans. It was a wildfowler's paradise, until the bird populations had been hunted down to dangerously low numbers.

The government and several philanthropic millionaires had finally intervened, combining forces to preserve as much of the wetlands as they could, fighting off the constant encroachment of real estate developers. The Back Bay Refuge was now home to a resting and nesting place for not only an abundant array of water birds and passerines, but also a menagerie of wildlife. Otters, white-tailed deer, mink, rabbits, possums, raccoons, and fox were common sights. Even feral horses and pigs, loggerhead sea turtles, peregrine falcons, and bald eagles were occasionally spotted.

I felt as though I could run all day, putting in mile after brisk mile through the shifting sands of this unchained landscape. I ran through the sparse woodlands of live oaks and loblolly pines. Through the shrublands of wax myrtles, blueberry, bayberry, and wild black cherry bushes. Past the smartweed and spikerushes that lined the muddy trails where the cottonmouth snakes and ghost crabs hide.

It truly was a refuge, a time and place where I felt closest to God and to my true self. The perfect setting to clear my head and sort through all the information I'd gathered earlier that day. What did it all mean? When I distilled everything I'd learned that morning, here's all I really knew: somebody had been stung by something highly venomous, possibly an Irukandji jellyfish, and nobody thought it was a good idea that it showed up in the newspaper.

As I turned for home and felt a north wind suddenly freshen in my face, I kept asking one overriding question: if we truly were dealing with Irukandji, how in the world could something native to the waters of Australia end up in the beaches of Virginia? I recalled Dr. Bethesda's anecdotal evidence of Irukandji making their way to Florida in the bilge water of a ship. That theory begged further investigation.

# Chapter Fifteen

I could hear whooping from the end of Little Island Pier from the moment I stepped out of my car in the parking lot. It was that joyous sound that meant rod tips were bending.

The blues were running, and the boys were taking advantage. It also meant I was in for an easy night. With action like that, tomorrow's column would write itself.

"Slow night?" I asked the group innocently, as almost everyone on the LIP was either reeling in another bluefish or affixing another chunk of herring to a hook and trying their luck again.

"We're slayin' 'em, Mac!" hollered Topper. "Somebody go fetch me a bigger cooler!"

"What are you using?" I asked Rubes.

"Chunks, pin rigs, spoons, they're hittin' everything. You could toss a jellybean out there and they'd chomp it. B.B. King hasn't seen this many blues!" Rubes always showed particular delight when I jotted down notes as he was talking. I didn't know if he rehearsed his answers to my questions, but I knew he loved seeing his name in the paper, and consequently he was consistently quotable.

After I'd gathered enough details and flavor for my article, I asked the one question to which I really wanted an answer. "I know this is a long shot, but any of you guys remember any ships from Australia passing through these parts recently?"

I noticed Lyman, sitting in his usual spot and heretofore uninvolved in the bluefish brigade, spun his head around and momentarily caught my eye. For some reason my question had piqued his interest. The rest of the boys reacted with a *how could you not already know that?* kind of look.

"Absolutely!" yelled Topper. "Who could forget that? That's the biggest thing to happen on the LIP since they put in the new wash sink!"

I withstood howls of laughter from the gang and pressed on. "What are you talking about? What happened?"

Rubes took over. "Back in February, there was this huge cargo ship that ran aground, right over there." He pointed to the south of the pier. "It was like 600-feet long. I think it was the *Cudmore*?"

"Yep," nodded Topper. "*Cudmore*. I remember seein' the name painted on the side. Never forget it. It was the night I caught that king mackerel, remember that? That thing was thirty pounds, blistered the reel! I'd rigged me up a treble hook with a—"

Rubes cut him off and continued the historical narrative. "Anyway, we all stared at it for a coupla days, wondering if she was gonna break loose and crash into the pier. It woulda taken out the whole thing. Remember that, fellas?" They all nodded and murmured affirmation. "And I remember seeing on the news that the *Cudmore* was out of Australia. Don't know how it got here, or where it was headin', but it sure had folks in a lather for a coupla days. Coast Guard, Hazmat, salvage teams, you name it, they were out here."

"What finally happened?"

"Somehow they got it refloated and tugged it away. But it was touch and go there for awhile."

I was scribbling notes as fast as I could. Rubes sensed that his name might be making it into yet another column in *The Bay Breeze*.

I wandered back to the middle of the pier, where Lyman sat in his usual spot. I'd noticed that no matter what the conditions, he always fished facing south toward False Cape. He never said so, but I sensed it was so he didn't have to look at the garish condos just north of the pier that had somehow managed to make it through the zoning board. It was the only visual blight on the entire island, and Lyman hated the sight of them. They were ugly any way you looked at them, so Lyman chose not to.

I sat down next to him. "How's it going?"

"Fine. Good night to be out here."

"Seems to be."

Lyman smiled and whipped his line into the water. "Why don't you go ahead and ask me what it is you want to ask me?"

I could have feigned innocence, but there was no use. As always, Lyman Gregg was a step ahead of me. "I took your advice and looked up Irukandji. I've been diggin' a little deeper into it."

"And what have you found out?"

"That there's something fishy going on. Pun intended."

"I don't disagree."

"Where'd you hear about them?"

Lyman glanced over his shoulder. "It was 1953. I was in the Navy, comin' back from Korea. We stopped off in Australia, a town in Queensland called Cairns. Some of the guys went swimmin', and got stung by somethin' terrible. One of the corpsman on the ship thought these guys were havin' a heart attack, but since it was three of 'em all at the same time, I figured it had to be somethin' more than that."

"What happened to them?"

"They shot 'em up with morphine, but I know one of the guys didn't make it. Survived a war, but couldn't survive a jellyfish you can't even see."

"And you believe they were stung by an Irukandji?"

"Yep. That's what the locals called it. Irukandji. Named after a tribe of Aborigines." Lyman shook his head with a pained expression. "I'll never forget the pain those guys were in. It was awful. They were screamin' like they was all getting' jabbed with a red hot fire poker. So when I saw that guy screamin' the other night with that same kinda reaction, that's the first thing I thought of. And then you put that together with a cargo ship from Australia running aground, in the same place where the guy was stung? That's gotta be more than just coincidence."

"But how'd Irukandji get to Sandbridge?"

"Easy," said Lyman. "Bilge water."

Dr. Bethesda has raised the same possibility during my visit to the Marine Science Center. "So how would that work?"

"Every vessel has what they call a bilge. It's basically the bottom of the ship, where any water that doesn't drain off the side finally ends up. Seawater, rainwater, urine, oil, pretty much everything ends up there. When it gets too full, you have to pump it out. One cubic foot of water weighs about sixty-two pounds, so when the ship ran aground, the first thing they'd do is pump out the bilge water to lighten the load and free it from the sand bar."

I nodded in understanding. "So they pump the bilge water out of the cargo ship, that bilge water from Australia contained Irukandji, and now they're introduced into our local waters. Is that what you're telling me?"

"You got it."

I let out a low whistle as I soaked it all in. "Wow. Not good."

"You got that right. Not good for anybody."

"But it all makes perfect sense."

Lyman drew in a deep breath and focused his gaze out over the water as he rubbed the stubble on his chin. "Well. . . not quite."

"What do you mean," I asked, sensing his response was laden with deep meaning.

Lyman rested his pole in the notch on the railing and reached down for his notebook. He flipped through the pages like someone searching for the next hymn in church. He handed the open notebook to me. "Read that." I looked at his entry for February 9th. It detailed the conditions on the morning the *Cudmore* ran aground. Lyman kept his eye on his line even as he talked. It was clear he'd committed it to memory. "Low tide was at 10:17 a.m. That strike you funny?"

"Not really. Should it?"

"Someone want to explain to me why in broad daylight, a cargo ship that big would get this close to shore at low tide? Don't make sense."

"You've clearly thought about this before tonight."

"Quite a bit, in fact."

"Maybe the captain was asleep at the wheel. Or drunk."

"At ten o'clock in the mornin'?"

"Maybe it was a medical condition," I surmised.

"Maybe. Or maybe they did it on purpose."

"Why would you run aground on purpose?"

"Don't know. I just know it don't add up."

"So have you told the authorities about any of this?"

Lyman shook his head with vehemence. "Nope. That's for somebody smarter than me to figure out. I'm just a simple fisherman."

I nodded quietly, but I didn't really agree. I wasn't sure there *was* anybody smarter than Lyman Gregg.

"I got faith in ya, Mac. If there's somethin' to all this, you'll find out."

"I'm trying. I have a few pieces to the puzzle, but haven't put it all together yet."

"You will. You will."

I knew I would joust with insomnia that night. My own bilge was a filthy pool of dread, excitement, and ignorance over what I might learn about a deadly jellyfish taking up residence in the peaceful waters of a tourist town. The only way I could stem the rising tide of apprehension was to focus on Grace. My weary soul always ran to her. I transported my consciousness back to a trip we'd taken together to the wine country of Napa, California. I filled the vacuums of uneasiness with the aromas of oak barrels and coriander seed, blended with Grace's soothing perfume. I reached for a letter.

> My darling Seth,
> You are the music that fills my life. You are the rhythm that makes my heart beat. . . makes it race, causes it to skip. You are the lyrics that I hear all day long. . . a melody in motion. Here's the big reveal in all of this. . . if you haven't loved the way we love, if you haven't felt the way we feel, if you haven't explored the layers deep beneath your surface where emotions run white hot, if you haven't found that one person with whom you can share *everything*. . . your hopes, your dreams, your fears, the raw, naked core of your being, if you haven't found your soul mate, then you've never really heard the music. I love that you gave me music lessons.
>
> All my love,
> Grace

I listened to the distant waves crashing on the beach and tried to hear their music.

# Chapter Sixteen

Tracking down the address of one of the stinging victims in the medical records I'd photographed in the files in Dr. Hartog's office was not as straightforward as I had hoped. His name was Kenneth Batterbee, and he listed his residence on the medical form as 3257 Colechester Road. I assumed this was a single family dwelling. Sipping my morning coffee and looking at the street numbers as I drove a mile and a half down Colechester, I realized the address I was seeking was for the North Bay Shore Family Campground. I pulled past the unmanned front gate at the entrance and felt my heart sink as I saw dozens of RV's and popup campers crammed into the sprawling confines of the campground. One address covered them all.

The stern woman at the main office brusquely informed me that she was not at liberty to divulge the names and specific locations of the campers, guarding such precious secrets like launch codes. I nodded that I understood, and resigned myself to a long morning of knocking on aluminum doors and tent flaps.

After nearly an hour of asking around for Kenneth Batterbee, and deflecting defensive questions like *who wants to know?* and *why? what's he done?* I finally found my man. He was the lone occupant of a small camper in a section of the campground dubbed Piersons Point. The rounded metal of the aging Shasta was a mildewed white with faded yellow around the bottom third.

"Yeah, that's me," answered the man in his early forties. It sounded more like a confession than an introduction. His accent indicated he was either Australian, South African, or a New Zealander, but I couldn't quite place it. He was wearing a sleeveless undershirt and dirty jeans as he stood in the doorway of the camper with a cup of coffee and a fresh cigarette. He looked like he'd just woken up, and his gravelly voice added to the evidence. His unshaven, swarthy face had the washed-out look of someone who was either slightly hung over, or just recovering from the flu. He pushed back an untamed shock of black hair to get a better look at me. "Who are you?" Batterbee stepped out of his camper and faced me head on. He was easily six foot two and had the strong, seasoned triceps of a longshoreman.

"My name's Mac Rellman. I'm a reporter for *The Bay Breeze*." Batterbee recoiled a little. I'd seen that trepidation a thousand times before. As soon as you tell someone you're from a newspaper, they have one of two reactions: either they're glad to see you because they've done something noteworthy and are thrilled to get the recognition, or they have something to hide and they're immediately fraught with suspicion because they're worried you're going to expose them. Batterbee fell into the latter category.

"No comment," he said tersely, shaking his head for emphasis.

"I haven't even asked you a question!"

"Doesn't matter. I don't have anything to say to no newspaper reporter. So bugger off." He turned to retreat back into his camper.

"Did you get stung by a jellyfish last week?" I threw the question at him like a lightning bolt from the blue. It grabbed his attention as he stopped mid-step and whipped his neck around.

"Why you askin' me about that?"

"Is it true? Did you get stung?"

"That's not somethin' I can talk about."

"*Can't* talk about it? Or *won't* talk about it?"

He paused. "Both."

Despite his reluctance to talk, Batterbee stood in place. I sensed that he wanted to tell me what happened to him, but something was holding him back. I tried a friendlier approach, mixing in a white lie.

"Look, I already know you got stung. I spoke with Dr. Hartog the other day." I saw alarms go off in Batterbee's eyes when I mentioned Hartog's name. I continued. "I'm not trying to cause you any trouble. I just want to know what happened, and if it's something people need to know about."

Batterbee wet his lips and rubbed the bristles of whiskers on his jaw. He looked around to make sure nobody was eavesdropping. His demeanor softened as he spoke in a hushed tone. "Listen, mate, I'd like to help you out, but I can't. I can't afford to."

"What do you mean?"

Batterbee gestured to his camper. "Obviously I'm not a rich man. So when someone offers to pay your medical bills, and gives you a little bonus on top of that to keep your mouth shut, you do it. So I don't have anything to say. I'm sorry."

I nodded as if I understood his dilemma and agreed with him. "Did they tell you they were worried about what it would do to tourism if anyone found out what happened to you?"

He nodded back. "Somethin' like that. Yeah."

"I understand."

Batterbee scratched his head and started to formulate another sentence, but then decided he'd said enough. He exhaled loudly and disappeared back into his camper.

Back in my car, I looked at the photos I'd taken in Dr. Hartog's office that were stored in my phone. The second stinging victim he'd treated was named Margaret Doolan. Her address was in the 1100 block of Pacific Avenue in Virginia Beach.

That address turned out to be The Belmont Inn, a typical beach motel. I sat in the car for a few minutes and observed the area, thinking I might get lucky, but there was no activity except for a maid going from room to room on the second floor. I ventured into the lobby and rang the bell for the clerk. An older balding man emerged from the back, chomping on a sausage biscuit.

"Yeah?" he said with an exasperated look.

"Excuse me, but I'm looking for a woman named Margaret Doolan. Do you know if she's still a guest here?"

"Got no idea," he said with crumbs falling out of his mouth. He looked at me with a blank stare, as if to indicate that this conversation was already over.

"Could you perhaps check the guest register?"

"Sorry. We don't give out names. If they pay their bills, we leave 'em alone."

I tried a different tactic. "I owe her some money. I'd like to find her."

He didn't bite. "If you really owe her money, then I'm pretty sure she'll find *you*."

"I guess you're right." I could tell this wasn't going anywhere. I scribbled my new phone number on a piece of scrap paper and handed it to the clerk, who held it in his greasy fingers and examined it at arm's length. "Well, if you happen to see her, please tell her that I have her reimbursement check and I'll be glad to drop it off when it's convenient."

"Will do," said the clerk, stuffing my number in his shirt pocket. He gave me a two-fingered salute and disappeared back into his room. I had no idea if my message would be delivered or if its next stop was a trashcan, but at least I had made the effort.

I spent the rest of the morning in a cramped back room at *The Bay Breeze*, wading through the paper's archives in the morgue. Back issues weren't stored on a computer in such a small operation, so manual labor was the only way to get your hands on this forgotten history.

My hands were barely stained with printers' ink when I came to the issue I was seeking. . . February 10. The headline was basic and bold:

## BARGE RUNS AGROUND

I jotted notes as I scanned the copy, while at the same time thinking that *The Bay Breeze* could definitely benefit from a more ingenious headline writer.

The article stated that the *Cudmore* had originated in the city of Perth, Australia. It had left Western Australia in October, carrying a load of garnet to be used for sandblasting at the shipyards in Newport News.

I skipped ahead a few issues for follow-up stories and read where they'd quoted a man named Duncan Danforth, the financier of the operation. I wrote down the name and circled it, a reminder to delve deeper into his background.

I heard the annoying chomp of his carrot before I saw Munce's tiny shadow invade my space. "Whatcha workin' on?" he spewed out through orange teeth.

I gave him a cursory glance, just enough to acknowledge his presence, but not enough to condone it. "Oh, just reading up on the local history. Thought it might spark some story ideas on slow days."

"You runnin' out of material already, MacClellan?"

I wanted to turn around and smack the smarmy look right off Munce's face, but I restrained myself. "No, in fact I'm working on a series of pieces about a tiny little fish in a tiny little pond." I couldn't tell if Munce had the slightest clue that this was a veiled reference to him, and I didn't care. The only way I could maintain any shred of self-respect was to covertly mock him, even if it meant I was the only one in the room who got the joke. I constantly walked the balance beam of desperately needing to hang on to a job I actually enjoyed, while working for a man I detested.

Munce moved closer and looked over my shoulder. "Why you interested in the *Cudmore*?"

"Like I said, just trying to catch up on the local history. I heard some of the guys on the pier talking about it and thought I'd check it out."

I really didn't sell my answer, and Munce didn't buy it. "MacClellan, I don't know what you're workin' on here, but I'm not payin' you to do news. You do fish. Got it? Fish. They have scales and big, bulging eyes. Look into it. Ocean's full of 'em."

Munce's condescension was more than I could stand. I stood up and faced him at close range, enjoying the fact that I towered over him by nearly a foot. "What if it's a news story that impacts public health? Would that be worth a few inches in the sacred annals of *The Bay Breeze*?"

"What are you talking about, MacClellan? What about public health?"

I decided to tip my hand. Sooner or later I'd have to get Munce's permission to run with the story, so I might as well get on with it. I took a deep breath. "There are rumors. . . I repeat, just rumors. . . that there's some kind of highly venomous jellyfish off the waters of Sandbridge Beach."

"That's crazy."

"Maybe. But I've been looking into it a little and there might be something to it."

"Oh yeah? How's that?"

"I know of at least one man who's been stung. There may be more. I've really just poked around a little in my spare time. Maybe if you'd assign me to work on this full time, I could—"

"No way!" Munce shook his head and waved me off. "There's no way we're gonna be any part of spreadin' rumors like this. Forget it. Do you remember what happened after *Jaws* came out? People wouldn't go in the water for years!"

It struck me odd that Munce used the same reference to *Jaws* as Dr. Hartog. True, it was the perfect analogy. . . dangerous sea creature strikes fear into small coastal town. . . but in my mind, the response to deadly jellyfish should be the same as to a rogue shark on the loose: warn people to stay out of the water. "Don't you think we have a responsibility to at least look into this?"

"No! Can you imagine the panic you'll cause if this gets out? Do you have any idea what that would do to the tourist industry?"

"Shouldn't we be more concerned about what a poisonous jellyfish would do to the actual *tourist*?"

"You're overreaching, MacClellan. It's probably just a Man-O-War. I'm not yelling 'wolf' in a crowded theater."

I ignored his mixed metaphor and pressed my case. "It's not a Man-O-War. It's not a stingray, it's not a sea snake. Something in the water is putting people in the hospital and I think we should investigate it."

"You have no proof of that. And I'm not here to facilitate whatever personal redemption you think you might get by tryin' to scare up a story that isn't there. Now go do the job I pay you to do, or go look for another one." Munce bit his carrot with purpose and stalked out of the room.

*How do you not go after a story like this?* I asked myself, thinking that Munce was an even bigger buffoon than I'd imagined. No wonder he'd never made it very far in the newspaper business. What's worse, *I* worked for *him*. For that humiliating fact alone, I was glad nobody I cared about knew where I was currently employed. I knew one thing. . . I was going to get that proof.

As the sun started to fade into the clouds hovering over the Back Bay, I had just finished a grinding six-miler at a torrid 6:25 pace on the hard-packed sand next to the shoreline. I was starting to make my way through the band of heavy sand that led to the path back to my condo when Jenna appeared from nowhere on her Beach Patrol ATV. It was almost as if she'd been waiting on me. I had to admit she looked very impressive perched on her Honda Recon four-wheeler, complete with a very official looking radio. Her red one-piece bathing suit revealed a chiseled body that had clearly spent a lot of time lifting weights and swimming laps.

"Hey! What are you doing out here?" I asked as I approached, heaving to pull fresh air into my burning lungs.

"Just checkin' on old men in danger of keeling over. I've got a portable defib unit in my jump bag if you need it."

I laughed from deep in my aching chest. "Just get me to my wheelchair. I think I have almost a full canister of oxygen left."

"Still think you can improve your lung capacity by running, marathon man?"

"Beats the heck outta paddling in the water, Aquagirl."

"Go ahead, mock away. But I bet you dollars to doughnuts I can hold my breath longer than you."

"Not likely. I've got lungs the size of dirigibles."

"I'm ready to go, right now."

"Not fair. I just ran six miles."

"Typical runner. Afraid you'll lose."

"Let me get my heart rate down below a hundred beats per minute and I'll dust you."

"No way a road jockey is ever going to beat a swimmer in an aerobic competition. No way."

"I think you've been out in the sun too long. You're delirious."

Our banter was interrupted by two elderly women who emerged from the path coming off of Sandfiddler. I knew them only as Mildred and Stella. They looked like sisters, but I wasn't sure. All I knew about them is that they were year-rounders who lived somewhere near me and they treated me with B-List celebrity status because they loved the recipes in *The Fish Finder*.

"Mac!" squealed Stella. "Crab stuffed halibut? Out of this world!"

"Thank you! Glad you enjoyed it."

"You need to come up with something for sea bass," said Mildred. "That's our favorite!"

"Yes, ma'am. I'll work on that!"

"Have a nice evening!" they both said in near simultaneity.

"Thank you, ladies! You too!" They scooted away in their comfortable shoes for their usual evening stroll across the sand.

Jenna shook her head in annoyance as she witnessed the exchange. "What's the deal with the manners, anyway? Is that your thing?"

"My *thing*? What do you mean?"

"You know, your thing. How you pick up girls. Some guys play the bad boy card, some guys try to play it really cool. . . you apparently like the 'nice guy' approach."

"First of all, that's not my *thing*, as you call it. I don't have a *thing*. And secondly, since when was being nice a character flaw?"

"It's not, but you're *too* nice. I don't trust you."

"*Too* nice?"

"That's right. It's unnatural."

"So let me see if I understand what you're saying here. If I weren't so nice, then you'd trust me more?"

"I didn't say that."

"Yeah, you kinda did."

"All I'm sayin' is that you come off as a little insincere. Rehearsed. Like you want something."

"Sorry. I'll make a point to scale back on the kindness and decency."

"You know what I mean."

I shook my head with an insincere smile. "I really don't."

"The bottom line is, nobody is that nice. At least nobody I know."

"And from where do you know most of the people you know? A bar?"

Anger shot through her veins as she absorbed the blow. I was immediately sorry I'd said it. "I apologize. Now *that* wasn't nice."

"Thank you for proving my point. People are only nice if they want something. I call it 'church nice.'"

"'Church nice?'" I asked. "I've never heard that term."

"That's because I made it up. I used to work with a woman who would be all nice and polite on Sunday morning at church, but then surly the rest of the week. Didn't talk to us, didn't even know most of our names, but when she needed a favor, she never had a problem asking for one. I hate that kind of person."

"So how do you know when someone's actually nice, or just being 'church nice,' as you call it?"

"I can always tell," said Jenna with complete certainty as she inspected me from head to toe like a horse at auction.

"Not always."

"You'll have to prove me wrong."

"You're assuming your opinion of me matters."

"And you're pretending it doesn't." Her eyes twinkled as she turned the key on her ATV and wristed the throttle. "Besides, I'm not sure I really like nice people," she yelled over the revving of the engine. She sputtered off in the opposite direction on her four-wheeler, but I noticed she turned around to catch one more glimpse of me. I wondered why.

As night fell on the sky of early May, the lights of Little Island Pier strained to make their presence known as a heavy canopy of mist descended over Sandbridge. It was as dark as a noon shadow. Visibility was barely fifty yards when I stepped onto the planks. Nobody else was on the pier, not even Lyman. There wasn't a breath of wind, and barely a sound traveling across the cloaked night air. I felt like the subject of a Friedrich painting. A wanderer above a sea of fog, alone and isolated in the face of the sublime forces of nature. I leaned against the railing, clasped my hands together, and stared into the white nothingness. The ocean smelled of salt and sadness. As I stood on the plain where the mist joined forces with the mystical, I let my mind wander back to a similar night nearly two years ago in San Francisco.

They'd lost my luggage somewhere between Atlanta and California, but I didn't care. I had everything I needed, sitting next to me in the rental car. Grace and I had flown into San Francisco that morning and were now on our way to the wine country of the Napa Valley.

It wasn't long before I was not only slightly lost, but also managed to get the five-speed transmission stuck in reverse when we stopped for directions. Grace continued to smile and laugh. By now she knew I was not smooth, not suave, and not really all that smart. What a comfort to know that I could just be me, as inept as I was at times, and Grace still loved me.

We drove through the California countryside, going where our whimsy led us. A windmill reminded us of the things dreams are made of.

For no real reason other than it's what we "felt," we found our way to an Art Deco hotel in uptown Napa, checked in, and wandered the streets. A perfect dinner of steamed mussels and crème brûlée put the capstone on a perfect evening.

The village square was filled with the music of two classically trained violinists. We danced under starry skies worthy of Van Gogh, uncaring that everyone was watching. We had come to realize that other people loved to see us in love.

The next morning we were back in the car, driving through endless fertile acres of vineyards. I looked over at Grace, illuminated by the refracted sunlight pouring through the window, and I remembered again how lucky and proud I felt to be there with her. We had no real idea of where we were going, but somehow we got there. We stopped at a small winery in Yountville and two more in Pope Valley. After a generous sampling of Merlots and Pinot Grigios, we settled in to a quiet café with a view of Lake Berryessa. There was one place in the entire world that day that was perfect for two people in love, and we were basking in it. We poured out our hearts over long-stemmed wineglasses, talking about regrets of our past, and hopes for our future. I'd never felt such a perfect peace as I did during those two hours. I just had a feeling that we'd be back there someday.

It was time to head back to San Francisco. I was driving, Grace was navigating. The team that always found their way.

That night, as we leaned over the side of our hotel balcony and stared across the lights of the city, I wondered how many other love stories were taking place at that very moment, a space in time I will always remember.

We would fly home the next day, never separated by more than a few inches. Parting in the airport in Atlanta was nothing short of excruciating, but if that was the price to pay for our time together, so be it. I'd do it again, and again, and again.

There's no possible way to adequately describe how I felt when we were together. It was like someone who wakes up one morning and suddenly discovers they can play the piano *really well*. One could only understand our relationship if they'd experienced the same thing, and I didn't know of anyone else who had.

In the end, the trip wasn't really about exploring new territory or sampling full-bodied wines. It was about us. The simple joy of being together and enjoying each other's company and conversation during an intermission from the overly busy reality of our lives. It was a chance for two people who are separated by miles and circumstances to finally be inseparable, and to just be us. Where our next journey would take us, I couldn't guess. I only knew I'd go anywhere, as long as she was by my side.

"*I should have been driving that car*," called the same haunting voice that echoed in my head night after night as I dwelled on her car accident in Ireland. "*If only I'd been driving. . . if only I'd been driving*," it repeatedly screeched. Like the pounding surf, the voice was powerful and incessant.

The piercing *kuk-kuk-kuk-kuk* call of a passing willet snapped me out of my trance. I'd spent enough time courting loneliness for one night. I wanted some company.

My headlights dealt a glancing blow to the wall of fog as I made the short drive down Sandpiper Road to the Baja. The parking lot was half-full, confirming my long held theory that no matter what the weather, some people will somehow always manage to make it to an establishment that serves alcohol.

As I'd guessed, and truthfully hoped, Jenna was at the bar. She sat alone with just her murky thoughts and a fresh whiskey sour.

"Mind if I join you?"

The hint of a pleasant smile actually crossed her face. She gestured to the bar stool next to her. "Have a seat, marathon man. What brings you out on a night like this?"

I didn't want to tell the truth, that the walls of my condo were starting to close in on me. "I realized this morning that I was fresh out of vermouth. Thought they might have some here. Turns out, I was right."

Jenna smiled a little more broadly. "Yep. This is your lucky day." She gestured to Trey, who was already in tune to my presence. "Get this man a fresh vermouth. Make it a double. On me."

Trey knew she was joking, but didn't share in our quiet laughter. He'd already reached for a pint glass and was pouring me a frothy Guinness.

He slid it in front of me without a greeting. I took a sip, licked the bubbly brown residue off my upper lip, and nodded my approval.

Jenna shook her head in mild disgust. "I don't know how you stand that stuff. Looks like used motor oil topped off with sea foam from low tide."

"Nectar of the gods," I rebutted. "And four million Irishmen can't be wrong."

She rolled her eyes. "I suppose. To each his own." She raised her glass and clinked it with mine. It was the first overt sign of friendliness I'd ever seen her make, to me, or anyone else. We both took a sip and exhaled with enjoyment.

"You ever hear the name Duncan Danforth? Know anything about him?"

"Of course. Everyone on the island knows Duncan Danforth. Australian. Richest guy around. Why you askin'?"

"Just curious. Saw his name in the paper."

"Yeah, he's pretty well known by the locals."

"Where'd he get his money?"

"Little bit of everything, I think. Imports, exports, real estate, buncha stuff. Guy owns a ton of land around here. Seems like he's always tearing down trees and building something. I'd say that most people around here don't like him. In fact, they hate him."

"Why?"

"Because he keeps turning our dunes into developments. If it were up to Danforth, we'd have condos, hotels, and go-kart tracks up and down the whole place. Nobody wants that."

"Do you hate him too?"

"I actually feel sorry for him."

"Why's that?"

"He's kind of a tragic figure. His father-in-law died in a sailing accident last year, and his wife was killed in a house fire back in September. All the money in the world can't make that kind of pain go away." Jenna's eyes wandered off as she took a hard swallow of liquor. She never ordered a Cosmo or Strawberry Daiquiri or some other typically feminine cocktail, but always a whiskey sour. It was clear to me that she drank to numb some deep-rooted pain. She sipped again and abruptly changed the subject.

"Why is a smart guy like you working as the fishing reporter at a Podunk newspaper?"

It was my turn to drink away some pain. "That's kind of a long story."

"Foggy nights are made for long stories. I got no place to be. I doubt you do either."

I let out a low whistle that emanated from pursed lips, wondering if sharing my tale of woe was a good idea. I knocked back a healthy dose of Guinness and took a deep breath. "Where to begin?" For the next four or five minutes, I explained in streamlined fashion how I'd lost the love of my life in a car accident and then how I'd gotten myself fired from my dream job at the *Herald* just a few months later. Jenna soaked in every word, and seemed to feel sorry for me.

"Tough break," was her succinct response as she patted my shoulder twice.

"Yep. Tough break." We simultaneously drank to my sorrow, like someone toasting the recently dead after an Irish wake.

"What was she like? What did you like about her?"

"Oh man, what *didn't* I like?" I thought about it for a moment. My list was a long one. "Grace always dressed well. From that first time on the beach in that blue sundress, I just really liked how she dressed. She didn't spend a lot of money on clothes, but she was always put together well. A skirt, slacks, jeans, usually a colorful top, flats, and always the minimum of makeup and jewelry. She looked as good in flannel as she did in pearls. 'You never have to apologize for being overdressed,' she used to say."

"You loved her because you liked her outfits?"

"Obviously it was a lot more than that! But she *was* cute."

"Was she a runner, too?"

"No. She loved yoga. But whenever she'd come to visit, she'd come and watch me race. She'd sit in the bleachers and either take pictures or sketch all the people at the finish line. She was a big supporter of my running addiction."

"What did you do to support *her*?"

"I listened to her."

"That's it? Just listened?"

"Yep. It's kind of a lost art among men these days."

Even as I spoke those words, I noticed Trey moving within closer earshot of our conversation. He seemed to deliberately linger at our end of the bar, wiping down the counter a little longer than usual as we talked.

"Listened to what?" asked Jenna.

"To her ideas, her opinions, her dreams. Everything. Her work, her art, her family, places she wanted to visit. I just loved hearing her talk. Some nights I'd just sit on one end of the couch in the dark, and she was on the other end, and we just talked."

"That's it? You just *talked*?"

"Yes. Just talked. And listened."

"Impressive. She was lucky to have you."

I shook my head. "More like the other way around."

"Don't put yourself down. Any woman would be lucky to have you."

I laughed sardonically. "Oh yeah. What woman could possibly pass up a guy who barely makes minimum wage and lives in a one bedroom condo with no view of the water, not even the swimming pool, and spends most of his free time wallowing in grief? I agree, that's a *very* attractive package."

"It might be to some people."

"Not when they find out I write about tuna for a living."

"Agreed, not that enticing. But at least you're nice. And funny."

"Wait, did you just admit that I'm nice? And funny?"

"Excuse me, my mistake. Funny is too strong a word. More like amusing. Mildly amusing."

"I'll take it. I admit, my humor's an acquired taste."

Her tone switched to serious. "You know, one of these days you're going to have to let yourself fall in love again."

I shook my head and stared into my glass. "I doubt it. I'm not sure I will ever want to."

Jenna looked at me with mild disgust and finished her cocktail with a single swallow. Trey was immediately there with a fresh one.

"What about you, Jenna? Any lost loves to talk about? Any current loves?"

I noticed Trey homed in on our discussion with even keener interest.

"Nope. Too busy."

"I don't believe you."

"Oh really? And why's that, Dr. Freud?"

"I think you just like to put up a good front. You're like the paint on a beach cottage. . . each coat with its own history, standing up to the winds and sand and sun. . . then freshly painted over to look new. . . but underneath, lots of layers, lots of history."

"You're *way* off."

"Am I?"

"I'll have you know I do just fine." She tossed back a gulp of her cocktail.

I left it at that. I certainly didn't have room to comment on other people's love lives. I turned to face her, changing the subject. "The night I met you, you said something about an 'anniversary story.' What were you talking about?"

Jenna took a deep breath and mulled over her response. "Well, as long as we're sharing, I might as well tell you."

I could sense that this story had a great deal of pain attached to it, but Jenna had just enough alcohol in her system to relax her inhibitions.

"I used to be cop."

It was not at all what I expected. "*You* were a police officer?"

"Yeah. Dad was a cop, grandfather's a cop, brother's a State Trooper, uncle in the FBI. . . it's part of the Czarnecki DNA. I always wanted to go into law enforcement. Kinda felt like I was upholding the family tradition."

"So what happened?"

Jenna puffed out one burst of sardonic laughter and looked at the ceiling with a wistful smile. "Just a little over three years ago I was serving a warrant on a guy who'd violated a 50-B."

"Protective order?"

"Exactly. The guy was a first-class wife beater. Got drunk and knocked his wife and kids around all the time. She finally had enough of it, so she moved out and took out a 50-B. That of course made him furious, so he tracked her down and went over and beat her senseless. So I go over to arrest him." Jenna took a long pause. Her chin started to quiver as she replayed the next chapter of the story in her head. Across the bar I could see Trey's head shaking almost imperceptibly, silently begging her from a distance to not continue. She took a small sip of her whiskey, composed herself, and began again. "He's drunk and belligerent, but it's all pretty routine. I'm starting to cuff him and read him his rights when suddenly he just explodes." She softly rubbed her right cheek with the fingers of her left hand as she stared straight ahead and narrated. "He caught me in the jaw with his elbow, then he hit me with a roundhouse in the temple. I went down." Her voice fell quieter, wavering. Her eyes glassed over with the tears of haunting remembrance. "When I came to, he was gone, and so was my gun. I knew what was going to happen even before I got the call." She stopped and hung her head, squeezing her eyes shut as if to blot out the ending of the story.

I gently touched her shoulder. "What happened?"

"He'd gone over to her house. Killed her. Killed the two kids. Killed himself. With *my* gun." Jenna bit her bottom lip to fight back the torrent of tears she'd dammed up in a reservoir of self-loathing.

"It wasn't your fault, Jenna."

"Yeah, it was. Entirely my fault. For lots of reasons. I should never have taken that call by myself. I shoulda called for backup. I wasn't strong enough to handle that guy if something went wrong. Obviously."

"So did you quit because of that?"

She shook her head. "Didn't quit. Fired."

"They fired you for that? But cops get overpowered all the time!"

"Word got back to the Chief that I'd been having a beer with lunch at Margie and Ray's when I took the call. So the next day, badge and gun. . . gone. Poof." She brushed away a tear and forced a plastic smile. "First Czarnecki to ever tarnish the family honor. As you might imagine, Thanksgiving dinners aren't much fun."

As Jenna swirled the ice in her whiskey sour, I think we both noted the irony that it was a casual beer at lunch that launched her descent into functioning alcoholism.

"I'm sorry," was all I could think to say.

"Don't be. Nothing I can do about it now."

Trey kept a watchful eye on both of us as we wallowed in our shared misery.

"So how about it?" Jenna blurted out in a much happier tone.

"How about what?"

"Seeing who can hold their breath the longest. Stud-muffin swimmer girl versus broken down runner boy. I'm callin' it 'the Aerobic Olympics.' Loser buys the next round."

Considering that Jenna apparently didn't actually pay for her drinks at the Baja, courtesy of Trey, I didn't see how she was really risking very much, but I had no choice. It may have appeared to onlookers to be nothing more than a casual bar bet, but in my mind I had been thrust into the position of defending the honor of runners everywhere and I simply could not back away from the challenge. "That's a go!" I said with gusto, feeling the same adrenaline rush that I got before any athletic competition. I was already hyperventilating in preparation.

"Okay, rules are simple. On the count of three, we suck it in. First one to exhale loses. Deal?"

"Deal."

"Trey!" she called in a loud voice to the end of the bar. In a terrible acting job, Trey looked around as if trying to discern the origin of the voice. He finally let his expression transition from confusion to recognition and ambled our way.

"Whatcha need?" he asked, as if he didn't already know.

"We're gonna hold our breath in the ultimate test of fitness. You count us down and keep the time."

Trey nodded. "All right. You guys ready?" We nodded. "Ready, set— go!" Jenna and I sucked in the deepest breaths possible through our mouths and filled our lungs. She tried to stare me down like an arm-wrestler, but I wasn't buying into the intimidation. I locked my gaze straight ahead in silent stoicism, trying to relax and let the seconds tick by. The one minute mark was easy. I could feel my heart beating, but no discomfort. I glanced at my watch. Ninety seconds came and went. At the 1:45 mark I could feel it. A pulsing in my temples. A slight burning in my chest cavity. I shot a glance at Jenna, clenching her jaws to prevent the air from escaping. At the two minute threshold I realized I wasn't as aerobically fit as I thought. It was the same painful oxygen debt you feel in the last 200 meters of a mile race. Your body craves fresh ether to replenish the blood cells, but you can't provide it. At 2:15 I tightened my abdominals, hoping to eke out a few more seconds. Mercifully, Jenna shattered the silence with a mighty blast of carbon dioxide. I released my lungs a second later. Heaving for breath, I pumped my weak right arm in triumph.

"I rest my case," I gasped. "Along with the rest of me." We both placed our crossed arms on top of the bar and buried our exhausted heads on top of them. I was in no condition or mood to collect my free drink that night.

"I want a rematch," came Jenna's muffled voice from underneath her arms.

"Funny. . . I thought that *was* the rematch. I do believe that makes me two for two, if you count the first time you tried to outrun me."

"I don't." Still lightheaded, I got up to leave. "Where you goin'?" asked Jenna.

"I'm going out to get some air. Literally. I'll see you 'round." Jenna waved me off, too exhausted to do much more.

I slipped across the street and let the night come over me as I stood in the cold sand next to the pier. The light of the nearly full moon was spread across the water, making the surface light up like sheets of phosphorescent linen. The view took me right back to Charleston, and a night of gazing up at the moon with Grace. I fished around in my pocket and dug out the small shell I'd found during our first meeting on Folly Beach. For some reason, I took the shell with me everywhere I went, like a talisman to ward off evil. As a lucky charm, it hadn't really fulfilled its promise, but I kept it anyway. I wondered what had happened to the other half. I turned up my collar against the chill of the night air and headed back to my car. Time to go home.

My column that night was uninspired. It opened with the line, "You can't tie good knots with braided line—fact or fiction?" After banging out twelve inches of copy on the virtues of Stren knots, Uni knots, and Albright knots, and their desirability for joining braid to a mono leader, I felt as though the subject had been adequately covered. The irony that these knots were perfect for bottom fishing was not lost on me. I turned off my computer and sat in the darkness of my lonely condo with the window open. I could hear the ocean. It provided symphonic accompaniment to her voice as I read one of her letters.

My Darling Seth,
Despite all obstacles, certain people do belong
together because they complete each other. . . so
despite the facts of life, I continue to dream about
the days ahead, all the while growing closer, falling
more deeply in love. Two people who spent years
meandering through life, then took a leap into the
unknown, and discovered that perfect mate, the one
our souls had always known existed, but with whom
the stars had not yet aligned. And while the stars
are still shifting into place, it is with certainty that I
can say "it is you I love, now and forever."

Always,
Grace

I turned off the light and let my loneliness linger in the darkness.

# Chapter Seventeen

I was awakened the next morning by the buzzing of my phone on the nightstand. I looked at the screen and didn't recognize the caller's number. For a quick second in my groggy state I imagined it was Grace calling me. . . this had all been a terrible dream. The insane fantasy was immediately dashed.

"Hello?" I said, sitting up and shaking away the cobwebs of restless sleep. No response. "Hello? Who is this?" Still no voice. Dead air. "This is Mac. Who's this?" There was an inordinately long pause on the other end and I could actually hear someone breathing, as if they were summoning the courage to say something, but then the line went dead. My head was starting to clear away the fog of slumber as I tried to sort it out. It didn't seem to be your typical wrong number. I immediately called back the number on my screen, but nobody picked up. I could only think of one possibility.

A half-hour later I was back at the Belmont Inn on Pacific Avenue in Virginia Beach. I could see through the glass doors of the lobby that it was a different clerk on duty. A young girl. I might have more luck with her than I did with Mr. Greasy Fingers.

I ran across the street to a giant beach store and bought the cheapest purse I could find. I walked into the lobby and looked as cheerful as possible. "Good morning!" I chirped.

"Good morning!" she echoed back. "Need a room?"

"No. I found this purse when I was walking through your parking lot. The I-D inside says it belongs to Margaret Doolan. Is she here?"

I prayed the young girl wouldn't stop to think how I could possibly track down someone at a hotel from their I-D card. It passed right over her. Whenever a person thinks they're helping someone, they're generally eager to oblige, and she was more than helpful.

"Well aren't you nice! You know most folks these days wouldn't do that. They'd just keep whatever they found. I know. I lost my wallet once at a club in Norfolk and never did get it back. I swear, people these days just ain't as honest like they used to be. You know what I mean?"

Seeing as how I had just lied to her, I was less than enthusiastic in agreeing, but I nodded in affirmation of her world view. "Oh yeah. I hear ya."

The young clerk quickly flipped through the guest registry. "Doolan. . . Doolan. . . here she is. Room fifteen. Second to the last one on the left, next to the ice machine."

"Thank you."

"No, sir, thank *you* for doing the right thing. You're a true gentleman."

I knocked on the door to room fifteen. After a fairly long wait, the door cracked opened five inches, the brass security chain holding it back. A woman in her early thirties with no makeup stood on the other side of the narrow opening. The deep lines on her face seemed to be reflective of what appeared to have been a hard life. She looked like someone who'd hitched her wagon to a dying star, perhaps an aspiring country music singer who didn't make it in the recording industry, but instead ended up carving out a long career as a waitress in an all night diner. She didn't look well. "Are you Margaret Doolan?"

She paused before answering, sizing me up. "I'm Maggie. Who are you? You the guy who claims he owes me money?"

"Uh. . . well, that wasn't exactly true."

"Didn't think so. So why are ya snoopin' around for me? What do you want?"

"I want to ask you about a jellyfish sting."

Her eyes darted beyond me with furtive glances around the parking lot, as if looking to see if we were being watched. She started, then stopped. "They told me not to —"

"Not to say anything?"

"Please go." She could have easily slammed the door in my face, yet she didn't. I felt like she wanted to talk but fear prevented her.

"Who is *they?*"

"I can't talk to you. You have to leave now." Still, the door remained open.

"May I come in?"

Maggie scanned the parking lot again, then hurriedly unlatched the security chain and ushered me inside with a nod of her head. She slammed the door, then peered through the drawn curtain to make certain there was no movement outside.

I leaned against the dresser and immediately noticed the numerous prescription bottles on the nightstand. Maggie sat on the end of one of the beds and lit a cigarette, her hand trembling like it had palsy. She closed her eyes as she inhaled and bellowed out a cloud of fresh smoke.

"I'm scared," she whispered through the haze.

"I can see that. I'd like to help you. Why are you so scared?"

"They just made it clear that if word got out, they'd come lookin' for me."

"Can you tell me what happened?"

Maggie took another long drag off her cigarette. "I was down at False Cape, hoping I might see some wild horses. I always loved horses. I used to ride some growin' up." She stared at the floor with a wistful look, perhaps thinking about the innocence of her childhood. "Anyway, it was hot, so I walked down to the water, took my shoes off, and waded in. Next thing I know somethin' stung me on the leg. It was like I'd been shot. The pain? Oh my Lord, it was like fire shootin' through your skin. Next thing I know I wake up in a doctor's office."

"Dr. Hartog?" I asked.

She looked up. "Yes! How'd you know that?"

"How'd you get there? Who took you?"

She paused, thinking of an answer. "Well I don't really know. Good question. I guess somebody musta drove me there, but I was in so much pain, I don't really remember."

"And was it Dr. Hartog who told you not to say anything about this?"

"No, it was another guy. I don't know his name. I just remember he looked really important. You know, rich. Cufflinks, fancy watch, that kinda guy. And threatening. I could tell he meant it." She paused, then shook her head. "The trouble is, I feel like somebody oughta know about this. If there's somethin' out there in the water, then other folks need to be warned. Nobody should go through what I went through."

"I agree. That's exactly what I'm trying to do."

She narrowed her eyes and cocked her head slightly sideways. "Who are you, anyway?"

"I'm a reporter for a local paper."

A sudden sense of alarm washed over Maggie as she leapt off the bed and started to pace. "A reporter? No! I can't be talkin' to a reporter! They'll. . . they'll come for me! They'll know I'm the one who talked!"

"Don't worry. I'll keep you out of it. I promise."

She rubbed her weary forehead. "Ya know, I save up all year just to come down here for a coupla days of vacation, just to get away, and now I'm in this mess. Unbelievable. Just my luck. Now I don't even have gas money to get home."

I pulled out my wallet and gave her twenty dollars. "Here, go get something to eat. And don't spend it on cigarettes."

She took the money, although somewhat reluctantly. "Thank you. And you swear you're not gonna tell anybody we talked?"

"Promise."

She pocketed the twenty. She seemed a little calmer as she took a final drag on her cigarette and snuffed it out in an overflowing ashtray on the nightstand. "You should probably go." I nodded and quietly left the room. My encounter with Maggie Doolan reminded me of why I became a journalist. It was to give a voice to the voiceless, even when they were too frightened to talk. She was right. If there was something dangerous in the water, people needed to be told about it. I was determined to be that voice.

My next stop was to the offices of the Virginia Beach city government on Courthouse Drive. I wanted to know more about the mysterious Duncan Danforth, and sifting through property tax records and business licenses was the easiest way to do that. I'd spent more time than I care to remember bent over public files trying to glean information from someone's financials. It was like mining for gold; painstakingly slow, but usually turned up a valuable nugget or two.

After several hours, I'd pieced together a decent dossier of Danforth's background, at least what was available in the public domain. I discovered that many of Danforth's holdings were scattered across "shell" companies, which immediately sent up red flags. Any businessman who operates through shell companies is almost always hiding something, either from the IRS, or law enforcement. Within his various companies, Danforth had extensive real estate holdings, including, to my surprise, the condominiums where I currently resided. As a few of the puzzle pieces fell into place, I was starting to think I might know who the rich man in the cufflinks was who threatened Maggie Doolan.

It was almost six o'clock by the time I got back to Sandbridge and pulled into the parking lot of my condo. Plenty of daylight left to get in a long run and still make it the pier before sunset, the angler's version of "happy hour."

As I walked in and tossed my notepad and keys onto the kitchen table, an icy chill ran up the nape of my neck. I didn't know exactly why, but I sensed someone else had been there, or perhaps was *still* there. Maybe it was the trace aroma of cologne, or something imperceptibly out of place that only registered in my subconscious. Raw instinct told me something was different. I was not alone. I froze in place. The skin on my scalp tightened as that innate sense of peril washed over me. I could feel my heart pumping faster as pure adrenaline surged through me, urging fight or flight. "Hello?" I called out, not sure whether I really wanted a response. I slowly backed up toward the door, developing a plan to slip quietly out to my car, retrieve my cell phone, and call the police. As I wrapped my sweating palm around the doorknob, I suddenly jumped with shock as if lightly touched with a cattle prod.

"There you are!" came the voice from down the hall. A half-second later, a man in a tailored suit appeared in the living room, rubbing his moistened hands together to dry them. "I was just in the back freshening up. I've been waiting quite a while. Wasn't sure you were ever coming back from your errands."

I was still locked in one spot, my hand refusing to let go of the doorknob, as he approached me and extended a handshake.

I knew exactly who he was before he ever said his name. Gold cufflinks, a thickly knotted tie on a spread collar, and eyes the color of mild insanity. "I'm Duncan Danforth," he said with a crisp Australian accent.

I let go of the doorknob and shook his hand, more out of forced habit than purposeful intention.

"I know."

"And you're the famous Seth MacClellan."

It confused me that he used my real name. I hadn't heard it spoken aloud in months. "What are you doing here? What do you want?"

He forced a smile. "I believe that it is *I* who should be asking *you* that question. What do *you* want?"

"What do you mean?"

Danforth sat down in the living room as if he were the host and I were the guest. "Word has it that you've been doing a little research on, how shall I put it—current events. And also doing a little checking into me."

"What makes you think that?"

"Let's not pretend, Mr. MacClellan. My information network is vast. I know everything that takes place on my island."

"You mean you have spies?"

"I prefer to use the term 'resources.' And I think you will find me to be extremely. . . resourceful." Danforth looked down at his hands, nervously clicking his thumbnail against his middle finger. "And so I will ask you again, Mr. MacClellan. . . what are you up to?"

I finally moved away from the door, but remained standing. I wasn't entirely certain the danger was over, but I was determined that Danforth not sense my fear. "I'm a reporter, Mr. Danforth. It's simply my job to know who the key players are. Just doing my due diligence."

"I see. How admirable." Danforth drummed his fingers on the arm of the chair and emitted short bursts of air past his lips, measuring his next words. He stood up and turned his back to me, gazing out the window. "Mr. MacClellan, I have a vested interest in making sure people want to come to Sandbridge Beach and spend their money. Tourist dollars are the lifeblood of the local economy, and without them, life here is unsustainable. You obviously understand that wild, unsubstantiated rumors of stinging jellyfish tend to be at odds with my objective, so if you're trying to go down that road, you need to touch the brakes, turn around, and move on to something else that's more your speed. Like what kind of bait they're using to attract flounder." He spun around to face me with piercing eyes. "Am I making myself clear?"

"So you want me to ignore a potential public health hazard and just walk away. Is that what you're asking?"

"I'm not asking you. I'm telling you. Leave it alone."

"I don't know that I can do that."

"I strongly suggest you find a way." Danforth moved closer and squared up to me, face to face. "There are *lots* of health hazards on this island, Mr. MacClellan. 'Twould be a shame if one were to befall you."

"That sounds like a threat."

"Interpret it as you wish. But I'm a businessman, Mr. MacClellan, not a hooligan. And I'll let you decide if our business ends here, or if it becomes necessary that we meet again. Goodnight. Sleep well." A crocodilian smile swept across Danforth's face as he brushed past me and slipped out the front door. The intimidating chill he left behind was palpable. It had been awhile since I'd had my life threatened and I couldn't convince myself that I wasn't unnerved by it. Before, I'd had the corporate safety net of a major newspaper to fend off such unpleasantness. Now I was alone. An unprotected dune against a hurricane. I really didn't want to cross paths again with Duncan Danforth, genuinely concerned that our next meeting might end differently than our first.

# Chapter Eighteen

Rattled by my encounter, I skipped my nightly run and sought refuge at the Baja. I felt as though the company of strangers would be better for my jangled nerves than the solitude of running. An infusion of alcohol probably wouldn't hurt either.

I sat down at the bar and flagged Trey's attention. He nodded in understanding and immediately poured a Guinness, the foamy head of the stout creeping just up to the rim of the pint glass. I swiveled my neck, looking for Jenna, somewhat surprised she wasn't already there. Trey walked over and slid the pint glass in front of me.

"She's not here."

"I see that. I guess it's kinda early."

"What do you want with her, anyway?" asked Trey with a tinge of accusation.

"I just wanted to talk to her." I continued to scan the bar.

"I don't mean just tonight. What are your intentions with her?"

"What?" I focused my full attention on Trey. I replayed his last sentence in my head and suddenly made sense of it. "Trey, listen to me. It's not like that."

"What is it then?"

"Look, I can tell you have feelings for her. But trust me, I am not a threat. I have absolutely no romantic designs on Jenna. She's just a friend, and that's all. And that's the honest truth."

"That's not the problem. The problem is, she's falling in love with *you*."

I had no response. I had never considered the possibility that Jenna's view of me wasn't identical to my perception of her. I didn't think my actions toward her had promoted anything more than just a simple friendship. In fact, I wasn't even certain that the woman even *liked* me, much less anything beyond a casual affinity. I sat there in queasy silence, trying to sort out this vexing new piece of information. I thought of Grace, and how much I still loved her. How I could never love anyone else, ever. I believe the triumphant or tragic code of the cosmos is that you're only granted one soul mate, and Grace was mine. *Had* been mine. Past tense. It's a harsh reality to confront the notion that not only *would* I never fall in love again, but that I *couldn't*. I don't know how long I sat there attempting to process the nugget of news that had just been delivered, but I snapped out of my mild trance when Trey whistled softly to regain my attention. He angled his head and darted his eyes to the door of the bar, signaling me to keep quiet. As if on cue, Jenna walked in and twisted her way through the crowd to get to the bar. Trey already had a whiskey waiting for her.

"Hey!" she said brightly as she sat down and acknowledged Trey's prompt service with a nod of her head. She seemed friendlier than usual, or so I imagined.

"Hey," I replied in a much more somber tone.

"What's eatin' you?"

"We need to talk."

"Okay, let's talk. What about?"

"Someplace quieter."

"Ooo. Sounds serious," she said with an impish smile.

"It is."

"All right then, let's go talk." Jenna tossed down her drink like it was lemonade on a balmy afternoon. I abandoned my Guinness, only half-empty. I threw a ten on the bar, and she got up without paying. Under Trey's watchful eye we hastily exited. Considering his recent revelation, I could only imagine what Jenna thought might be the topic of our discussion.

We walked across the street, took off our shoes, and made our way through the soft sand down to the beach. Moon shadows covered the night sands as we moved north, away from the lights of the Little Island Pier. We made our way to the shoreline, leaving distinct footprints in the pliant sand of the water's edge. It was the first time I ever noticed Jenna walking more like a carefree girl than a stoic woman, weaving rhythmically along, each footstep crisscrossing over the axis of her torso. I sensed a smoldering chemistry, but only on her side.

"So what do you want to talk about?" she asked, playfully punching me in the shoulder.

"It's about the Irukandji."

"Oh. We're back on the jellyfish, are we?" Her deflation was visible.

"I got a visit from Duncan Danforth tonight."

"What? Are you kidding?"

"Wish I were. He was waiting for me inside my condo."

"Whoa, wait a sec, back up here. Duncan Danforth... *the* Duncan Danforth, was inside your condo?"

"Yep."

"How'd he get in?"

"Well, he owns the place. That might explain it."

"What did he want?"

"He warned me to leave the Irukandji story alone. To walk away. Forget it ever happened. And he more than hinted that it would be in the best interest of my long-term health to do so."

"Why? What's he care?"

"I'm not entirely sure, other than just money. Tourist dollars. He seems to think that news of a deadly jellyfish might be bad for business. Imagine that."

"Wow. Duncan Danforth breaks into your condo to threaten you. That's kinda creepy. How did he even know you were investigating?"

"Good question. I think maybe he has people down at City Hall who watch out for him. Who knows."

"So what are you going to do?"

"I don't know. Right now I'm a little rattled by it all. But I swear, the mere fact that someone like Danforth is so intent on quashing the story tells me that there *has* to be something to it. And I just don't think I can leave it alone."

Jenna shook her head. "You're playin' with fire, Mac. Not just matches. A flamethrower."

"I know. I know." I closed my eyes and rubbed my open palms over the worry wrinkles of my face, trying to exhale away the anguish.

"I don't know what to do," I whispered above the steady din of the incoming waves.

We walked for at least two minutes in silence, cloaked in the ambient noises of nature. Jenna finally spoke. "Why are you so bent on getting to the bottom of this?"

It seemed like an easy question, especially for an investigative journalist. The standard reply should have included something about "truth" or some tired bromide about "the public's right to know." That may have been part of my motivation for pursuing the story, but the honest answer was much more complicated. Much more selfish. I dug my hands into my pockets and looked up at the blanket of stars in the night sky. "I guess I think this story might offer me some measure of redemption. Maybe it won't bring me all the way back to the man I used to be, but it's at least a foothold out of the quagmire."

"Redemption," repeated Jenna after a long pause. "I can relate."

"Can you?"

"Why do you think I'm a lifeguard? My mistake cost three people their lives. Not just their jobs, Mac, but their *lives*. So now, every time I pull someone out of the water, it's a little measure of redemption. It'll never make up for what I did, but it's at least a start. We're very much the same, Mac."

"I suppose."

"Why do you love to run?" she asked.

"I don't know. I just do. Keeps me in shape."

"I don't believe that."

"What don't you believe?"

"That you run just for your health. The way you run. . . and the way you *look* when you run? You love it for a lot more than just keepin' your cholesterol down."

"Maybe you're right."

"I know I'm right. I just don't know *why* I'm right. You gonna tell me, or do I have to drag it outta you?"

"Is this a conversation or an interrogation?"

"It's just me trying to understand you."

I exhaled and looked out across the water. The light from the lamps on Little Island Pier was shimmering on the water below like the iridescent scales of a million shad. I wasn't sure how much I wanted to share with Jenna. I had no reason not to trust her, but I didn't feel like opening my heart too widely to someone I really wanted to keep at arm's length. On the other hand, it had been so long since I'd let anyone penetrate the fortress I kept around me that perhaps it was time for more than just the superficial conversation to which I'd grown so accustomed.

"I was an only child. I had great parents, but my father was gone a lot. He was a photographer for the Associated Press. He made a name for himself in Vietnam, always willing to take risks to get a great shot, so he was in high demand. He had a wall covered with awards. I used to go into his office at home and just stare at them, imagining what he'd gone through to get just the right angle in exactly the right light at the precise moment in time. I'd always worshipped my father, but it wasn't until I was touring the Newseum in Washington and I saw one of his pictures prominently displayed that I realized the breadth of his talent and industry. He could have rested on his laurels, but he kept trying to top himself. He went all over the country, all over the world, chasing the next big story and trying to tell it in pictures. And then one day, when I was in fifth grade, he didn't come back."

"What happened?" said Jenna, almost afraid to ask.

"Wish I knew. He was working on a story in Brazil and he just vanished. Not a trace. We never found out what happened, and Mom certainly didn't have the money to pursue it. After awhile, we just quit talking about it. She went about the day to day work of raising me, working two jobs, making sure we had enough money for footballs, baseball gloves, movie tickets, and pocketknives. . . all the things that make up a little boy's life. We just moved on."

"But she never really got over it. . ."

"No, she never did. She was used to being alone when Dad traveled, but this aloneness was altogether different. I could hear her crying in the shower some nights, perhaps believing the sound of the cascading water would drown out the anguish that poured out of her. Mostly she suffered in silence, never wanting her pain to become mine. She died seven years later, the day after I graduated from college. I'm the only person I know who attended a graduation and a funeral in the same week. I've been alone ever since." I quit talking and Jenna instinctively kept quiet and let me sit there, alone with my thoughts. I guess my mother figured her job was done and she couldn't stand to live without Dad anymore. Only now do I understand the wretched pain of missing someone that much. Perhaps that's why I loved blending in with Grace's family. I had parents again, plus brothers and sisters I'd never had. I missed all of that. I turned my wandering attention back to Jenna. "So then, you're asking yourself, what does all that have to do with why I love to run?"

"Yeah. What's the connection?"

"After Dad died, I quit team sports. I just wanted to be alone. I really wasn't the kind of kid who wanted to sit in my bedroom and read books, so I turned to the only physical activity that you can do by yourself. I put on some old sneakers and I started running. I found out I loved the solitude of it. It was cathartic. I felt free. I ran hard, just trying to clear my head, to feel the release of endorphins and flush away the pain through my pores. And I also discovered I was pretty good at it. One day after gym class, where I'd dusted the whole school in the 600 yard fitness test, the track coach, Mr. Privette, brought me into his office and gave me a pair of real running shoes. Adidas Gazelles, I'll never forget 'em. They were slightly used, but man, those things felt *good* on my feet. A couple days later, Coach Privette asked me if I'd like to try out for the Cross Country team. I said yes. And I loved it. I got pretty good without really intending to. Coach never really pushed me, he just coaxed me. And so running became my safe harbor, my reason for being, and it remains so. You certainly can't afford a therapist on the salary of a newspaper writer, but if you combine some good shoes, some nice headphones, and a lotta miles, it accomplishes pretty much the same thing."

We sat in silence, staring out at the dark tableau of beach and breakers, lost in thought. Although Grace didn't really believe me when I told her, in recent years I'd really run for her. She inspired me to train harder, and was always the angel on my shoulder during races, especially the marathons. She was always in the right place at the right time along the race course when my legs were growing weary. A vision of lovely. Clapping, smiling, spurring me on. "I love you! I'll kiss you at the finish line!" she'd yell above the din.

I would always sprint to the end with the excitement of knowing she was there. I searched the crowd for her face but she always spotted me first. Grace made me feel like her hero, which made all the miles of training worth every step. I would hold her hand as I limped back to the car or hotel, exhausted, but feeling like we accomplished something together. She massaged my aching legs and told me she was proud. I always ran for her.

A piercing whistle and subsequent explosion two hundred yards down the beach captured our attention as somebody set off a large bottle rocket. It was a common sight and sound in Sandbridge. Fireworks with a report were illegal in Virginia, but unless it became a nuisance, nobody did much to enforce it. The world was getting to be that way.

The brilliant burst of sparks immediately took me back to a trip I'd taken with Grace to Pamplona, Spain. At precisely midnight, as we walked along the cobblestone streets sharing a bottle of sangria, fireworks rocketed up into the night sky above the steeple of an ancient church. Of all the moments I treasured of our time together, that image remains the most enduring. Grace's beautiful face looking up into a cobalt blue night, with streaks of glitter and color raining down overhead. While the rest of the inhabitants of the medieval city were craning their necks to soak in the shower of sparks above, I was watching Grace. Heaven and earth had collaborated on a lustrous work of art, and she was the point of focus.

The next morning she'd waited for me after my lunacy of running with the bulls. She ran into my arms in tears, relief pouring out of her eyes. It dawned on me now that Grace was always waiting for me. Whether I was crossing the finish line at a marathon, or late to dinner trying to meet a deadline at the paper, she was always patiently waiting. Was she still?

"Where'd you go?" said Jenna, interrupting my time travel.

"Huh?"

"You drifted away. Where were you? With her again?"

"Oh. Sorry."

Jenna changed the subject to lighten the mood. "Did I tell you I quit smoking?"

"No! That's great! When?"

"Two weeks now. Lungs already feel a lot better. In fact, I'm ready for our rematch."

"Holding our breath?"

"Uh huh. You promised me a rematch."

"I don't remember any such promise."

"Scared?"

"Hardly."

"Then let's do it."

I reluctantly agreed as we both scrambled to our feet and dusted off grains of sand. "All right, but this is the last time."

"You say that now. Wait 'til you lose, then you'll come beggin' for a rematch."

"Kinda like you're doin' now?"

"Stop talking and start inhaling."

Secretly, I was thrilled by the competition. I had been working on my lung capacity in hopes that she'd challenge me, and I was about to spring the trap. I set the timer on my watch as we both filled our chests with the salt air and braced ourselves for the anaerobic suffering that was about to invade our blood cells. Again, one minute was no trouble for either of us. Jenna looked especially comfortable. Quitting smoking was agreeing with her. At ninety seconds, still no real signs of discomfort. I looked at my watch. Two minutes were gone and neither of us was backing down. Jenna narrowed her eyes in suspicion and brought her face within inches of mine, trying to discern if perhaps I was cheating by silently breathing in through my nose. After lingering in my space for an inordinate amount of time, she finally backed away. The seconds ticked by, seemingly slower than the normal pace of time: 2:15, 2:30, 2:45. Places on the stopwatch we'd never seen before. Three minutes approached. My muscles ached. Darts of blackness were stinging my brain: 3:05, 3:06, 3:07. Mercifully, Jenna gave up and a squall of carbon dioxide shot forth from her exhausted lungs. I held on for two more seconds, just for triumphant emphasis, then let go and joined her in heaving for breath.

"You cheated!" she finally mustered, bent over and sucking in oxygen.

I walked in small circles, my wrists resting on the crown of my head. "No I didn't! You were right next to my face!"

"I mean, you've been *practicing!*"

"Well, so have *you!*"

Jenna shook her head, partly to disagree, but mostly to reinvigorate the blood flow.

"You okay?" I asked.

"I'm a little woozy."

I moved closer and bent over to get a better look at her face. She was trying to open her eyes as widely as possible to shake off the lightheadedness from her oxygen debt. I'd seen this at the finish line of a hundred races. Someone who'd pushed themselves to their limit, and perhaps a little beyond. Jenna leaned forward and pressed her flagging body into mine, her lungs still fighting to replenish their stores. She nestled her head into my chest and I instinctively wrapped my arms around her in protective fashion, like a blanket around a sick child. She closed her eyes and gradually approached a normal rhythm of breathing. Even so, she didn't pull away. She seemed to find peace in the close human contact, and I wondered when was the last time she'd allowed herself to enjoy such a basic indulgence. Though I didn't know her all that well, I knew that Jenna was broken inside. She was like a fireproof safe that contained only jagged glass. Untouchable on the outside, unmendable within.

She moved her head a few degrees and pressed her ear firmly against my chest. "Your heart's not broken. I can hear it. It's working just fine."

I laughed softly, wishing that were true. I closed my eyes and thought of Grace. I remembered how much I loved to hold her and soak in her goodness. How I missed her healing touch. How I ached to wrap my arms around her again and lift her off the ground.

Jenna's lips were on mine before I had any sense of what was happening. My eyes flew open and saw her face pressed into mine. I violently pulled away like a hand touching a hot stove and backtracked in the sand.

"I'm sorry!" I blurted out. "I can't!"

Jenna was wounded, embarrassed by her advance. She crossed her arms and looked away. "Why not? Because of her?"

"Yes! Because of her."

"Everything you do is because of *her*!"

"Well, I'm sorry. That's just the way it is. I've never pretended otherwise."

She turned to face me, her awkward rebuff now being converted into anger. "You're in love with an ideal, Mac. It's not real anymore."

"It's *very* real."

"Don't delude yourself. You have this woman built up in your mind to where she's perfect, and *nobody* can live up to that."

"You're right. Maybe she's not perfect, but she was perfect for me, which is why I can't have a relationship with anyone else, because nobody else can live up to that. And I'm not asking anyone to try."

"How long has it been, Mac? A year and a half? Two years? When do you start living again?" I had no response. Jenna shook her head in frustration. "You're pathetic."

"Maybe I am. But I can't expect you to understand. You never met Grace. If you had, you'd see why I feel this way."

"You can't keep living like this, Mac. You can't be in love with a ghost."

"What do you care?" I shot back with growing anger. I was immediately sorry I'd said that, knowing perfectly well why she cared. We stared at each other in the darkness. Jenna shook her head again and started to back away. "I need a drink. See ya round, Mac." I started to offer up an apology, for what I don't know, but I left it alone. She turned around as she continued to walk away. Even from fifty yards away, I could see the tears glistening in her eyes. Jenna broke into a run and vanished beyond the dunes.

I stood alone in the sand, sorry that I'd wounded her, but more unsettled by the toll our exchange had taken on my own raw feelings. On more than one occasion I'd told Grace that I couldn't live without her. I was starting to believe that was true.

Sleep was a stranger that night. My scene with Jenna on the beach replayed itself over and over. I felt as though I'd handled it poorly, but I couldn't imagine what else I could have done. Coupled with that was my unnerving encounter with Duncan Danforth earlier that evening. Each blast of sea wind on the window screen and every creak in the floorboards seemed to be a harbinger of danger. It was the darkest hour before sunrise when I rolled over and turned

on the lamp on my nightstand. I reached into the suitcase under my
bed and unfolded another letter.

>My Dearest Seth,
>I miss you. I ate the last blueberry muffin, danced to
>the beach music you left behind, organized my new
>paints, and remembered. When we get older, remind
>me again of this visit. Remind me of our airport
>embrace, our walks, our joy rides. Remind me that
>we both scored an "eleven" on the happy scale.
>Nothing would matter if you weren't next to me,
>holding my hand. Life with you is magical. I can't
>wait to look into those blue eyes again.
>
>Always and forever,
>Grace

I closed my blue eyes, now riddled with red, and fought off the
impending sun.

# Chapter Nineteen

Sleep, even just a few hours of it, has a way of solving problems. The subconscious can sift through the entanglements of daily difficulties without the distractions of the external world. When I woke up the next morning, a course of direction had presented itself, and I immediately knew what I had to do. The hour for redemption had arrived.

With strong coffee to wash away the fog of fatigue, I channeled all my energies through my fingers and onto my keyboard. With a self-imposed deadline, I started to bang out a rough draft of the story of the Irukandji. I flipped through the copious notes I'd gathered in recent weeks and the computer screen quickly filled with the narrative of my investigation as I knitted the fragments of the story together in chronological order. The grounding of the *Cudmore*, the mysterious stinging of Kenneth Batterbee and Maggie Doolan and their treatment by the evasive Dr. Hartog. I included snippets of my conversations with ambulance driver Walt Kwiatkowski and Dr. Bethesda at the aquarium. Admittedly, my story raised as many questions as it provided answers, but it was a start. Every journalist knows that *The Washington Post*'s first revelatory story about Watergate was a basic below the fold staff piece about a break-in at the Democratic National Committee offices, initially dismissed as a "third rate burglary." Woodward and Bernstein would soon turn it into blockbuster headlines, and two years later a Presidency was toppled. I vividly remembered a journalism professor who'd used white chalk on a blackboard to reveal that the same letters were used to spell "words" and "sword." My cutlass had been drawn.

I saved the Irukandji story onto a thumb drive. Exhausted from eleven hours of poring over notes and transcribing them into newspaper copy, I turned off my computer and set my alarm for a two hour nap, then fell into bed and let my heavy eyelids succumb to gravity. I drifted in and out of fitful sleep as I waited for the dark before dawn.

It was just after midnight when I pulled into the offices of *The Bay Breeze*. As on every Sunday night, there was only one other car in the parking lot. I knew it belonged to Hank Shaw, the late night Metro editor. It was his job to put the paper to bed. It was going to be my job to get rid of him. I walked cautiously through the shadows to the passenger side of his car. Looking around one last time, I knelt down, unscrewed the plastic cap on his tire's valve stem, then pressed my thumbnail against the needle to let out the air. The *hisssss* was muffled by the swirling breeze, not that there was anyone around to hear it. In less than a minute, the tire was nearly flat.

As I walked toward the building, I turned up my collar to fight off the fresh spits of rain and a pushing wind of a late night thunderstorm, the first bad weather we'd had since I'd arrived at Sandbridge. It felt like a harbinger, heralding the lightning storm I was about to create.

I moved quickly to the side door and swiped my key card. It was something I'd done dozens of times before in the previous months, but tonight it was different. It felt clandestine. I wasn't entirely sure if what I was about to do was illegal, but at this point, I didn't care. I was driven by good intentions and the overriding principle that the public needs to know, and that was all that mattered. I was flinging a fistful of sand into the giant machine, hoping some of the grit would bring the gears to a grinding halt.

I was sweating profusely from mental unease as I walked upstairs to my office. I checked my watch. 12:09 a.m. Timing was critical. The paper went to bed at exactly 12:30 a.m., and not a second later, meaning all the local articles had to be in and edited, cutlines for photos and headlines written, and the latest scores and wire copy updated. Sunday nights were always the slowest. All the local stories had been in for hours and all of the East Coast ballgames were over. Some wire copy might need some proofreading and freshening up, but that was about it. All the late night editor had to do was sign off on the final proof from the layout guys, release the pages to the printer, and five minutes later, the presses were rolling. That gave the printers enough time to print the edition, bundle it, and get it out the door for 4:00 a.m. delivery. If you didn't release the pages by 12:30 a.m., the guys at the printer would call and bless you out. They wanted to go home, and the late night editor was standing between them and a warm bed. First, I had to get rid of Shaw.

"Hey, Scrim, how ya doing?" I said breezily as I walked into the pale fluorescent light of the newsroom. Hank "Scrim" Shaw was the grizzled veteran of the newsroom. He was probably only forty but looked sixty from a lifetime of hunching over keyboards and filling his lungs with the smoke of non-filtered Pall Malls. He'd spent years on the city desk at *The Baltimore Sun* and was a walking spellcheck when it came to proofreading copy. I had no idea why he was working at such a small shop like the *Breeze,* other than he just loved living at the beach and this job was simply a means to an end.

"What are you doin' here this late, Mac?" he said, barely looking up from his computer.

"Oh, just catchin' up on a few things. You about done?"

"Yeah. Just waitin' on the final proof from layout." He checked his watch.

"I hope it's soon. You might want to get that tire changed before the rain starts coming down any harder."

Shaw looked up for the first time. "What tire?"

"Your right front. It's flat. I assumed you knew."

"Aw, man, are you kiddin'?" He checked his watch again. I checked mine. 12:11 a.m.

"No. It's pancaked."

"Oh, great. I want to get home. I've been here all day." Agitated, Shaw checked his watch again. He looked at the phone, willing it to ring. "We're always the last in line with those guys, ya know? I get my stuff in at 10:30, and still, always the last to get my pages. I miss the old days when we did it ourselves."

"I could change it for you, save you some time. You might want to get outta here before the storm starts blowin' down trees."

Shaw stood up and exhaled loudly, torn between his duty as the editor, and wanting to get home on a rainy night. He checked his watch again. "Tell you what. . . would you mind just taking the call from layout, then releasing the pages to the printer? That'll save me twenty minutes."

"Sure. Glad to."

"Oh, man, thanks." He grabbed his jacket off the back of the chair and checked the pocket for his cigarettes and keys. "I gotta get outta here. Wife gets worried on nights like this."

"I understand. I'll take care of it."

"Thanks, Mac."

Shaw stuffed an unlit cigarette between his lips and headed out the door. I felt a little sickened knowing that I was sending a good man out into the wind and rain to fix a tire that I'd flattened, but it had to be done. I couldn't dwell on it because I now had a narrow window of opportunity and I had to get busy.

I couldn't believe how nervous I was as I logged on to start the process. It took me three tries just to insert my thumb drive into the computer. A half-minute later my article on the Irukandji finally popped up. Sweat from my palm dripped onto the mouse as I highlighted the copy and saved it into the system. I forwarded it directly to layout. 12:16 a.m. I picked up the phone and called layout. No answer. It continued to ring. 12:17.

In the "old days" that Hank Shaw referred to, layout was all done in-house, and was incredibly primitive. The copy was walked over to a paste-up room, put through a waxer, then literally stuck onto lined paper. The page was then photographed and sent on to the printer. In the digital age, all the layout work was now done at a remote location, in our case Arlington, Virginia, that handled as many as a dozen other papers. I was counting on that distance and detached corporate mentality for my plan to work.

Still no answer. I put the receiver on the desk and ran to the far window looking out over the parking lot. I could barely make out the figure of Hank Shaw pulling out a spare tire and jack from the trunk of his car. I ran back to my desk and kept waiting for layout to answer.

"C'mon, c'mon." I hung up and redialed. It rang, but still no response. 12:19. Deadline looming. I ran back to the window just to make sure Shaw wasn't coming back in. He was putting a wrench to the lug nuts. As lightning tore across the night sky, I felt even worse that I was putting him through this. From across the room, I could hear my phone being answered.

"Hello?" came a voice crackling through the handset. "Hello?"

I raced across the newsroom and lunged for the phone. "Yes! Hello! Layout?"

"Yeah. Who is this?" The voice on the other end was clearly annoyed by the intrusion.

"This is the *Breeze*."

"Why you callin'?"

"I have a late change. Breaking news."

"Are you serious?" Annoyance was turning into anger. "We're like five minutes away from deadline and you're changing something?"

"I'm sorry. But it's a big story." I glanced at my watch. "And it's more like ten minutes."

I heard an audible sigh and then a long pause. I could only imagine the shaking head and rolling eyes on the other end. "Okay, what is it?"

"I just sent it over. We'd like to play it on the front page above the fold."

"If it's such a big story, why did you wait to the last minute?"

His attitude was grating on me. The layout team at *The Atlanta Herald* would bend over backwards to accommodate late changes. Fresher was always better, and they knew it. This new generation just wanted to get it done and go home. I was about to launch into a sermon about old school journalism, but I had to tread carefully. I didn't want to push too hard or he'd start asking more questions. I also realized his apathy worked in my favor. The last thing I wanted was for anyone in layout to pay attention to the actual written words.

"I'm really sorry about that, but we're dealing with this storm down here and we've had a few computer problems. Listen, you can just kill what's there. The new piece should fit. It's only twenty-five inches, so you don't even have to mess with a jump page. Easy enough."

"Yeah. Easy. So says the guy who doesn't have to do it." There was another long pause. 12:22. The boys in printing were firing up their presses. My window was closing quickly.

"Look, I'm gonna get hammered by my boss if I don't get this—"

"All right, all right. Just chill. I'm doing it right now."

"Thanks. I owe you one."

"Yeah, how many times have I heard that?" I could hear him breathing hard as he dragged and dropped my story into the layout.

"How big you want the headline?" he asked.

"Is there room for 72-point font?"

"I suppose." Another long pause. 12:24. Clock ticking.

"Done," he announced after two minutes. *That's it?* I thought. *We argued for three minutes over something that only took you two minutes?* I was seething with self-righteous anger and about to say those very thoughts out loud when the brash voice on the other end of the phone hit me with the verbal equivalent of a left hook. "What's the headline?"

"The headline?"

"Yeah, you know, those large words on the top of the story? All the good papers use 'em these days. Any thoughts?"

I ignored his sarcasm and drummed my fingers on the desk in a mild panic as I tried to come up with a headline. You want something eye-catching, because a good banner headline sells more papers out of the rack than anything else. It can't be too basic and dry like *The Wall Street Journal*, but it shouldn't be over the top like *The New York Post*. As I sat there and urged my tired brain to come up with something borderline clever, I developed more respect for headline writers at the major dailies, whose sole job was to come up with three to five carefully crafted words that tantalized readers into consuming the story below. Why hadn't I taken care of this before? *Come on, Mac. . . just put down anything! It doesn't matter!* But it did. This was going to be the most important story of my life and I wanted the headline to be as good as the body of the article. *Deadly Jellyfish Jeopardy. Coastal Menace Means Trouble. Hidden Danger for Swimmers. No! Terrible. Boring. Come on, Mac, think!* 12:25. I was wasting precious time. I closed my eyes and rubbed my temples, vainly trying to conjure up just three more words.

"How about Killer Looms in Infested Island Waters?"

"Way too long if you want 72-point."

"Okay, how about. . . um. . . Trouble for Swimmers?"

A derisive sigh came through the line. "That's your big breaking story? Seriously?"

"Just give me a sec..."

"Hey, I'm back."

I whipped around and leapt to my feet, feeling the shock of the sudden intrusion blitz through every vessel of my vascular system. It was Shaw. "Geez, Scrim, you scared the crap outta me!"

"I can see that. Sorry!"

"It's okay." I was certain he could hear my heart pounding as I cupped my hand over the receiver. "Why'd you come back? You need help with the tire?"

Shaw sat down at his desk and brought his computer back to life. "No, it's fixed. I called home to tell them I was on my way and my kid told me she needed something off the internet for some school project due tomorrow. The thunderstorm knocked out the power to our neighborhood, so here I am, racking up more father-of-the-year points." He started banging away on the keyboard. "Did layout call back?"

"Uh, yeah. All good."

"Thanks for covering for me." Shaw leaned forward to read the pages popping up from his online search. "What happened to the good old days when we just wrote a book report in longhand?"

It was 12:26. I needed to slap a headline on the piece and be done with it. I sat back down and tried to reset my brain from the jolt it had just received. "You still there?" I asked the irritated soul in layout.

"That would be a yes. Do you have a headline, or don't you?"

I refocused. *Danger Lurks Offshore. Horrible.* 12:27. If I didn't come up with something right away, the printers would call. Shaw would answer. I'd have some awful explaining to do.

Shaw shattered my concentration. "Hey, Mac, you know anything about Gallipoli? All I'm gettin' are movie reviews."

"Look up Dardenelles," I responded to Shaw.

"What?" came the voice over the phone.

"Thanks," said Shaw.

12:28. The angry voice in layout started to speak. "Okay, listen, I'm just gonna send the original—"

"Killer Stalks Sandbridge," I blurted out.

"What's that?" said Shaw, his eyes married to the computer screen.

I ignored him. "You get that?" I asked layout.

"Got it. Thank you," he replied with utter contempt. "It's in. Sending it on. Now then, are there any other major breaking stories that lack headlines I need to know about?"

"No. We're good. Thanks." I hung up at exactly 12:29. All I had to do now was hit SEND, emailing the printer and releasing the pages for the Monday morning edition. In less than five minutes, ink would be hitting blank newsprint and transforming it into mass media. By first light, the beach community would be informed of the perils of the Irukandji, and lives would be saved. But as my finger hovered over the keyboard, I was suddenly gripped by the queasiness of self-doubt. Was I sure I was doing the right thing? In those last few seconds as the deadline approached, I recalled with great clarity the fallout from a story I'd done on a prominent Atlanta physician who'd been committing insurance fraud by charging for services that were never rendered. Not only did he go to prison, but his wife lost her position as an administrator at a private school. Numerous local charities, sports teams, and cultural events lost their funding because his generous checks suddenly stopped coming. His four children were shamed so badly they finally had to move to another city to escape the humiliation of their father's misdeeds. I hadn't anticipated the extent of the ripple effect. But at the end of the day, it was all dirty money, and even though some good came out of it, it was still a crime that needed to be exposed. As I ran it through my mind, I knew a story about deadly jellyfish would impact the tourist industry in Sandbridge, but then again, so would dead bodies from lethal stings. I knew in my heart I wasn't just doing this story to salvage my career. This was truly for the greater good. I was saving lives, and it was entirely up to me, because frankly, nobody else had the guts or the resources to do it. I glanced at the clock. Ten seconds until the deadline. Nine... eight... seven. I hit SEND. Redemption.

# Chapter Twenty

I woke up early and ran the two miles to the Sandbridge grocery, where the morning edition of *The Bay Breeze* was nearly sold out. I bought a copy and swelled with pride when I saw my rogue article in print. I hadn't attached my byline to the piece, but I didn't care. I realized that the parking lot was full of people reading my words, and slowly shaking their heads in quiet disbelief. It was probably the same scene at breakfast tables all across the island. It was my Woodward and Bernstein moment. They had Watergate, I had the waters of Sandbridge. I knew my exposé would save lives. I also knew it would get me fired.

As I expected, Paul Munce's nasally voice was on my voicemail when I got back to my condo and turned on my cell phone. As I filtered through his tirade of four-letter words, I got the message: I was summarily and immediately relieved of my duties at *The Bay Breeze*. I didn't care. I wore my dismissal from the newspaper as a badge of honor. I had fallen on the sword in the name of investigative journalism, and the world would be a better place for my sacrifice. Because of my mighty pen, an army of scientists and marine biologists would descend on the beaches of Sandbridge like soldiers on the sands of Normandy. Because of me, the elusive and deadly Irukandji would be discovered and eradicated. The local ecosystem would be restored. Lives would be saved. All because of me.

I walked to the beach and looked out over the waves, wondering what changes were in store now for Sandbridge. As it would turn out, I had no idea.

# Part Two

# Chapter Twenty-one

I could not have possibly foreseen, nor even imagined, the local cataclysm my story would cause. The minute my piece on the Irukandji hit the newsstands, and was subsequently picked up by the Associated Press and disseminated worldwide, the phones started ringing incessantly at the local real estate rental companies. Each caller was the bearer of the same bad news: *cancel my reservation at Sandbridge. . . there's no way I'm taking my family to a beach that's teeming with venomous jellyfish.*

Within hours, the entire summer rental slate had been wiped clean. Nobody was coming to Sandbridge. The domino effect of the cancellations spread quickly. Restaurants were suddenly empty. Gift shops had more clerks than customers. Laundry service, equipment rentals, produce stands, golf courses, bait and tackle shops, all washed away in a tsunami of fear.

The greater impact was about to come in a second wave. Because the vast majority of the homes on Sandbridge Island were vacation rental properties, and suddenly there were no renters, the bottom fell out of the local housing market. The precipitous freefall in market prices was going to plunge the unprepared and over-leveraged into bankruptcy. Without the rental income, the owners could no longer afford to keep their properties. Many of them were already perilously close to being underwater with the overbearing terms of their subprime lending and adjustable-rate mortgages. I had simply provided the tipping point, the final push into foreclosure. "For Sale" signs popped up overnight like dandelions, the owners scrambling to be first in line to get out from under the burden of a massive mortgage payment on their million dollar beachfront rental homes. Properties were listing for less than twenty-five percent of their appraised value in this desperate fire sale. It was like a run on a dying bank, with account holders willing to take just pennies on the dollar of their investments. But even in the dark valley of rock bottom prices, nobody in their right mind was going to buy a house built next to deadly water. Nest eggs were going to be wiped out, futures dashed. All because of me.

For the next two days, I holed up in my condo, tossing and turning at night and then sleeping away every hour of daylight. I ignored Jenna's phone calls, and even refused to answer the door on the two occasions she dropped by to check on me. Paralyzed by grief and uncertainty, I simply didn't know what to do next. And so I did nothing. My only escape came from running. I slinked into the dark night for hours of joint pounding and mind numbing miles. It was the only way I could find to put one foot in front of the other. I was never running toward anything, only running away from a recent past so twisted and haunting that I couldn't begin to wrap my weary mind around it.

When the last morsel of food was gone from my refrigerator and cupboards, I realized it was time to move on. I didn't know where, but I knew that *anywhere* was going to be better than my current situation. Maybe now was the time I booked passage back to Europe. I could find menial work to support myself and vanish entirely from the English speaking world. Perhaps I could work in a vineyard in Italy. Grace and I had always dreamed of going to Tuscany on our honeymoon. It would provide the perfect ironic setting in which to immerse myself in self-loathing. If only Grace could see me now, to see how far I'd fallen since our first meeting on Folly Beach. Thank heaven she couldn't.

As I packed my meager belongings and prepared to leave Sandbridge, the despondency I felt was crushing. This was far greater than anything I'd felt after my debacle at the *Herald.* That had only affected a handful of people, principally me. The collateral damage I'd caused this time impacted tens of thousands of people. Maybe I'd saved a few lives, or at the very least a few trips to the emergency room, by warning everyone about this public health threat lurking in the water, but at what cost? I tried to convince myself that it wasn't *me* who had ruined their lives, but rather it was the *story*. The blame for the sudden panic should rest on the message and not the messenger.

Could I have gone about it another way? Was I so bent on redemption that I forged ahead without anticipating the cascading economic impact? Too late for such musings in hindsight. It was water over the dam, and I was drowning in it.

I decided to go for one last run. I would run along the beach down to the Little Island Pier, perhaps see the boys from a distance, then flip around and cruise home on Sandfiddler Road. A tailwind pushed me along as I ran south towards the pier and the Atlantic surf was kicking up into whitecaps. These were the early warnings of a nor'easter storm pushing down from New England. The strong northeast winds would soon collide with the warm air and moisture from the Gulf of Mexico and create a storm every bit as powerful as a Category 1 hurricane. I was getting off the island just in time.

As I ran along the hard-packed sand near the shoreline, I was struck by the eerie absence of activity. It was like the dead of winter, only worse. The sands were lifeless and devoid of color. No sunbathers, no surfers, no umbrellas or beach chairs. Not even the enigmatic Melvin playing chess with himself. All gone. All because of me.

As Little Island Pier came slowly into focus, I could see there was only one person fishing in the darkened waters. Lyman Gregg. Something brought that man back to those weathered boards day after day. A purpose. A mission. A calling. I admired the passion Lyman had for living, and I wondered if I'd ever reclaim it for my own tormented soul.

I didn't want Lyman to see me, so I gave him a waving farewell from a distance and then made a hard right and ran through the soft sand and exited the beach onto Sandfiddler. I picked up the pace on the hard pavement, knowing these were my last steps on the island. Despite the pain I felt, this place would always hold fond memories. It had cradled me and provided a measure of healing for my lacerated heart. I had made good friends with the boys on the pier, and of course Jenna. I had developed a much deeper appreciation for the divine beauty of nature. Above all, I had learned a lot about life, mostly that I still had a great deal more to learn.

As I ran past the empty driveways and decks of the rental houses, a fresh focus was suddenly cast on the blur of recent events. What had been a "For Sale" sign in a front yard a few days ago was now crossed by a banner reading "Under Contract." A half-block later, another "Under Contract" sign tilted in the strong breeze, and then two more. As I slowed my gait, I realized there were at least a dozen beachfront houses on this one street that had been snapped up in recent days. Something had suddenly and drastically changed to create a seismic shift in the local real estate market. But what, or who, was behind it? Who in their right mind would knowingly buy such damaged goods? Either they didn't know why the local housing market had tanked, or for some odd reason, they didn't care. It made no sense.

Infused with curiosity, I sprinted home through a twenty mile an hour headwind from the northeast, showered off, and jumped in my car.

I sat at the end of the bar at Margie and Rays, nursing a Land Shark Lager as I turned on my laptop. The real estate agent's name on the "Under Contract" signs along Sandfiddler was Bev Coleman with Seaford Realty. Her name just *sounded* like a real estate agent, and she looked like one too when I found her picture and contact information on the agency's website. I turned my back on the rest of the bar and gave Bev a call.

"Seaford Realty, this is Bev Coleman speaking," answered the pleasant voice on the other end. "Can I help you?"

"Bev, my name is Jake Barnes. I saw a house for sale a couple days ago on Sandfiddler Road and your name was on the sign."

"Do you remember the address?"

"It was 3023 Sandfiddler. Near the intersection with Bonita."

"Oh, I'm sorry, that's already under contract."

"Oh," I sighed, trying to ooze with disappointment. "That's too bad. I really liked that house."

"Yes, it went under contract yesterday."

"Shoot. Wish I'd gotten there first. Can you tell me who made the offer?"

"No, I'm sorry. I can't divulge that."

"Well can you at least tell me how much the offer is?"

"Sorry. We don't do that. It's against the law."

"Is there some place I can look it up? City Hall or something?"

"I'm afraid not. Until the sale goes through, I'm the only one who has that information."

I sighed heavily into the phone. "Oh man, my wife is going to be so disappointed. She loves that house."

"Are there some other properties you might be interested in? I have quite a few listings. If you could tell me about what price range—"

I interrupted her sales pitch. "What if I put in a backup offer, you know, in case your buyer doesn't work out?"

"You are certainly welcome to do that, but it's not likely to fall through."

I kept working on her, trying to wear her down. "If I did make a backup offer, *then* can you tell me who I'm bidding against? I'd at least like to know if I have a chance. I'd hate to get my wife's hopes up and then disappoint her."

"Again, I'm not at liberty to say. I could lose my license."

"And you said there's no place to look up who's making the offer?"

"I'm afraid not. The only place the buyer's name is listed is on the 'offer to purchase' form, which only a few of us at the agency have access to. It's all to protect my seller, just as I would do with you," said Bev, as politely as possible. "I'm sorry, Mr. Barnes. I hope you understand."

"Oh well. Rules are rules." There was a long, awkward pause as I tried to figure out another avenue of questioning in what was turning out to be a dead end.

Bev broke the silence. "Now then, the rules are different if it's for sale by owner. . . they can tell you whatever they want, but as a licensed agent, I'm bound by the laws of the real estate association."

I sat up straight, tuning her out as my brain was quickly rewinding what she'd just said. *The rules are different if it's for sale by owner. . . they can tell you whatever they want.* Her words had instantly given me new life.

Bev was still talking. "As I said before, I have multiple listings on the island that you and your wife might—"

I hung up, inoculated with fresh adrenaline. I left a five dollar bill under the half-empty Land Shark and hit the door running.

I sped back to the island and turned onto Sandfiddler. Within less than a mile I saw what I needed: a sign reading For Sale By Owner. I pulled in the driveway and knocked on the door. A shirtless man in his early 50s answered, already looking annoyed that I'd intruded. He looked and sounded like former military.

"Hi," I offered, as politely as possible. "I saw your sign and wondered if the house is still on the market."

He frowned slightly as he sized me up. "Why? You tryin' to steal it out from under me too?"

"I'm not sure what you mean, sir. Has somebody already made an offer?"

"If you want to call it that. They're offerin' about twenty percent of what it's worth. It's a joke." He stepped outside and spit angrily. "Everyone around here's panicking because of this jellyfish thing, and they're all trying to bail out. It's insane."

"Are you gonna take the offer?"

"No way. I pumped my life savings into this place. I'm not gonna let some carpetbagger slide in here and lowball me. So unless you got a really good offer, you best be movin' along." He spit again.

I frowned and nodded in agreement with him. "I tell ya, that makes me really mad when people take advantage like that." I spit, trying to prove I was as angry about it as he was.

"I know, right? This mess could wipe me out, and these crooks could care less. They just want to rip me off. Vultures."

"Exactly. Vultures." I shook my head in disgust, letting him know I was completely on his side. "Can I ask who made the offer?"

"Some corporation."

"You remember the name?"

"Not sure. Hang on a sec." He spit again, then disappeared into the house. He returned a few moments later with a single sheet of paper. He slipped on a pair of reading glasses and pointed to the name on the first page of the offer as he showed it to me. "There. That's them."

The name on the paper was Cleito LLC. How clever, I thought. The name was clearly a tribute to Plato's Cleito; wife of Poseidon, the King of the Sea, the mother of Atlas, and matriarch of the rulers of the mythical Atlantis. Obviously a great deal of thought went into the selection of that title, whoever had come up with it.

"Ever heard of 'em?" asked the homeowner.

"Can't say I have." *Not yet,* I thought to myself. I started to back away. "Thanks for your time. I appreciate it."

"You interested in the house? I'd be willing to entertain a reasonable offer."

"*Very* interested," I nodded as I headed back to my car. "I'll be in touch." I saluted him for some unknown reason as I hopped in my car and rolled away.

I sat in the parking lot of the Sandbridge grocery store and fired up my laptop. It took less than two minutes on the Commonwealth of Virginia State Corporation Commission's website to find Cleito LLC. I scrolled down to see if I could attach a name and face to the mysterious company. My heart nearly collapsed when I saw it: Duncan Danforth. Suddenly, all those "Under Contract" signs made perfect sense. Like a ravenous shark, Danforth had swooped in and placed offers on dozens of distressed beachfront homes on Sandbridge, getting them at rock bottom prices, all through Cleito LLC. After I recovered from the sickening reaction of my initial shock, I quickly did the math in my head. In the fire sale frenzy, he'd swiftly put offers on properties with an estimated tax value of close to a hundred million dollars for an investment of just over twenty million. All minimum down payments, all executed within a three day span. It was as if Danforth had been sitting on the sidelines with cash in hand, fully anticipating that the local real estate market was about to crash. More like *knowing*.

As I scanned the other holdings of Cleito LLC, the news went from bad to worse. Nothing makes the hair on the back of the neck of an investigative reporter stand up more quickly than a situation that at first glance appears to be the product of pure coincidence. We do not readily believe in the randomness of life. When peeling back the layers of a crime or a cover-up, what may appear to most people to be two isolated events, rarely are. They are dots that require you to connect them. When I saw the address on one of the properties in the Cleito portfolio, I knew immediately it could not be coincidence: 105 Tuscany Drive. The rhyming address of the office of Dr. Dirk Hartog, who treated the Irukandji victims. The building was owned by Duncan Danforth.

A sickening knot began to grab my stomach, that same feeling of nauseated distress you get when you're fifty miles from home and suddenly realize you forgot to turn off the oven. The tourniquet would soon twist tighter as I pored over more documents. I saw an address on Princess Anne Drive that I also recognized. It was the building that headquartered *The Bay Breeze*. Duncan Danforth also owned the newspaper. "No, no, no, no, no, no," was all I could manage to utter in a heaving whisper. I was sick beyond repair.

# Chapter Twenty-two

A cold rain was falling as I sped away from the island, not entirely sure where I was going first. I leaned forward in the driver's seat and clutched the very top of the steering wheel with two sweaty palms, the same way you'd drive through a blinding blizzard. The synapses in my brain were in rapid-fire mode, the neurons overloaded with all the dots I was trying to connect. What did it all mean? How was it that the dirty fingerprints of Duncan Danforth were on everything I'd touched? I fought off the awful memories of my mistakes at *The Atlanta Herald* and tried to focus on the new problems in front of me.

My first stop was Dr. Hartog's office at 105 Tuscany Drive to see what he might know. Closed. No cars, no sign out front, no activity whatsoever. I jumped out and peered through the blinds of the front window. The reception area was completely empty. The furniture that had been there just weeks before had vanished. The pelting rain from the nor'easter's outer bands was coming in sideways, soaking me, as I started to visibly shake with emotion. Nothing made sense as I stood at the intersection of confusion and nausea. I knew something was horribly wrong, but I couldn't fit any of the pieces of the puzzle together. *What is happening?* echoed through my weary soul as I pressed my forehead against the hood of my car, feeling the heat of the engine against my muddled brain. I was in a daze, trapped inside a nightmare where I couldn't wake up. *Think, Seth, think. Focus on the facts. Think.* Some clarity finally arrived.

My mind flashed back to that same parking lot a few weeks before. Any good reporter can learn more about a person from just looking at their car than you can from actually talking to them. Cars don't lie.

That vehicle will tell you how much money the driver makes, their favorite color, and if they care enough to fix dents and scratches. Are they neat, or is the floorboard covered with wrappers from fast food restaurants? Is there a Starbucks cup in the cup holder or a bargain brand soda can from the grocery store? The stickers on the bumper or back window will tell you their favorite social causes, favorite bands, favorite teams, political leanings, philosophy of life, and even the places they've visited. For some reason, some people want the entire motoring public to know they've seen Luray Caverns and Rock City. Most importantly, you can also figure out where that vehicle is usually parked. . . in a gated community, a company parking deck, a military base, or perhaps a college campus. I distinctly remembered the Old Dominion parking sticker on the green Honda Civic that had been parked in front of Dr. Hartog's office. The nervous young girl with the crimson in her hair should be easy to find.

Less than an hour later I was on the campus of Old Dominion University in Norfolk, flipping through the pages of recent yearbooks in the Admissions office. It took only fifteen minutes before I spotted the distinctive picture of the "receptionist" I'd encountered a few weeks earlier at Dr. Hartog's office. I now had a name to go with the face. Hayley Wozniak. Drama major.

I wandered over to the University Theatre where summer-school students were constructing a set for Shakespeare's *The Tempest*. I approached a young man in tight jeans and vintage sneakers, slapping paint on plywood.

"Excuse me. I'm looking for Hayley Wozniak. They said she might be here."

"Who are *you*?"

"I'm a casting agent. I need someone for a commercial we're shooting. National spot. I saw her headshot and thought she'd be perfect."

I now had his full attention. "National spot? Wow! That's big time!"

"Yes it is. Do you know where I can track her down?"

"I'm pretty sure she lives in Foundation House."

"Where's that?"

"Over off 49th. But you're more likely to find her at the Borjo."

"Borjo? What's that?"

"It's a coffeehouse off of Monarch. She works there most afternoons."

"Thanks."

"Man, I hope you give her the part. Hayley's really good. Awesome actress. She can play anything."

"So I hear."

Minutes later I pulled up in front of the Borjo at 45th and Monarch, right next to the green Honda I'd seen at Hartog's office. Through the window I could see Hayley, wiping back the beads of sweat on her jet black pageboy hair as she labored over a hissing milk steamer. I was still reeling with bewilderment over the bizarre cascade of recent events, but I collected myself enough to enter the coffee shop and present myself as calmly as possible.

"Hello, Hayley."

As soon as she looked up and our eyes connected, I could see the blood drain out of her sallow face. You could tell that her first instinct was to abandon her duties as barista and make a run for it out the back door, but she quickly slumped her shoulders in resignation.

She turned to the girl next to her behind the counter. "Can you take over for a minute?"

Moments later we were seated at a table in the corner of the coffeehouse. My instincts had been right about our first encounter at Dr. Hartog's office. She *had* been lying to me. But not for the reason I thought. Hayley was trembling as she looked straight into the tabletop and confessed her sins.

"They told me it was an acting job. They gave me lines to rehearse and everything. But when I got there and saw there weren't any cameras, I knew something was wrong."

"But you did it anyway."

"They'd already paid me. A lot. I needed the money for school, so I played the part and went home. I had no idea what they were doing. I still don't." She looked up, fear in her eyes. "Are you like some kinda private detective, or something?"

"Kind of."

"Am I in trouble?"

"Not if you help me."

"What do you want to know?"

"You said *they* hired you. Who's *they*?"

"A man and a woman. I don't know their names. I met 'em at a club one night. They asked me if I did any acting and it just kinda went from there."

"What did they ask you to do?"

"They said they needed someone to play the part of a receptionist, for some sort of hidden camera show, or something like that."

"And you said you'd do it, just like that?"

"Hey, when you're a broke college student-slash-actress, you'll take any job you can get. I know girls who've done a lot worse things."

"I can imagine. Okay, so you take the job. Then what?"

"It was easy. They coached me a little on what to say, and it went down just like they said it would. They said you'd come in and ask for the doctor, and I was supposed to appear to be nervous and incompetent, then send you in. It was easy."

I thought back to our encounter that day. "I must say, you're a *very* good actress. You definitely pulled off nervous and incompetent."

She nodded in appreciation. "Thank you. Actually, I *was* really nervous, so I suppose you shouldn't give me too much credit."

"Anything else you remember?"

"Yeah. The minute you left the office, the guy who'd hired me rolled up in a rental truck and started loading the office furniture back into it. I remember the truck said *South Bay Rentals* on the side. He told me to get lost, so I did."

I wrote it down. "That helps a lot. Thanks."

Hayley looked up for the first time. "Did I do something illegal? I can't afford to get in trouble."

"Nah. You're good. Nothin' to worry about."

She exhaled softly and nodded in thanks, her chin quivering as she fought back tears of relief. I sensed that this time she wasn't acting. She brushed back her black hair and exhaled again. "Who are these people?"

"I don't know. Yet."

# Chapter Twenty-three

Sometimes people will give you information you need or want because you bluff your way into it, concocting some pretense as to why they should reveal what they know. Sometimes they do it out of a sense of civic duty, believing they're helping to solve some crime. And sometimes they hand over information because they just don't care. I found the latter to be especially true at the beach. So many people here are working temporary jobs for rent and beer money and it makes not a whit to them if they let you come in and download the company's entire hard drive. Such was my luck when I walked into *South Bay Rentals*.

All I had to do was convince the young man behind the counter that two of my employees had rented a panel truck on April 30th and they'd lost the receipt. I just needed to know how much they'd spent so I could deduct it on my taxes.

"No problem, dude," as he stepped up to the computer. "April 30th, you said?"

"Yes."

A few mouse clicks later I had my answer. "I think this is it. It was the only truck that went out that day."

"Who signed for it?"

"Let's see. . . looks like Kenneth Batterbee?"

Batterbee. The guy I'd met at the campground with the Australian accent. One of Dr. Hartog's Irukandji patients. I was stunned, but couldn't show it. "Yep, that's one of my guys. Thanks!" I started to walk out.

"Hey, didn't you want to know how much it cost?"

"Oh, yeah. How much was it?"

"One hundred forty-nine bucks. That includes the tax."

"Got it. Thanks!"

With my windshield wipers beating back and forth, I raced through the strengthening nor'easter and made my way to the North Bay Shore Family Campground to reintroduce myself to Kenneth Batterbee. I stepped out of the car and wiped the driving rain out of my eyes, as if that would change what I was seeing. The cement slab where his camper had been on my initial visit was gone. Uprooted without a trace. I was fairly certain he hadn't left a forwarding address. I also knew in my gut that the distraught woman I'd met at the motel, Maggie Doolan, or whatever her real name was, had long since checked out. Probably moments after I'd left her.

I stood in the vacant lot and spun around in disbelief. A piercing rain tore through my clothes and chilled my skin. A paralyzing panic was taking over my body. I looked to the heavens, as if the answer would reveal itself in the storm clouds. *What was happening? Think.* I told myself again. *Sort it out. Think this through.*

I got back in my car and for no logical reason I called Paul Munce. I just needed someone to listen as I tried to sort through the perplexing labyrinth of recent events.

"Hello?" came Munce's irritating voice through the receiver.

"Paul, it's Mac."

"Mac MacClellan?"

"Yeah." I resisted the urge to say *how many Macs do you know?* "Listen, I know you're really mad at me right now, and I don't blame you, but there's something very strange going on and I just feel like the newspaper needs to know about it"

"How many times have I heard *that?* Everybody thinks the paper can solve their troubles. Make *your* problem *my* problem."

"Munce, can we skip the lecture just this once and let me tell you what's going on?"

There was an audible sigh of exasperation on the other end. "Oh, all right. What's got you so bent outta shape?"

"It has to do with the Irukandji story. I just have this gut feeling that there's more to the story than I reported. I think someone needs to dig into it."

"No way," shot back Munce. "Do you have any idea how much damage you've already done? You've single-handedly ruined the local economy! You need to slip out of town in the dead of night, before they come to your house with torches and tar."

"I know, I know, I screwed up in a big way. But I'm tellin' you, there's something fishy about all this."

"That's an unfortunate choice of words."

"You know what I'm saying. There's something terribly wrong here. I don't know what it is, but something's just not right. I really need your help."

"Hey, I tried to help you out when I gave you a job when nobody else would touch you, and look how you repaid me! Like I said, you need to pack up and leave town and change your name… again. It's over."

"At least hear me out," I begged.

"Sorry, Mac. You did this to yourself. The answer is no. Don't call me again."

He hung up. Call ended. I slumped down in the driver's seat and pressed my forehead against the steering wheel. During my years as an investigative reporter, I'd always been able to tell the difference between hitting rock bottom and hitting a dead end. I didn't feel like this was over. I wasn't ready to give up.

I leaned forward with fresh resolve, cranked the engine, and let my tires spew gravel as I drove out of the campground. Paul Munce was going to listen to what I had to say, whether he wanted to or not.

Thirty minutes later I was in front of Munce's house, a well-kept Cape Cod style home on 48th street just off Atlantic Avenue on the north side of Virginia Beach. There was a Jaguar convertible parked in his driveway with the sheen and color of black onyx. *Management certainly gets paid better than reporters* I thought as I pulled in behind it.

I leaned forward into the wind as I ran through the rain to the front door. I knocked loudly and waited. I had expected anger or dismay, but the look on Munce's face when he opened the door was one of sickening shock. "What are you doing here? I told you to leave town! Now get outta here!"

"Please! Just let me lay it out for you, then I'll leave you alone!"

"There's nothing you can say to me that I want to hear! You're poison, Mac, and I don't want anything to do with you. Now go, before I call the cops."

He tried to shut the front door but I shoved my foot in the way. "You can call the police, but I'm not leavin' until you hear what I have to say. Five minutes. That's all I want. Then I'm gone."

Munce shook his head vigorously. "Mac, I'm warning you. . . go! Now!"

Another man's voice came from behind the door. A voice with a rich, Australian accent. "Oh, let the man in. Surely we owe him five minutes after all he's done for us, don't you think?"

Munce exhaled in resignation and opened the door wider. Standing behind him, holding a snifter of brandy, was Duncan Danforth.

"Well, Mr. MacClellan. Our paths cross yet again. Please, come in."

I stepped across the threshold in stunned silence. The visual information being presented to my weary brain was not computing. *What in the world is he doing here?* The door shut behind me as I stood in Munce's living room, speechless and reeling.

Danforth smiled as he looked down into his snifter and took a small sip of brandy. "I suppose someone owes you an explanation."

I looked at Munce, trying to regain my footing after the staggering blow. He dropped his head and looked at the floor.

Danforth pointed to the couch, beckoning me to sit down. "Please, make yourself comfortable. Can we get you a drink? You seem. . . frazzled."

"I'll stand, thank you. You wanna tell me what's going on? What are *you* doing here?"

Danforth's face was creased with a smug grin. "I imagine it *is* a bit confusing, even for a man of your intellect." Danforth eased himself into one of the room's overstuffed chairs and crossed his legs, amused by the dramatic theatre he'd created. "Now then, where to begin?"

A sickening numbness invaded every cell in my body as Danforth revealed the unbelievable truth. He fashioned a villainous grin as he drummed his index and middle fingers against his chin and launched into a soliloquy that clearly delighted him. "Let's suppose you wanted to create a panic. . . a mass hysteria. . . how would one go about that? I imagine first you'd have to establish the threat, some sort of imminent public danger, then you'd have to find a vehicle with which to disseminate that information to the masses. The second part of that equation is rather simple, given today's social media. But the first part. . . inventing the danger. . . much more complex."

I was so dazed I was having trouble grasping Danforth's line of reasoning. "What are you trying to say?"

Danforth sipped his brandy and continued. "What if, for example, there was suddenly the threat of a deadly jellyfish looming off the coast. What impact might that have on the local psyche? I should think it would make one want to avoid the water. Perhaps avoid an entire island. Wouldn't you?"

The blurred lens through which I'd been viewing recent events was suddenly starting to come into sharper focus. "Are you telling me there never *was* any Irukandji?"

Danforth grinned and nodded. "Precisely."

I shook my head in dazed disbelief as I looked down at the twisted grain of the hardwood floor, now wet from the drippings of my drenched clothing. "The stinging victims. . . Dr. Hartog. . . none of it real?"

"Bravo, Mr. MacClellan. You catch on quickly! Fortunately for me, not *that* quickly."

"So you create this panic, run everybody off in fear, then buy up all the distressed rental properties in the fire sale."

"Exactly! And rather ingenious, wouldn't you say? For time immemorial, nobody has ever wanted to buy a haunted castle. You provided the ghost, and then did me the additional favor of telling everyone about it. All I needed was someone to light the fuse and then I stood back and watched the fireworks. Lovely sight. Just lovely."

My knees nearly buckled under the weight of Danforth's revelation. It was the same stupefying nausea I'd felt when I'd blown the Ludwig Oil story at the *Herald*, only a thousand-fold worse in magnitude. *How did this happen?* I asked myself. *How did I get duped yet again?* I knew the answer. I'd wanted to redeem myself so badly, to salvage my reputation and reclaim my shattered life. My mind quickly replayed snippets of scenes from the last few months. Munce handing me the security card to get into the newspaper office after hours, Lyman's musings about how on earth the *Cudmore* could have run aground in broad daylight, Dr. Hartog carelessly leaving his medical files for me to see, and on and on. I wondered how many other people like Hayley Wozniak had been actors in this grand conspiracy. Didn't matter now. I had gobbled up every morsel of misinformation that Danforth had left for me on this path to purgatory, and now I was paying a dear price for my blind ambition. My self-loathing transformed into anger as I raised my addled head and looked squarely at the agent of my misfortune. I pierced Munce with my furious eyes. "Why *me*, Munce? Why'd you set me up? What did I ever do to you?"

Munce hung his head and stared at his scuffed brown loafers. He looked more like a pitiful little boy than ever before. "I'm sorry, Mac. He caught me embezzling from the company. I was trapped. I had to play along."

"I see. You *had* to play along. You get caught with your hand in the company till and the *only* way you can see your way out of it is to ruin hundreds of lives, starting with mine. You're pathetic, Munce."

"Come now," Danforth chimed in. "Don't blame little Muncey. Don't you see? It *had* to be you. We needed the perfect storm of desperation, investigative skill, and the blind passion for redemption. After what happened to you at the *Herald*, we knew you were the right man for the job. There was really no other choice. We knew you'd pursue the story and we knew you'd find a way to get it into print, because that's who you are. Your dogged determination was the one thing we knew we could count on without fail." Danforth swirled his brandy and held it up to the light to gaze at its amber tones. "Of course, you probably realize by now that your getting fired from the *Herald* wasn't just a coincidence." He grinned madly, on the brink of laughter. "I think my favorite part of all that was naming him Harold. Harold? *Herald?* Don't you think that's pure genius?"

"Oh my God," was all I could think to say as my knees buckled underneath me. "You were behind that *too*? Unbelievable."

Danforth nodded with enthusiasm. "I'll take that as a compliment. And as you can now clearly see, my dear 'mackerel man,' you have been the most wonderful of messenger boys. Our puppet. A pawn with a pen. I want to thank you for all you did to make a plan come together, however unwittingly you went about it. Brilliant! Just brilliant, wouldn't you agree?"

I was seething. "You won't get away with it!" I yelled, casting my burning eyes at both of them.

"Oh, but we already have," said Danforth. "The damage is done, and the benefits are being reaped, all thanks to you. You can't unring the bell."

"You'll go to prison for this! I'll see to it!"

"For what? I've done nothing illegal. *I'm* not the one who dug up this crazy story about killer jellyfish. *I'm* not the one who crept into a newspaper office in the dead of night and changed the copy for the morning edition. *You* did all that! *You!* You are the author of all this wreckage and ruin. Nobody put a gun to your head and made you do anything. At least not yet." Danforth turned up his snifter and swallowed the last inch of his burnt wine, gasping for a breath as it burned his throat on the way down. He threw the glass at the fireplace, smashing it to bits.

"Hey!" snapped Munce.

"Relax," snapped Danforth with a hint of disgust for Munce. "I'm about to be worth a hundred million. . . I'll buy you a new set. I'll buy you a new fireplace. In fact, a new house. It's the least I can do after you delivered this buffoon to me."

My anger suddenly spilled over. For the first time in my adult life, I was moved to violence. I lunged at Danforth and wrapped my hands around his neck, trying to choke the life out of him. We tumbled backwards in the chair, spilling out in a furious heap onto the floor. Within seconds there were two burly arms latched onto me, dragging me away from Danforth. It was Kenneth Batterbee, who'd obviously been standing in the next room in case his muscle was needed. I heard a gun cock. The woman I knew as Maggie Doolan had it pointed directly at me. She was no longer the frightened creature I'd encountered at the hotel a few days ago. She had the hardened face of a career criminal, and held her weapon like someone who had pulled a trigger many times before. What a performance she'd given me that day. I couldn't decide who was the better actress, her, or Hayley Wozniak. I winced from the bitter irony that I'd given Maggie Doolan twenty dollars in gas money to help her on her way.

I slowly stood and raised my arms skyward to concede defeat. Danforth brushed himself off, straightened his tie, and smoothed back his tousled hair. "I know what you're thinking, Mr. MacClellan."

"Do you now?"

"Oh yes. You're telling yourself, 'this isn't over.' You're thinking you'll find a way to sort all this out. Justice. Am I right?" I didn't respond. Danforth stepped closer, his eyes flashing. "But you see, my dear boy, the only culpable party in all this is *you*. When those bankrupt homeowners start looking for someone to sue, they're going to come after you, not me. And they'll keep coming, until they bleed you dry. So your only way out of this is to simply walk away. I've already made it easy for you. There's no record of you ever having worked here. No real names, no tax records, no social security numbers, nothing. Not even a lease agreement or a utility bill. Your brief employment here was completely off the books, so there's nothing to trace. So I suggest you take full advantage of my discretion and disappear. Vanish. Start over with a new name in a new town. It actually works out well for both us." Danforth jutted his chin within inches of mine. "You've lost. I've won. Now go, before I *do* commit a crime." He turned his head with arrogant disgust and flicked the back of his hand through the air, like a despotic king dismissing an enemy from his court for beheading.

I stood motionless, dripping wet and powerless. Danforth was right. It was over. Like Cornwallis at Yorktown, Lee at Appomattox, it was time to surrender. I nodded in solemn defeat, turned and exited Munce's bungalow, and stepped into the blinding rain and gale force winds buffeting the Virginia coastline.

Sheets of rain covered the windshield as I sat in my car, disconsolate and immobile. In recent years I had cried a thousand tears, then a thousand more, but no anguish could compare to the wrenching melancholy of this moment. I thought of all the people whose lives I'd ruined. First Bynum Sherry, and now the hundreds of people who were going to lose millions in the real estate crash. I flashed back to the day of watching Melvin playing chess with himself. I had been the pawn, unable to anticipate my adversary's next move, and smote by the stronger piece. I couldn't bear the weight of the shame and grief. I was imploding inside, collapsing like a dying star turning into a black hole and caving in on itself. I would drive to the pier for the last time. It was time to say goodbye.

# Chapter Twenty-four

I was the only one on the Little Island Pier as the flanks of a powerful nor'easter storm were lashing the Tidewater area of Virginia. The torrential rains had shut down all outdoor activity. Swelling seas and deadly rip currents raged throughout King Neptune's domain. Winds at over seventy miles per hour made it hard to even walk. Flying grains of sand stung my face like taunting needles. I didn't care. I had come here to simply say goodbye to Sandbridge, a final farewell before I went in search of a new life, but the longer I stood in the maelstrom of wind and water, I started to think about leaving the whole world behind.

The damage I'd caused was irreparable. The problems I'd created, unsolvable. The intense pain that now coursed through me, unbearable. I replayed in my addled mind the series of events over the last two years that had taken me down the path to this despondent dead-end of the trail of wreckage I was leaving behind. I started to wonder from what height and at what rate of descent one would have to jump off this pier in order for the landing to be fatal.

I leaned forward on the railing, teetering over the edge. The wicked wind of the nor'easter howled and pressed against my neck, as if urging me off the wood and into the water. Nearly every night I had shared my soul with these briny waters. My hopes, my dreams, my fears. Mostly my fears. I had tossed questions into the misty marine layers, searching for answers. None ever came. Even on a night when my worries seemed to have a greater urgency, the sea held fast to its silence, other than to beckon me with a siren call that it harbored the only solution to all my troubles.

Water had always been the undercurrent of my lifeblood, my partner in the best chapters of my life story. Deep blue oceans, pristine lakes in the Blue Ridge Mountains, and whitewater rivers ripping through the valleys of West Virginia, Tennessee, and Georgia. Water flowed through every critical juncture of my life. And here I was again, drawn to its power, mystery, and danger.

Nobody really knows what heaven is. We all have our ideas, notions, and theories. We carry visions of an afterlife we may believe with all our heart, but nobody *really* knows. I think God intended it that way. Perhaps it's not the same for everybody. Maybe heaven is whatever you want it to be if you're lucky enough to get there. For me, heaven is where I'll see Grace again, and ultimately, find peace. That will be heaven. And tonight, I'm in a sudden hurry to get there.

I stepped higher, placing my right foot on the top railing. If the fifty foot drop to the hard water below didn't finish me off, then certainly the riptides spawned by the nor'easter would swallow up even the strongest of swimmers. If all else failed, I could count on becoming hopelessly ensnared in the unforgiving tangle of abandoned fishing lines and lures that lurked beneath the surface, wrapped through the pilings of the pier. At least that way it might appear to be more of an accident and not a coward's leap.

I pushed myself higher and stood on the top of the railing. There was nothing to hold me back. I took a deep breath, exhaled a final time, and closed my eyes. And then I heard a voice.

"It's a lot easier with a pole, ya know."

I spun my head around and saw Lyman Gregg in the shrouded lamplight.

"What?" I said, confused by the context.

"I said it's a lot easier catchin' fish with a pole, rather than jumpin' in and snatchin' 'em with your bare hands. I've tried it. Don't work so well. Pole's *much* easier. That's why ya see most folks usin' a rod and reel these days."

I remained standing on the top of the railing, now facing Lyman. I shook my head back and forth like a stunned boxer, struggling to wrap my mind around why he was there, and what he was saying. I stared at him blankly, unable to muster a single coherent sentence.

Lyman cocked his head to one side. "Well? Ya gonna be sociable, or just stand there all night? Get down here and let's sit a spell. Talk to me."

I gradually snapped out of my trance and focused on the voice coaxing me back into reality. I slowly lowered myself off the top railing and onto the timbers of the pier. I looked back at the churning seawater, then back to Lyman. "What are *you* doing here?"

"Thought I might wet a line, but mostly I just came out to look at the water. We don't get storms like this too often. Wanted to see it up close. Remind me of her power. Her fury. Her majesty." Lyman turned up the collar on his rain slicker and dug his hands into the side pockets. He walked over to the bench where his fishing gear was gathered and beckoned me to sit next to him. I joined him, trembling with emotion, mostly embarrassment. "Now then, you want to tell me what you were doin' standin' on the top of the railing?"

Our glances met briefly, then I turned away to look at the water. I spoke in a desperate whisper, fighting back tears. "I don't really know, Lyman. I'm kinda at the end of my rope."

"I can see that. And you thought divin' into the ocean was gonna solve all your troubles?" It was more of a commentary on my pathetic state than a question.

"I don't know. I don't know anything anymore. I've screwed up my life so badly I don't know what to do."

The whipping wind and rain of the nor'easter took a momentary respite from its fury as Lyman drew in a deep breath of salt air and stared straight ahead. "Tell me what's goin' on with you," he said softly, like a gentle pastor. "But first let's get outta the rain."

Moments later, we were sitting in his pickup truck, the rain sheeting down the windshield and the gusty winds buffeting the cab back and forth. I didn't know where to begin, but it didn't matter. For close to an hour I reiterated all the misfortunes that had happened to me. About my failings at *The Atlanta Herald*, the botched job with the Irukandji story, and Danforth's scheme to snap up all the distressed real estate. I sensed that Lyman already knew much of what I was trying to tell him. Word on the island travels fast, especially among the pier people. Lyman listened patiently to my ramblings, never once interrupting, only occasionally nodding to indicate he was still following my discourse. He waited awhile to speak after it was clear I'd finished my story. "I feel as though I'm partially to blame for this," said Lyman, drumming the top of the steering wheel with his thumbs.

"How ya figure that?"

"I'm the one who told you how a jellyfish from Australia could end up in Virginia from bilge water. I helped you put the pieces of the puzzle together. I didn't mean to, but I did."

"Come on, Lyman, there's no way this is your fault. It's mine. All mine."

"Ya know, accepting responsibility for your mistakes is noble. It takes a lot to admit you made a mistake. I admire that in a man. But shoulderin' blame for somethin' you didn't do, or for somethin' that didn't turn out the way you expected even when you were tryin' to do the right thing. . . well, there's no need for that. That's unproductive, plain and simple."

"What are you saying?"

"I'm sayin' that you mighta made a few missteps along the way, but there were other forces. . . other people. . . pushin' you down that path."

"What are you talking about?"

"I'm talkin' about Duncan Danforth. I wouldn't be the least surprised if he *ordered* that Australian cargo ship to run aground here, just to get us all off on the wrong track."

"The *Cudmore?* How could he do that?"

"Danforth is a powerful man. Worse than that, he's evil, and you met him at the crossroads of those two traits. He used you, just like he's been usin' other folk for years. Just be glad you're not dead. Like the others."

"Dead? What do you mean?"

"Well, look at the trail of death that follows him. First his father-in-law, then a few months later, his wife. I don't think that's a coincidence."

"I thought I read that Victoria Boyd-Danforth died in a fire."

"You, better than anyone, ought to know you can't believe everything you read." Lyman allowed himself a wry smile. I hung my head and snorted a quick laugh.

"What about Danforth's father-in-law. . . Morton Boyd. Sailing accident, wasn't it?"

"That's what they say, but it didn't happen that way."

"What do you mean?"

"I mean I read the story in the paper. . . your paper. . . and it didn't add up."

"I wasn't here then, so I don't know all the background. What didn't add up?"

"Well, for one, it was foggy that night. I'm talkin' pea soup foggy." Lyman reached behind the passenger seat and pulled out his weather Bible. He flipped the pages open to July 22, three years before, and the handwritten words *THICK FOG, NO FISH* were the only entries on the entire page.

"See, right there. I wrote it down. You couldn't see the end of the pier from here that night. Couldn't even make out any lights on the beach."

"Okay, so it's foggy. How does that relate to Morton Boyd's death?"

Lyman closed his notebook and cast his glance my way. "Ya basically need two things to create a thick blanket of fog. Moist air, and no wind."

"Yeah? So?"

"So, who in their right mind goes sailing when there's no wind, *and* zero visibility? I say nobody does, especially an experienced sailor like Morton Boyd. So I don't know what happened that night, but I don't think for a minute that it happened like they all say it did."

I felt that rush of adrenaline any good journalist gets when the purported facts of a situation don't mesh with reality. From the first day of class in high school journalism, reporters are taught to make sure their stories cover all the W's; who, what, when, where, and why. While the coverage of most news stories focuses on *what* happened, the good reporters are always far more interested in *why*. Whenever there's a giant question mark next to *why*, it means you need to start asking more questions. I was suddenly energized. I instinctively reached for a pen in my breast pocket, but there was nothing there. A small action, but Lyman still took notice. "So what do you think happened?" I asked Lyman.

"Can't say for sure. I only know that there's a lot that don't add up."

"Like what?"

"Well, think about it. . . the police said that Morton Boyd was killed by a blow to the back of the head. From what I read in the paper, best they could figure was the boom on the mast hit him when he was tackin'."

"Tacking?"

"That just means turning the bow of the boat so the wind changes from one side of the sail to the other side, while you switch over to the other side of the boat."

"So where's the problem?"

"The simple fact that when you're tackin', you're *facin'* the boom and duckin' underneath it to get from one side of the boat to the other, so if the boom was to hit you in the head, it's gonna be on your *forehead*, not the *back* of your head."

"Good point," I said as I scribbled mental notes.

"On top of that, for a boom to hit somebody *that* hard. . . hard enough to kill 'em. . . the wind woulda had to been blowin' mighty stout. Not that night."

I stroked my chin as I tried to visualize the scenario. "So what do you think really happened?"

"Can't say for sure. But I know it wasn't the wind that took Morton Boyd five miles down the coastline that night, *against the current*, I might add. Had to be a motor. Which kinda defeats the purpose of going for a late night sail, now doesn't it?"

"Wow," I said. "That all makes perfect sense!"

Lyman nodded in agreement. "I do know *one* thing fog is good for."

"What's that?"

"Makes a pretty good cover if you don't want anyone to see what you're up to."

"So you think Morton Boyd was murdered. Someone bashed him in the back of the head, then set him adrift and made it look like an accident."

"Didn't say that. I'm just sayin' there's no way it happened the way they say it did. No way. And from what I hear, there's a coupla things that don't quite jive with the death of Danforth's wife, either."

"Sounds to me like you're accusing Duncan Danforth of murder. Two of them."

"Maybe he did, maybe he didn't. But I know he sure had a good reason to push 'em both out of the way."

"What would be his motive?"

Lyman gestured south towards False Cape. "Land. Expensive land. Morton Boyd owned it, Danforth wanted it. He did what he had to do to get it. Simple as that."

"So you think Danforth killed Morton Boyd and his daughter to get control of beachfront property?"

"I think it's highly possible."

"Did you tell any of this to the police?" I asked.

"Nope."

"Why not?"

"Don't trust 'em."

"You don't trust the police?"

"Nope."

"Why not?"

"I have my reasons. And I think they're pretty good reasons. That's all I'm gonna say about that." Lyman crossed his arms. It was clear to me that this part of the conversation was over.

"Looks like I may need to ask a few questions."

"Yep," nodded Lyman. "Much of life is about unanswered questions. The hard part is decidin' which ones to keep askin', and which ones to let go." I sensed Lyman may have been talking about something else, but I didn't pursue it. "The first question is one you need to ask yourself."

I stared blankly out the window. "What's that?"

"Ask yourself what makes you happy. And you already know the answer."

"Really? You want to fill me in? Because right now, I don't see much out there to smile about."

Lyman stretched out his legs and crossed them in front of him. He adopted a wistful gaze. "You know what makes *me* happy, Mac?"

"I'm gonna guess fishing."

"That's right. Fishin'. Fishin' makes me happy. And you wanna know *why?*"

"Why?"

"Because I'm unhappy if I'm *not* fishin'. That's why I'm out here every night. I need to cast a line if I want to sleep at night."

"Okay, I know there's a reason you're telling me this. What is it?"

Lyman turned to look directly at me. "From what I know about you, Mac, there are two things that make you happy. One is diggin' up stories that right people's wrongs. You hold people accountable for their misdeeds. You're good at it, and it brings you satisfaction. That's why you got all bent up on that jellyfish story. It was the thrill of the chase, and it made you happy. Just like me tryin' to catch a Cobia off this pier every night. Rarely happens, but I come here every night with a bucket and bait and hope that this might be my night."

"So what are you saying?"

"I'm sayin' you need to get back to that."

"I just did. And look how that turned out."

"Let me ask you this. When I started tellin' you about Morton Boyd, the first thing you did was reach for a pen so you could start takin' notes. Now why was that?"

"I don't know."

"Yeah you do," Lyman continued, part counselor, part prosecutor. "Your blood started runnin' like you'd hooked a shark. Tell me I'm lyin' and I'll shut up."

I shook my head and looked down at the floorboard. "No. You're right."

"Of course I'm right. You love it, as much as I love fishin'. It's what we were born to do. And you need to go after Duncan Danforth. Hook him and reel him in. And ya got to do it right away, before he closes the deal on all those houses he's tryin' to buy."

"What? Go after Danforth? You just told me you think he murdered two people, and now you want *me* to go after him?"

"You have to get to the bottom of it. You're the only one who can."

"Why me? That's what police are supposed to do."

"Pshaw," uttered Lyman with derision. "They had their chance and they blew it."

"Danforth would crush me. I'll end up dead." I realized the irony of that statement just as it escaped my mouth. An hour ago I'd seriously contemplated leaving this world for another. Suddenly life seemed precious again.

Lyman narrowed his eyes and collected his thoughts. "Though I walk in the midst of trouble, thou dost preserve my life. . . thou dost stretch out thy hand against the wrath of my enemies, and thy right hand delivers me. The Lord will fulfill his purpose for me. Psalm 138. I memorized it when I was in the Navy. Got me through some tough days." Lyman turned and looked squarely at me. "Mac, your purpose on God's earth is to reveal truth, and by doin' so, vanquish the enemy. You have no choice."

"I suppose." I heaved a sigh, soaking it all in. I raised my head and looked at Lyman. "You said I loved two things. What was the other one?"

Lyman chuckled as a wry smile creased his face. "You really have to ask?"

"You're the one who brought it up."

"You know it as well as I do. You love a woman. I don't know her name, but I watch you out here at night, gazing out into the ocean, lost in time. I've seen that look before, when I was out to sea. Guys would stand out on deck and just stare at a thousand miles of endless water. They were always thinkin' about one thing... that girl back home. Sometimes it was the girl they was going back to, sometimes it was the girl they left behind. It's what kept 'em goin'. Kept 'em alive, if you ask me."

"Were you ever one of those guys out on that deck?"

"Oh, yeah. Most every night. And when I finally made it back home, I married her. She gave me forty-seven wonderful years together."

"Is that another reason you're out here every night?"

"I 'spose that's part of it. Miss her terribly. There are few things worse than the silence of an empty house."

"Yeah. I know all about that."

"The difference is, there's nothin' I can do about my situation. But you can."

"How? I don't even know where to begin."

"I just gave you a bucket full of questions about Morton Boyd. I reckon you could start by askin' a few. Maybe that'll get ya back on the right track."

I slowly nodded in agreement. "Maybe so." I drummed my fingers across the dashboard, trying to plot a course in my mind.

"You got a lot to live for, Mac. A precious lot. You got a good, long life ahead of you, with blessings around every turn. I know you're in a bit of a valley right at the moment, but if there's one thing I've learned from sittin' out here, night after night when the fish aren't bitin', it's that you got to always hold onto hope that things'll get better. Your life will get better, Mac. Startin' right now."

I nodded in agreement. "Everything with you is JLF, isn't it?"

"Yep." Lyman nodded back. "Just like fishin'."

I waited a long time before I spoke again. I could already feel a tremendous weight being lifted. "Thanks, Lyman. For everything."

"Don't mention it. Now then, you best get on home and get some sleep. You've had a hard day and a worse night. Besides, all this talkin' is scarin' the fish away."

I grinned and forced a laugh out of the depths of my diaphragm. How far I'd come in just a few hours. "Goodnight, Lyman."

"Night, Mac."

I got out of the truck and filled my lungs with the wet, night air and slowly walked away through the driving rain, leaving the old man alone with only his hopes and his distant memories. As I turned around, I could see him leaning back in his seat with his eyes closed. He was in another time and place, and finally, so was I. I turned back and walked on. I had a lot of questions to ask, many of them of myself.

When I got back to my condo a short time later, another unpleasant surprise awaited me: I'd been evicted. Not officially, but in reality. All my belongings were stacked up in a heap on the front stoop, subject to the vagaries of the wind and rain. Nothing was missing as far as I could tell, but it was quickly becoming a sodden mess. My key wouldn't fit in the door. Danforth and company worked fast. Ironically, they'd left the Canon camera I'd been issued on my first day on the job. I figured I'd keep it as the sum total of my severance package from my brief stint at *The Bay Breeze*.

As I stood there helplessly and tried to figure out what to do next, the power went out, and what little light there had been from streetlamps and porch lights immediately vanished. The entire island was instantly plunged into a murky darkness, disorienting and eerie. Ironically, the sudden loss of electricity seemed to jolt me into action. I quickly put all my belongings in the car, which thankfully didn't take very long because I didn't own much these days. I sat behind the steering wheel, dripping wet from rain and sweat, and tried to think. With the worst of the nor'easter fast approaching, I didn't have many options. I was afraid the road onto Sandbridge Island might already be washed over and I'd never make it to a hotel. Nor did it seem like a good idea to try to ride out a dangerous storm in a car at sea level. I felt like I had only one choice, at least for the short term. I threw the car in reverse, spun away from the condo, and drove north on Sandpiper. I made my way back to Sand Bend Road to some vacant rental properties that backed up to the canals on the bay side. I looked for one with a garage, so I could keep my car out of sight from the year-rounders.

I chose a house off of Back Bay Crescent that was further off the street than the others. I pulled deep into the driveway and jumped out, leaving my headlights on so I at least had a little illumination to guide me. The garage door was locked, but the garage was attached to the house, so if I could get inside, I could access it that way. With only a four inch flashlight from my glove box to scare off the oppressive darkness, I felt my way around the back of the house, testing every window and sliding glass door in hopes one had accidentally been left unlocked. No such luck. I hated to do it, but I felt I had no other choice than to force my way in. I used a paving brick to crack the glass pane just above the window lock, trying to inflict as little damage as possible on the premises. I reached through and unlocked the window, pushed up the bottom section, and crawled through like a common burglar. It felt good to get out of the cold rain, but that was the only aspect of my crime that brought any comfort. I'd violated the sanctity of someone's home, and it didn't sit well. I rationalized that since it was a rental, they were accustomed to strangers within their walls, that it was more of a business property than a sanctuary, and perhaps that would make my unholy trespass more palatable. I promised myself that I would leave an anonymous note and some cash for repairs, explaining my predicament and the extenuating circumstances that forced me to break into their home. Hopefully they could understand.

I stepped over the shards of glass and grabbed a pillow off the bed and stuffed it into the opening of the broken pane to keep out the sideways rain. With the dimming beam of my flashlight, I made my way into the house, only briefly surveying the surroundings. It smelled a little musty from disuse, but the cozy furnishings helped ease my accelerating anxiety over having just committed a felony.

I found the door to the garage, rolled up the door by hand because the power was out, and pulled my car inside, all in a matter of ninety seconds. I went back in the house with one duffel bag of clothes and my precious tweed suitcase, drew a deep breath, and contemplated my next step.

The house had no food, no drinks, not even bath towels or linens. There was just enough hot water left for me to take a quick shower and warm up. I dried myself off with some paper towels from the kitchen.

Finally back in dry clothes, I tossed my belongings into the first bedroom down the hall. By now it was close to two o'clock in the morning. I took stock of my situation: I was homeless and jobless, and about to ride out a leviathan of a nor'easter in a house that was powerless. But unlike the Seth MacClellan of earlier that night, I was no longer hopeless. I was no longer aimless. Lyman had literally rescued me from the brink of desperation and given me new life. I knew what I should do with my second chance, and if I could survive this storm, I was ready to get started on the journey. As I sat there in the lonely crush of darkness, the case-hardened truth was abundantly clear: I had nothing left to lose.

By the light of a vanilla scented candle I found in the kitchen, I laid down my weary head on the bare mattress and read a note Grace had written me as I was embarking on a trip to do a story on government corruption in Haiti Even though it had been my suggestion, I wasn't entirely certain that I really wanted the assignment. Much of that angst was because I didn't want that aching feeling of missing her.

My darling Seth,

All glory comes from daring to begin. The next few
weeks will be among the most challenging, exciting,
and defining days of your life. I want you to know
that you are not going it alone. I am with you. As
your partner, I promise you that I will kneel down
for you every night and send up prayers. So sail away
from the safe harbor. . . catch the trade winds in
your sails. Explore. Dream. Discover. I pray for your
safe passage home. . . you will be missed more than
you know.

Until I see you again,
Grace


Her words of advice and encouragement took on greater meaning
than ever before. I carefully folded the letter and snuffed the candle.

# Chapter Twenty-five

No one I know has ever slept through a nor'easter. They have only *tried* to sleep through one. I tossed and turned as the nasty gale blew through with winds approaching seventy miles an hour, expressing its anger in mighty gusts and sheets of hard rain. At times it felt like the structure around me was going to collapse as it swayed in the potent wind. The worst of it moved through about 4:00 a.m., howling with fury at every board and beast in its path. Soon enough, the back end of the storm was moving across the island with no regard for life or tree limbs. With no access to a weather report, all I could do was exist fearfully in the storm's domain and count the hours until the fury subsided. The declining winds of daybreak were a welcome relief for my jangled nerves.

By noon, the last of the outer bands had finally blown through and made way for a bluebird sky. I didn't dare venture outside for fear of detection by the neighbors, but peering out the window I could see the streets were still partially flooded and the ground was littered with branches, roof shingles, and the remnants of porch furniture that hadn't been tied down.

The power was still out and I assumed it would be for the foreseeable future. I lined up every candle and matchbook I could find in case I was in for another night of pitch. I took the batteries out of the television remote and refreshed my flashlight. I would have to add that sin to my letter of confession.

For the first time since I'd left him on the pier, I wondered how Lyman had made his way home through the storm. I assumed a grizzled old Navy man could handle it. I couldn't wait to see him again and thank him.

Somewhere between my conversation on the pier with Lyman and the last gasps of the storm, my self-loathing and impotence had converted into anger and impetus. I'd had only fits and starts of sleep, but I met the day with new resolve, my mind clearer and stimulated through a renewed sense of purpose. Uncovering the truth was once again my driving force. I wasn't certain where my journey was going to begin, but I knew it would end at the tarnished throne of Duncan Danforth.

Even though I was physically exhausted from all the upheaval, and a night of buffeting winds, I was now invigorated by the challenge before me. Lyman had given me so many new paths to follow, but I wasn't sure how to attack the maze I was now about to enter. I flipped to a fresh page on my reporter's pad and jotted down all the avenues of new questions that demanded exploration and explanation. Two of them stood out above the others: *What really happened that night to Morton Boyd? What really happened to Victoria Boyd-Danforth?* I had a gut feeling that Duncan Danforth might be the answer to both.

I decided to work the Morton Boyd problem first. It had been days since I'd had any contact with Jenna. The awkwardness of my rebuffing her romantic advances was still a wall between us, but I needed her counsel. I put on my running shoes and slipped quietly out the back door of the house.

It felt good to run, even as I splashed through vast pools of standing water that had not yet seeped into the sand. I headed to the beach, where the shell seekers were out in force, reaping the bounty of churned up seawater.

A few miles up the sand I found Jenna patrolling the beach across from the Sandbridge grocery, clearing away debris that had washed up in the storm. There were a handful of people dotted distantly along the shoreline, but for the most part it was just the two of us.

"Hey," I said quietly as I approached. My voice drifted across the light breeze and found her ears. She looked up, first in surprise, then in dismay.

"Hey back."

"Any trouble riding out the storm?"

She went back to dragging an old section of someone's fractured dock closer to the dunes. "Is that why you tracked me down? To check on my well-being?"

"Not entirely. I need your help."

Jenna channeled whatever simmering anger that was inside her and started to drag the waterlogged wood in earnest. I grabbed an end and helped her haul it up to the dunes.

"What can you tell me about Morton Boyd?"

"Why do you want to know about him?"

"Just curious. Did you know him?"

"Didn't really know him. Just knew *of* him. Everybody here does. Or did."

"Can you think of any reason why someone might want to kill him?"

Jenna abruptly stopped. "What? What are you talking about? I told you, Mr. Boyd died in a sailing accident."

"Maybe, maybe not."

"What are you saying?"

"That perhaps his death wasn't an accident."

"Who in the world would want to kill Morton Boyd? Everybody loved the guy."

"It might have something to do with the land conservancy."

"What about it?"

"Guess who owns it now? Duncan Danforth."

Jenna crossed her arms and stared down at the sand, trying to fit the pieces together. "So when Morton Boyd died, what happened to the land conservancy?"

"I don't know yet. I'm just starting to dig into it."

"Man, you just don't know when to let things go, do you? Still looking for redemption, aren't you, Mac?"

I lowered my head and dragged my right foot across the sand. "I think that when there's a chance that someone got away with murder, somebody ought to look into it."

"And it just has to be you, doesn't it? Can't let the police handle this one, can you?"

"It's my experience that police don't always—" I stopped short, even before Jenna could interrupt me.

"Police don't always *what*, Mac? Don't always get their man? Let justice slip through their fingers? They blow it? Is that what you're saying?"

The next sentence escaped my mouth before I'd thought it through. "Are we still talking about *my* mistakes, or have we shifted over to *yours*?" When I saw how my words wounded Jenna, I immediately regretted them. "I'm sorry. I didn't mean that."

"Go away, Mac. I can't help you."

I shook my head in disgust over my own callousness. "Again, I'm sorry. Not myself lately. I'll leave you alone." I apologetically held up my hands and turned away. I'd only walked ten feet before Jenna called after me.

"By the way, I quit drinking."

I turned back, genuinely pleased by the revelation. "Really?"

"Yeah. Apparently I make bad decisions when I'm less than sober."

"About that—"

"Forget it. I made a mistake. Stupid."

"It wasn't stupid."

"Okay then, how about foolish? Silly? Pathetic? Any of those work?"

"Come on, Jenna, stop it. It's not a big deal."

"Easy for you to say. You're not the one who thrust yourself onto someone else like a seventh grade girl."

"Look, it's not you. It's—"

"I know, I know, it's Grace. It's always Grace. You don't need to explain."

"I've never been anything but honest about that. I've never led you on, have I?"

Jenna took a deep breath and softened her defensive posture. "No."

"Then why are you mad at me?"

"I'm not mad. Just embarrassed. And maybe a little jealous."

"I'm sorry. That's all I can say."

"Look, if you want to know more about Morton Boyd, go talk to a guy named Rob Martinez. He's a Park Ranger, down in the preserve. He worked with Boyd for years. He can tell you all you need to know."

"Thanks, Jenna. I'll see you around, okay?"

"Doubtful."

I waved meekly, then turned and took off on foot. It was a good five miles to the Ranger Station in the preserve, but I would cover it quickly. It felt good to run free.

There are few professions more noble than Park Ranger, and few that are lonelier, so after spending weeks on end with nothing but rabbits and snakes, Park Rangers are generally eager to talk with any human form. I found Rob Martinez wading through a stand of cattails, picking out pieces of dirty Styrofoam and tossing them into a trash bag. Because they spend so much of their time in solitude, Park Rangers seem to have keener senses than the general population in terms of sound and movement, and Martinez noticed my arrival long before I'd gotten anywhere close to him. He waved in acknowledgement, then continued to scoop out the bits of flotsam and jetsam that had been snagged in the marsh grasses of the Back Bay.

Dripping with sweat, I made it to the edge of the water before speaking. "One man's trash is another man's lunch hour spent picking it up."

"You know it," said Martinez. "I would give a year's salary to the guy who can invent a biodegradable beer cooler. Every time we get a big storm, my marshes become the final resting place of every inconsiderate boater who chunks his litter into the water. Bane of my existence." He kept plucking out the shards of foam.

"My name's Seth MacClellan. I'm assuming you're Rob Martinez?"

"That's me," he answered in a friendly tone. "What brings you all the way out here?"

"I'm friends with Jenna Czarnecki. She told me you might be able to help me."

"Now there's a name I haven't heard in awhile. How is ole Czarnecki these days? Still got a seat reserved at every bar in town?"

"Actually, she quit drinking."

Martinez finally quit picking up the floating litter and turned to face me. "Really? Wow. That surprises me. That's great, actually. Shame what happened to her."

"Yeah. She's been through a lot, but seems to be coming out on the other side."

Martinez waded back to the shoreline and stepped up onto solid ground, dragging a full bag of trash behind him. "So you said you thought I could help you. In what way?"

"I wanted to ask you about Morton Boyd."

"What about him?"

"How he died."

Martinez narrowed his eyes and sized me up. "Who are you? You a cop?"

"No. Just a reporter looking for some answers to the world's great unsolved mysteries."

Martinez made a *clucking* sound with his tongue and teeth and looked out across the Back Bay while he mulled it over. He tossed the heaping bag of trash over his shoulder like a peddler and moved past me. "You like coffee? I got a pot brewing at the station."

Minutes later we were sitting on hard chairs at the Ranger Station, drinking strong black coffee that Martinez had percolated on an old Coleman camp stove. He served it in metal camping mugs with a speckled-blue enamel. I couldn't help but think how much Grace would have loved their color. Martinez was doing most of the talking.

"A few months after Mr. Boyd died and his estate was settled, his daughter, Victoria, had come down here to look over some plans for improving the hiking trails. She loved it down here, and we'd gotten to be pretty good friends over the years. Anyway, I'd walked over behind the shed to wash up a little bit and that's when Duncan Danforth showed up and they got into an awful fight. I'm pretty sure he didn't know I was here, based on the way he was screamin' at her."

"What did he say?"

"Well, best I can tell, when Victoria inherited the land conservancy from her father, Danforth assumed they would develop it into beachfront real estate. It's gotta be worth millions. Tens of millions, maybe. But Victoria held her ground, and was pretty adamant that this land was going to remain a wildlife preserve. Man, you never heard two people go at it in public like those two did that day."

"Do you remember anything specific they said?"

"I remember her saying something about her father having the good sense to leave the land in a trust that Victoria controlled, and Danforth couldn't get to it. I think that's what set him off."

"How did they leave it?"

"Danforth said something to the effect of 'this isn't over', then jumped in his fancy Jaguar and sped off. Dirt and rocks flyin' all over the place."

"Did that surprise you?"

"What? That they'd fight like that in public?"

"Yeah. Were you surprised?"

Martinez drew a long breath and sipped on his coffee. "I'm not sure how much to say. Are you quoting me on any of this?"

"No. This is totally off the record. I'm just doing a little research, that's all." I held up my empty hands. "You'll notice I'm not writing anything down."

Martinez nodded. He warmed up our coffee with a short pour as he collected his thoughts. "Victoria used to come out here when she was upset, which was a lot. This was *her* refuge as well. One time she was particularly upset. She just started talking, pouring it out, like she just had to get it off her chest. She told me she honestly believed that Danforth might kill her one day."

"Why?"

"She'd found out he'd taken out a four million dollar insurance policy on her. That, plus he wanted this land so badly. She immediately apologized and said she didn't really mean it, but I could tell she did. She was afraid of him, and for good reason."

*Danforth Murdered Victoria!* was the headline that flashed through my brain, but remained unspoken.

"You say 'with good reason.' What do you mean?"

"Again, we're off the record here?" I held up my empty hands again to reassure him. "Well," continued Martinez, "let's add it all up. Danforth makes a cool four million dollars just in life insurance money from Victoria's death, to go along with a coupla million in insurance I'm sure he got from the house burning down. So on top of what he already has in the bank, he suddenly has another six mil he can use as fresh capital to start buying up all those foreclosed properties. Let's say, grand total, he's got ten million to work with.

You can make a lot of down payments with ten million bucks, startin' with that huge oceanfront mansion he bought for himself. Have you seen that place? *And*, on top of all that, he ends up with control of all this land we're sittin' on. And none of that happens unless Victoria is dead."

"You think he killed her?"

"Can't say. I just think it's an awful lot of coincidences. I just don't believe that someone that evil can also be that lucky."

I was starting to realize that luck had nothing to do with Danforth's fortunes. "And do you know if Danforth has any plans for this land?"

"I've heard he's already applied for rezoning permits. I saw some of the paperwork. I think the name of the company is Cleeto, Clayto, Clyto? Somethin' like that. He'll have to jump through a ton of environmental impact studies before he can ever move a spade of dirt out here, but with his money, he'll win in the end. The rich guys always do." Martinez looked out the window at the swaying reeds and marshes with wistful eyes. "All this unspoiled beauty, and in a coupla years it'll be strip malls and condos. Cryin' shame."

I nodded slowly in agreement and finished my coffee. Martinez picked up the pot and held it up. "More?" he asked.

"No thanks. One cup was enough. You brew it pretty strong out here in the wild. I know cowboys who couldn't choke this down."

He chuckled as he topped off his mug. "Yeah, that's become part of the job. This time of year, I'm here from early in the morning until the middle of the night. Takes a lotta caffeine to keep movin' forward."

"What keeps you here so late?"

"Poachers."

"Poachers? What kind of poachers?"

"People raidin' loggerhead sea turtle nests. Their eggs are a big black market item on the internet these days. We're gettin' into the egg laying months, so I'm out there on the water a lot this time of year. We got fourteen nests this year, each will have about ninety eggs, and it's up to me to babysit all of 'em. I can't keep the foxes away, but I can sure scare off some guys trying to make a quick buck. Some places in South Carolina have entire organizations that protect loggerhead nests, but here, it's just me and my boat. Hence, lots of coffee!" He raised his mug and took a hot sip.

Our conversation jogged my memory back to a trip Grace and I had taken one summer to Hilton Head Island, and the beat of her caring heart. She'd read somewhere that artificial lighting along the beach discouraged female sea turtles from nesting, and confused their hatchlings when they were born. Grace couldn't bear the thought of baby turtles mistakenly wandering inland to face the unseen perils of predation and busy seaside streets, so she spent the better part of one night unscrewing light bulbs from planked walkways leading down to the water. She even went so far as to go up to several houses and ask the residents to either turn off their lights or at least draw their curtains so as not to disorient the hatchlings. Most people would have reacted with resentment or even torrid anger over the intrusion, but something about Grace's innocent sincerity immediately won them over, and within minutes, it was 'lights out' up and down the short stretch of Carolina coastline that was now within Grace Chastain's ecological purview. The endangered loggerheads were safe for another night. The fragile ecosystem would survive. There was hope for the world. How I loved her heart and wherever she decided to share it.

After thanking Martinez for the coffee and his time, I stretched for a few minutes as I absorbed the new information he'd provided about Victoria, trying to make the pieces fit into the intricate puzzle that was still without clearly defined edges. Highly energized by caffeine, I took off on foot back towards civilization, very much alone, and my mind focused more on the conundrum than the concrete.

I ran back to the rental house on Back Bay Crescent and slipped unnoticed in the back door. There was still no electricity, and thus no hot water, but after twelve miles of running, the cold shower felt rejuvenating. However, I was increasingly worried that Danforth would hunt me down if I stayed here much longer. I would have to think about new accommodations.

I drove back to City Hall and delved into the records again. Based on what Martinez had told me, I found Cleito LLC and discovered Danforth's holding company was the sole proprietor of a sizable parcel of undeveloped oceanfront property immediately adjacent to False Cape State Park. Morton Boyd's dream of a nature preserve had in fact become Duncan Danforth's vision of a gated community.

That night, with the power still out on the island, I surfed the internet on my phone, praying the battery would last a little while longer. I sifted through the archives of *The Bay Breeze* and *The Virginian-Pilot* in Norfolk, looking for articles about the death of Victoria Boyd-Danforth. The basic facts were cut and dried, devoid of any emotion: Victoria Boyd-Danforth had died in a fire the night of September 15 at her beachfront home in Sandbridge. Investigators determined the blaze was caused by a space heater accidentally igniting some long curtains in her bedroom. No foul play suspected. The house was declared a total loss. Tax value of the home was listed at just over two million dollars. I jotted down the name of the lead fire investigator and made a note to contact him.

The archives contained dozens of articles referencing Victoria Boyd-Danforth, mostly highlighting her social life and charitable work in the Tidewater area. I found her wedding announcement, accompanied by a photo of her with Duncan Danforth. Perhaps I was reading too much into it, but she didn't seem to be beaming with the radiant smile of a happy new bride. I sensed distress, even then.

My phone battery suddenly died and my screen went black. A clear signal it was time for bed. By the light of a wavering candle on the kitchen counter, I pulled out a letter from Grace.

> My Darling Seth,
> I can't smell the aroma of wisteria or a Sweet Surrender rose or salty ocean air without thinking of you. I can't taste shrimp and grits or Italian food or crème brûlée without picturing you across the table. I can't see an airplane streak across the sky without hoping it's you coming to see me. I can't wake up in the middle of the night without immediately reaching for you. I can't see moonlight or a sunset without immediately sensing that feeling

of secure warmth you bring me. I can't experience anything anymore without wishing you were there. And I can't see a future without you in it.

All my love,
Grace

I blew out the candle and listened to the wind.

# Chapter Twenty-six

When I awoke the next morning, the electricity was mercifully back. I charged up my phone, treated myself to my first hot shower in days, then packed the car with what little I'd brought inside the house. I left the homeowners a note begging forgiveness while invoking the "any port in a storm" clause for seeking refuge, and left enough cash to cover the cost of the broken window and the pillow I'd ruined by plugging up the hole of the shattered windowpane. My life as an intruder was over.

There are a host of eyes and ears in a beach community. Legions of people who are daily eyewitnesses to everything that goes on in the shifting sands of renters and year-rounders. Mailmen, lifeguards, sanitation workers, maintenance men, pizza delivery boys, even surfers, all have a front row seat to the daily opera of the island. I started putting out feelers amongst the cast of regulars, asking anybody who'd listen if they knew anything about the death of Victoria Boyd-Danforth that hadn't already been reported in the papers. I was mostly met with indifference, but a few of my inquiries were treated with suspicion and perhaps even a little fear. I could sense that nobody wanted to tangle with the omnipotent Duncan Danforth, even from a considerable distance. I persisted nonetheless, having few other options for gathering information. I figured that if I cast my net widely enough, I just might catch something. JLF. Just like fishing.

I needed to talk to the investigator who looked into the fire at Victoria Boyd-Danforth's house. He told me over the phone he could meet right away. I called Jenna as I headed to the fire station.

"Czarnecki," came the voice over the phone in a clipped, matter-of-fact tone that reeked of *I'm too busy to talk to whoever this is.*

"Jenna, it's Mac." There was a long pause that indicated she still wasn't over her anger and embarrassment. It didn't make what I was about to ask her any easier.

"What do you want?" she finally answered, again with a terse cadence.

"I was wondering if I could stay at your place tonight."

"What? You want to stay with *me?* You gotta lotta nerve, MacClellan."

"Listen, I know it's a little awkward, considering everything that's happened, but I'm really in a jam. I got evicted from my place. I just need a place to crash one night until I can sort this out."

"Fine, fine. Yeah, you can stay with me. As long as you need to."

"Thanks, Jenna. Big favor."

"I'm working the late shift tonight so I won't be home until after midnight. Where are you gonna be? I'll get a key to you."

"I'm going to the fire station right now. You anywhere close?"

"I'm in Virginia Beach right now."

"I'll be down at the pier tonight. Probably around five or six."

"Good enough. I'll see you then. And Mac?"

"Yeah?"

"Take care of yourself."

"Thanks. I will. See ya tonight."

She hung up. After just a few minutes on the phone with her, I felt immeasurably better about my relationship with Jenna. I didn't see her in a romantic light, but I *liked* her. That wasn't what she wanted to hear, but it was the truth, and perhaps she was starting to appreciate the fact that I had been brutally honest. I also admired her greatly for not flinching when I told her I might be in serious danger. Perhaps it stirred the protective nature of the police officer still embedded in her DNA. Hopefully she didn't see this as a prelude to rekindling her romantic intentions. For whatever reason, I was grateful to be sleeping in a place where I entered through the front door and not through a broken window.

Minutes later I was at the Sandbridge Fire and Rescue. I parked around back, suddenly much more aware of my surroundings and the new dangers that may be lurking. I entered through the giant bays where they kept the imposing optic-green trucks of Engine 17, sparkling clean under their metallic yellow striping. Dark green lockers lined the walls of one side of the garage with the firefighters' turnout gear of caramel-brown canvas pants and jackets, black helmets and rubber boots, strategically placed so it could be accessed and donned within a matter of seconds.

I was greeted at the side door by fire investigator J.D. Campbell, whose name I'd seen in several articles about Victoria Boyd-Danforth's death. I had to take a chance that he wasn't in Duncan Danforth's pocket.

"You Seth MacClellan?" he asked, extending a friendly handshake.

"That's me. You Campbell?"

"Call me J.D. Just don't ask me what it stands for."

Moments later, in a small conference room, Campbell pulled out a sheaf of documents from a well-worn accordion file and spread the papers and photos out on the table where we were standing. I'd seen dozens of fire investigation reports in my early days as a general assignment reporter, and this was pretty standard fare. Time, date, location, a description of the scene, witness statements, evidence collected, along with diagrams and photographs. Campbell reiterated the basic facts I'd already read in the paper: a space heater ignited some curtains, and Victoria didn't wake up in time to escape. No accelerants found, no signs of arson, no signs of forced entry, and a final conclusion that the fire was accidental. Case closed.

"Did you ever consider this fire to be suspicious?" I asked Campbell as I sifted through the documents.

"I think *every* fire's suspicious until I can prove it otherwise," he quickly replied. "And I'll admit, this one had a few questions that needed answers."

"Such as?"

Campbell pointed to one of the pages. "Well, for starters, why didn't a two million dollar home have a working smoke alarm? The place had a state-of-the-art security system, but no smoke detector."

"And what was the reason?"

"It had been disabled."

"How so?"

"Apparently she'd taken the batteries out. I don't know why people risk losing their homes and their lives just because they need a coupla AA batteries, but they do it all the time."

I remembered how I'd stolen the batteries from a TV remote just two days before and Campbell's explanation certainly made sense. I pressed on. "Why do you suppose she didn't wake up?"

"A lot of people sleep through fires. The smoke kills 'em before the flames ever do. Especially if they're impaired in some way."

"What are you saying? Was she drunk?"

Campbell fingered through the documents and pulled out a toxicology report.

"No. The only thing the coroner found in her system was an elevated level of progesterone."

"Do you know why?"

"Here's what we think. . . Victoria was most likely taking progesterone for hot flashes. It's something a lot of menopausal women do. One of the side effects of progesterone can be drowsiness, the same kind you'd experience with a sleep aid, which would easily explain why she never woke up when her bedroom caught on fire." The hair on the back of my neck prickled. *Wait. Why would a woman having hot flashes be using a space heater?* I kept my sudden ruminations of that thermal paradox to myself, feeling stronger now that Lyman's suspicions of foul play were more than just conjecture. "So what's your interest in this case, anyway?" asked Campbell.

I knew Campbell was going to ask me that question at some point and I was ready with a plausible answer. "Oh, nothing too serious. It's just one of those stories that everyone on the island still talks about, and I figured I should familiarize myself with it as much as possible. When you're fairly new to an area, you have a lot of homework to do."

"But didn't you tell me you were just the fishing reporter?"

That's what I'd told him over the phone, conveniently omitting the part where I'd just been fired. I continued to lie. "I am, but tryin' to move up in the world. I'd like to work on something a little more challenging than spinner baits, you know what I mean? Like you, going from just putting out fires to figuring out what started them."

Campbell nodded in agreement, accepting my explanation. "I hear ya. A man needs a challenge."

I continued to peruse the photos from Victoria's bedroom, which was mostly a charred mess of wooden house framing and a box spring. The eight-by-ten-inch pictures were fairly sharp and I could discern a few items that hadn't been consumed by fire, like a brass picture frame and a porcelain lamp. As I studied one particular photo in greater detail, something seemingly insignificant caught my eye. It was on the floor, near a window, about the size and shape of a thick bar of soap. It appeared to be electrical or mechanical in nature. The plastic housing that had been around it was melted away, but the electrical prongs were still clearly visible.

"What's that?" I asked Campbell, pointing to the dot on the photo as small as an eyeglass screw.

"Hmmm. . . don't know." Campbell looked through several documents listing evidence and didn't seem to find anything to match the object in the photo. He held the photo closer and examined the image again. "Looks like maybe it's part of an alarm clock? Or a charging station of some sort? Can't tell. Any guesses?"

"No. Probably nothing." I put the photo back on the table, doing my best to burn the image in my mind. "By the way," I asked Campbell, "where was Duncan Danforth the night of the fire?"

"He was out of town. Some big charity ball in Richmond, best I remember. Picked the right night to be gone, otherwise we might have had two victims. Lucky guy."

"Yeah," I answered, not really agreeing. I had already learned that all of Danforth's recent good fortune had nothing to do with luck.

As the sun lowered its head over the Back Bay, I made my way down to Little Island Pier. It was more crowded than usual. The nor'easter had kept a lot of the regulars away for several days and they were eager to get back to the water.

The old timbers of the pier looked freshly scrubbed after a natural cleaning from rainwater and blasting sand. All the regulars were already in place. Topper was holding court, espousing the virtues of his new arsenal of Calcutta Flashfoil Shad lures and how Got-Cha plugs couldn't hold a candle to them when it came to mackerel. Rubes was helping a young family untangle a bird's nest of crossed lines. Cat was showing off the new Daiwa Emcast Plus 6000 he'd just ordered from a catalog.

Lyman was off to himself, patiently awaiting the tug of his next catch. He was on the same bench where I'd seen him during my darkest hour.

"I see you survived the storm," said Lyman without taking his eyes off his line. I wasn't sure if he meant the nor'easter or my emotional collapse. Perhaps both.

"Yeah. It's been an interesting few days." I took a seat next to him on the bench and we sat in silence for a few moments as Lyman slowly reeled in his line. I finally breeched the quiet. "I took your advice."

"Oh yeah? What advice was that?"

"I've been digging into Victoria's death. You were right. There's a lot there that doesn't quite fit into the official version of events."

Lyman nodded, as if that were something he already knew. "Such as?"

"Well, the official report says the fire was started by a space heater. The autopsy revealed that Victoria was taking progesterone, most likely for hot flashes. But who uses a space heater when your body is already overheating?"

"I've *never* thought it added up quite right." Lyman turned and looked me straight in the eyes for emphasis.

"What do you mean?"

Lyman rested his rod against the pier railing and reached down for the overstuffed notebook he always carried with him, his "fishing Bible." He flipped to a page with the date September 15, the night Victoria died in the fire. He traced his finger down a column and pointed to the handwritten number on the page and angled it into my view. "Look here. . . this was the temperature the night of the fire. Eighty-three degrees. Hot flashes or not, who's using a space heater when it's eighty-three degrees outside? Don't make sense." Lyman folded up the notebook, grabbed his rod, and *zinged* another cast into the deep blue.

"So what do you think happened?" I asked.

"I don't know. That part I can't quite figure out. But somethin' tells me somebody else put that space heater next to them curtains and turned it on, knowing full well they'd catch fire and she'd sleep through it. And I'm guessing it was Danforth himself."

"But he was out of town at a charity ball. Airtight alibi."

"Then maybe somebody did it for him. A guy like Danforth has enough cash to hire someone to sneak in there and flip a switch. You'd be long gone before the fire broke out."

I mulled it over, then shook my head. "No, I don't think so. Her security system was on, and there was no sign of forced entry."

"What if Danforth gave 'em a key and the code to disable the alarm?"

"Hmm. Now that's a thought." Excited by the theory, I pulled out my cell phone and quickly redialed the last number I'd used.

"J.D. Campbell," replied the voice on the other end of the phone.

"Mr. Campbell, it's Seth MacClellan again. Sorry to bother you, but I had one more question. Do you know if there were any interruptions in Victoria's security system that night? Is there any way to tell if the alarm had been turned off at any point?"

"We wondered the same thing. We had a theory that perhaps there had been a brief power outage and when it came back on, the surge might have caused the electrical malfunction. But I checked with the company that monitored her security system and they told me specifically that there were no interruptions. Once she set it, it stayed on until it was disabled by the fire. Why do you ask?"

"Oh, just curious. I was thinking that maybe someone else was there that night."

"No, don't think so. In fact, we canvassed the neighborhood. . . nobody reported seeing any other vehicles there or any unusual activity. Sorry."

"Well, thanks again for your help."

"Anytime. Have a good one."

Campbell hung up. I turned to Lyman. "Did you catch any of that?"

"Yep. That kinda shoots down my theory."

Again, we sat in silence, staring out at the sea and soaking in the gentle whistling of the sea breeze, the lapping of the waves against the pier, and the cacophony of sound from the other fishermen. I hung my head, approaching defeat. "Maybe the fire was truly just an accident, and I'm trying to add two and two together to make five."

Lyman glanced over at me with a slightly cocked head. "You really believe that? That it was *just* an accident?"

I shook my head and exhaled loudly. "I don't know anymore. I think maybe I've wanted to believe it so badly that I haven't been able to take 'no' for an answer. But sometimes you have to let the facts be your friend. What about you, Lyman?"

Lyman summoned up every wrinkle and crease in his weather-beaten face as he stared out over the ocean with a faraway look. "If there's one lesson I've learned in the cruel classroom of life, it's that facts don't always equal truth. So no, I don't think it was an accident, no more than I think Morton Boyd's death was just a sailing accident. You can show me all the official police reports you want, and I'll still never believe it."

"Hey," came the female voice behind me. I spun around to see Jenna standing there in her red lifeguard swimsuit and a small duffel bag slung over her shoulder. "I figured I'd find you here."

"Hello, Jenna. You look terrific!" I meant it. Sobriety agreed with her. Her eyes had a fresh sparkle I'd never noticed before. "Hey, let me introduce you to my friend. Lyman Gregg, this is Jenna."

Lyman stood up and graciously extended his hand. "Pleased to make your acquaintance."

"I feel like I already know you. You're kind of a legend out here."

Lyman smiled. "Only the fish stories are true."

Jenna reached into the duffel bag and pulled out a spare house key. "Here, you'll need this. I'll be home sometime after midnight. I made up the couch, and there's some leftover pizza in the fridge. I think there's a coupla beers in there too that I won't be needin', so help yourself."

I pocketed the key. "Thank you. It's just until I can find another place to live."

"No problem. What are friends for?"

"Czarnecki?" blurted out Lyman. Stunned by the outburst, I pivoted around and saw Lyman's gaze riveted on the white stitching on Jenna's duffel bag. Her name was sewn across the top in block lettering. "Your last name is *Czarnecki?*" repeated Lyman, a little more forcefully this time.

"That's me. Good Polish girl. And good job on the pronunciation. Most people—"

"You any kin to Lieutenant Raymond Czarnecki?" Lyman's voice was deepening with anger.

"Yeah. Ray Czarnecki's my dad. Why?"

Lyman abruptly snatched his rod off the railing and jammed it into his rolling tackle box, the untethered treble hook swinging wildly in the wind. He was packed up and ready to go in a matter of seconds. "Next time you see him, mention the name Roosevelt Gregg. Then ask him how he sleeps at night."

"I have no idea what you're talking about."

"Course you don't. I'd keep a dirty little secret like that to myself too." Lyman brushed past us and quickly walked away. We were stupefied by his sudden flash of anger. I'd never seen him like this, not even close.

"What's he talkin' about?" I asked Jenna.

"How should I know? I just met the guy!"

I shook my head in confusion, then chased after Lyman. "Hey, buddy, what's the matter? Help me out here. What was *that* all about?"

"Her father sent my brother to rot in prison. Because of a soda can! All because of a stinkin' can of Dr Pepper. That's all I'm gonna say. Now leave me be."

I watched Lyman roll his fishing tackle off the pier and into the parking lot. He threw it in the back of his rusty red pickup, slammed the door, and sped away. For a man who I'd only ever seen exhibit patience, kindness, and wisdom, his behavior was inexplicable. Lyman had a long fuse, but there was clearly a powder keg at the end of it.

Jenna came up behind me. "*That's* the Lyman Gregg you've been telling me about? What's with the hair-trigger temper?"

"I have no idea. What was all that about your father putting his brother in jail?"

"Who knows. My dad put a lot of people in jail."

"He was muttering something about a soda can. That ring any bells?"

"Nope. My father and I don't talk much."

"Strange. All very strange."

"Listen, I gotta get back to work. Let yourself in. See ya later." Jenna patted me on the back and headed off.

"See ya."

I left the pier and walked over into the jagged dunes holding in the waters of the Back Bay. The sun was sinking fast, like a blazing comet in slow motion. I stood there and absorbed its natural magnificence. The evening sky had the same color and hue as the night Grace and I had taken a sunset cruise down the Seine, posing for pictures as we glided underneath the stone arches of Pont Neuf. Even with everything swirling around me right now, all I could think about was Grace, and all the varicolored sunsets we had planned to enjoy together on a quiet porch somewhere. Perhaps she was painting it for me now.

Jenna lived in a tiny one-story rental cottage off Whiting Lane, circa 1965. Even though I'd been invited, I still had a feeling of the trespassing intruder as I turned the key to Jenna's home and stepped inside. Her place was Spartan and nearly devoid of color. She had the bare minimum of furniture and accessories, all modern and uninviting, that looked like it had all been purchased at the same store on the same day. There were no books on the shelves, no pictures on the walls, and no rugs on the hardwood floors. Her wine rack was conspicuously empty. It looked more like a hotel room than a home. The only personality in the living space was her mountain bike, parked in the middle of the living room.

I ate the ready-made sandwich I'd bought at the grocery, foregoing Jenna's offer for cold pizza, and drank both beers in the back of her refrigerator. I figured I was doing a favor for both her body and mine.

As weary as an old soldier, I sat there on the couch, listening to the pounding surf through the open window, exploding onto the sand like mortars in a distant war. Most nights the white noise from the roar of the ocean only exacerbated my insomnia. I was hoping tonight that in combination with the alcohol, it would lull me to sleep.

I reached for my collection of letters and pulled one out at random. It was something she'd written the day she'd sold her first oil painting.

My darling Seth,
My truer self has been allowed. . . not just allowed,
but encouraged to develop under your caring eyes,
nudging me to pursue gifts God gave me. I think of
myself as a very different woman these days, more
of what I was created to be. I can't wait for the next
time we melt into each other and savor the touch
electric.

Always and forever,
Grace

The words were almost too much to bear. I felt like I was falling
off an endless cliff, our dreams never to be realized. I stretched out
on the couch and reached back to switch off the lamp. I laid there
in the dark with the worn pages of the letter resting on my chest,
the paper pressing down on my heart like a great weight.

I was suddenly pulled back from the precipice of slumber by a
noise coming from the back door leading out to her patio. It was
erratic and purposeful, not the kind of random noise the wind would
generate. My first thought as consciousness came roaring back was
that somehow Danforth had figured out where I was and had sent
his minions to find me. The noise persisted. My heart racing with
new fear, I scanned Jenna's cottage to find anything that might
substitute for a weapon. There was nothing. No softball bat, no fire
poker, no golf club with which to defend myself. The only hard
object I could find was her bike helmet. I clutched it in my hand as
I crept through the darkness towards the back door. The sound of
movement outside intensified as I moved closer. I was clammy with
sweat as I slinked across the kitchen and approached the window
that faced the back patio. As boldly as I dared, I pushed back the
edge of the blinds and peered outside. There was just enough light
from a nearby streetlamp to discern shapes and movement inside
the small fenced enclosure. I didn't see anything, and now I didn't
hear anything. I stood there, hunched over in the midnight dreary,
each passing minute feeling more like five. Feeling braver, I stood
taller and adjusted my vantage point. I could now see a green plastic

trashcan tipped over in the corner. The wind freshened and the lid of the trashcan skidded across the cement, putting forth a hollow scraping sound. Forcing myself to feel a sense of relief, I surmised that the trashcan must have been the source of the disquiet. I gathered enough courage to open the back door and step onto the patio. Much calmer now, I walked over and reached down to turn the trashcan upright. As I reached down, a feral cat suddenly lunged from inside the container and took a swipe at me as he burst forward to freedom.

"*Geez!*" I yelled, falling backwards onto the concrete as the cat sank its claws into the soft wood of the fence and pulled his bony orange body up and over to safety. Heaving for breath from the shock, I sat on the cold pavement and gathered my wits. As startling as the encounter had been, I quickly realized how relieved I was that it was simply a hungry feline foraging for scraps and not something more sinister. I pulled myself to my feet and righted the trashcan, checking first to make sure there was nothing else inside that might leap forward. I reached down for the lid.

"What's all the commotion out here?"

"*Geez!*" I yelled again, louder this time, my adrenalized instincts forcing me to raise the bike helmet in my hand to defend against attack. I spun around and saw Jenna standing in the doorway.

I lowered my defenses as high anxiety turned to mild anger. "What are you *doing?*" I yelled at her.

"What do you mean, what am *I* doing?"

"Sneakin' up on me like that! You tryin' to give me a heart attack?"

"First of all, I wasn't sneaking up on you! I happen to live here! The better question is, what are you doing out here in the middle of the night with my bike helmet?"

Now I felt incredibly foolish. "Well, I heard a noise. It turned out to be a cat."

"And you were gonna whack it with a bicycle helmet?"

"I didn't know it was a cat when I came out here. I thought it might have been someone trying to break in."

Jenna oozed sarcasm. "Oh, I see. You were gonna whack *him* with a bike helmet. *Much* better plan. Maybe you could have used the trashcan lid as a shield."

I slammed the lid on the trashcan. "Hey, don't judge me. You weren't here."

"No, but I sure wish I had been. Man versus kitty cat. Epic."

"All right, all right, you had your fun. I'm going back to bed." I pushed past her and went back inside. She followed me into the living room.

"By the way, Mac, I keep a softball bat under the couch. Just in case."

"Gee, thanks. Next time there's a loose cat on the premises, I'll keep that in mind."

"Your nerves seem a little jangled, Mac. Like more than just a cat. You okay?"

"I'm fine. It's been a couple of rough days. I just need some rest."

When I got back to the couch, I noticed the love letter from Grace had been picked up off the floor and placed carefully on the end table next to the lamp. Obviously Jenna had seen it. I wondered if she'd read it. If so, I hoped it hadn't added to her pain. As I tried to casually fold the letter and return it to the tweed suitcase that harbored the handwritten history of my broken dreams, she revealed the answer.

"Why do you do that?" she asked softly.

"Do what?"

"Torture yourself like that."

I surrendered all pretense of denial. I sat down on the couch and tossed back my weary head, staring at the ceiling. "I don't really know. Sometimes I just miss her so badly, I want to feel the ache. I want to remind myself that I still have emotions, even if I don't use them much anymore."

Jenna sat down in the chair and rubbed her hands together. "Why don't you aim that emotion in a different direction? You can find that love with somebody else, Mac. Don't you think it's time to move on?"

"How do you move on from the love of your life?"

"But it's not reality! Nobody will ever measure up to this fantasy woman you've created because you won't *let* them!"

I closed my eyes and shook my head. My voice lowered to a whisper. "You're right. But I'd rather be tragically alone than settle for something less. I'm sorry."

"I'm sorry too. Goodnight, Mac." Jenna got up and started to walk away.

I lifted my head off the couch and sat up straighter. "Listen, I hear what you're saying. But last time I checked, you only get one soul mate."

Jenna stood in the doorframe of the hallway, her back still turned to me. I couldn't see her face, but I sensed there might be tears streaming down her cheeks.

"Maybe you're right," she whispered. "But maybe you're not." With that, she moved into the darkness of the hallway and disappeared into her bedroom, the door latching softly behind her.

# Chapter Twenty-seven

As dawn splashed sunlight through the windows of Jenna's cottage, I roused myself off the couch after a terrible night of half-sleeping and half-dreaming. Jenna's door was still shut as I trundled into the kitchen, foraging for something to eat. As I opened and shut doors to one bare cupboard after another, I heard a *click* behind me and noticed the coffee pot was suddenly going. The aroma of freshly brewed Arabica beans filled the air.

Three minutes later I heard Jenna's alarm clock go off. I felt the vibration of two feet hitting the floor and seconds later Jenna came in wearing nothing but her underwear. The absence of clothing revealed the rippled lean muscles of a swimmer, much more so than the one piece bathing suit she sported as a lifeguard. I averted my gaze and pushed my head deep into the refrigerator.

"Mornin'," she croaked in a throaty voice.

"Good morning. Sleep okay?"

"Like the dead. You?"

"My night was pretty much a series of short naps."

I could hear Jenna pour a large cup of coffee and take the first gratifying sip. "Mmmm. Coffee sure tastes better in the morning when you're not using it to cure a hangover."

"I agree. Nectar of the gods."

"I even treated myself to a new coffee pot last week. It's got a fancy timer on it that starts it going before I even wake up. I get outta bed, walk in the kitchen, and *voila,* coffee's sittin' right there waitin' for me. It's a beautiful thing." Jenna savored another taste of the earthy-brown liquid.

Suddenly, like a bolt from the blue, it hit me. I yanked my head out of the refrigerator, spun around, and stood transfixed on the coffee maker.

"What's wrong?" asked Jenna.

"Shhh!" I admonished, holding up my palm. Trembling with rising emotion, the fire investigator's declaration that *pictures don't lie* leapt into my head. I slammed my eyes shut and conjured up the images of the eight-by-ten-inch photos from Victoria's charred bedroom. I narrowed my conscious focus to the mysterious item on the floor with the electrical prongs. I turned and looked at Jenna, wild-eyed. "That's it! That's *it!*" I spouted in a hushed tone.

"What's it?" asked Jenna, puzzled over my sudden outburst. "And why are we whispering?"

I started to pace the kitchen, fitting the pieces together in my mind. "There was something peculiar in one of the photos from the scene of the fire, but I couldn't figure out what it was. It was something mechanical, about the size of my fist. I know what it was, Jenna! And I think I know how Danforth killed Victoria!"

Within minutes I was dressed and in my car driving to Lyman Gregg's house. I didn't know exactly where he lived, but I knew it was somewhere near Antioch Baptist Church in Pungo. I figured I would find my way there, then ask for help once I got into the general vicinity. I was counting on the fact that people who live out in the country are still well-versed in the dying art of giving good directions.

Lyman lived in the backcountry of coastal Virginia where the roads were named after old churches and sawmills, if they were named at all, and many of the mailboxes were made out of old tractor parts. It was a part of the world you had to be intentional about visiting, not someplace you just passed through, so everybody I drove by took a long look at the strange vehicle interloping on their corner of the map.

Soon enough, I came upon Antioch Baptist Church, a humble yet sturdy brick sanctuary with a freshly painted white steeple and an ample gravel parking lot. The most prominent feature was the hand-painted plywood sign posted on the front lawn. The freehanded block letters read:

FREE FISH FRY EVERY SUNDAY
EVERYONE WELCOME

As I slowly rolled past the church, I suddenly understood why Lyman Gregg fished with such purpose; he had taken it upon himself to feed the five thousand, and his talent for catching fish was undoubtedly God-given.

I only had to ask directions once, and even though my inquiry about Lyman's address was met with a hint of suspicion, the information was correct and led me directly to his residence. I found him in the backyard, hand tilling the soil of a modest vegetable garden. He saw me approaching quickly across the lawn, but never stopped pushing shovel into dirt.

"Hey, Lyman!" I called out breezily, hoping, or perhaps pretending, that there was no residual anger from our last encounter on the pier.

"What brings you all the way out here?" he asked flatly, as if I were a tax collector.

"I figured out how Danforth did it!"

Lyman finally stopped shoveling and looked me dead in the eyes. "You serious?"

"Well I didn't drive all the way out here to watch you shovel dirt."

Lyman looked around to make sure nobody was within earshot, and even moved a few steps closer to make sure. "What are you thinkin'?" he asked in a hushed tone.

"A timer!" I whispered as loudly as I dared.

"Timer?"

"Yes! An electrical timer, like people have on their coffee makers. But I'm talkin' about the kind that plugs into the wall, the kind people use to turn lamps on and off when they're not home so they can fool burglars. But in this case—"

Lyman finished my sentence as his eyes lit up with the lucency of sudden comprehension. "—somebody put a timer on the space heater!"

"Exactly! Somebody put the space heater next to the curtains, plugged it into a timer that's set to go on in the middle of the night, and *bam*! Heater cranks up, sets the curtains on fire, and it looks like an accident. They probably figure the timer will get burned up in the fire, and it almost does, except for a coupla gears and the electrical prongs. The proverbial smoking gun. Whaddya think?"

Lyman bit his lower lip and leaned his chin on the butt end of his shovel. "It sounds a little crazy, but I gotta say, *that* adds up."

"Yes it does. *And,* it brings Danforth back into it. Who better than him would know that Victoria was taking medication that made her drowsy? This way he could set the trap, and he knew she'd sleep right through it."

Lyman rubbed the stubble on his chin, trying to make sense of it all. "I don't know, Mac."

"What don't you know?"

"Your fire investigator said nobody came in or out of Victoria's house that night, right?"

"Right."

"And Danforth was out of town?"

"Yep. Spent the night in Richmond."

"For the life of me, I just can't figure out how someone set the timer."

"What do you mean? He could have gone in her house two days before and set it."

"I don't see how that's possible."

"I'm not following you, Lyman."

"He woulda had to have set the timer the same day as the fire."

"Why?"

"Simple. A timer's on a twenty-four hour cycle. If he'd set it to go off two days before, then it would have started the fire *two days before.* See what I'm sayin'? Whoever set it had to do it *that day,* and since Duncan Danforth was out of town, I don't see how he could pull it off."

I nodded as I let it soak in. He was absolutely right. "You know, you're pretty smart for an old codger."

"Even gray hair is still growin'." Lyman stepped back into the tilled soil and resumed digging. I realized I needed to do the same.

"Well, it's still just a theory." I jammed my hands into my back pockets and searched for the next conversation starter. "Whatcha planting?"

"Okra."

"Okra. Nice. I guess you can't serve up all that fish without a vegetable, now can you?"

Lyman shot me a sideways glance. I even saw the hint of a smile in his eyes. "No, that would be impolite. A good portion of hush puppies helps too."

I watched him work the soil for at least two minutes before I launched the next topic. "You want to tell me what put a bee in your bonnet on the pier yesterday?"

"That's none of your concern."

"Well, it kinda is."

"How ya figure?"

"You're about the only two friends I've got on the island. Actually, on the planet. It hurts me a little to see sparks fly between you two, and I have no earthly idea why. Neither does Jenna, for that matter."

"It's a long story."

"Well, seein' as how I'm both homeless and unemployed, I reckon I got time to listen to a long story."

Lyman turned over another spade of dirt, then suddenly stopped. He drew a long breath, never taking his eyes off the fertile ground below him.

Minutes later we were sitting on his back porch, sipping a tall glass of the best sweet iced tea I'd ever tasted. Lyman struck a rueful look as he stared out into the stand of pines that bordered his backyard. He took a long sip of his tea, then started in.

"Years ago, there used to be an old country store at the crossroads there in Pungo where everybody met on Saturday nights. They served homemade ice cream, stick candy, cold cans of pop in a washtub full of ice. My brother and I used to go there right regular, especially in the summer. When you think about 'the good ole days,' that was them." He took a long pause to collect his thoughts. "One night, there was a holdup at the service station about a mile down the road. The cashier was shot and killed. Pretty young girl, engaged to be married. Just tryin' to make a little extra money to pay for the wedding. I think they got away with about forty bucks." Lyman spit. I didn't dare interrupt, patiently waiting for the next sentence. "Cops investigated, couldn't figure out who'd done it. This was before they had security cameras and stuff like that. Nothin' to go on, so it looks like it was just gonna be one of them cases that never got solved. But folks 'round here wouldn't let it go. *Somebody* was gonna pay for that crime, by God." He turned to face me, his eyes flashing with the same anger I'd witnessed on the pier the night before. "That somebody turned out to be my brother, Roosevelt."

"How so?"

"Police said they found his fingerprints on a soda can at the scene."

"Is that true?"

"Yeah, it's true. Because they *put* it there!"

"I'm not following."

"One of those cops went down to the country store where we used to hang out, fished through the garbage can, and pulled out an empty can. They took it over to the service station and took a coupla photos that placed it at the crime scene. *That* was the extent of their evidence. Next thing you know, they're hauling Roosevelt off in handcuffs."

"How do you know all that?"

"I don't know it, I just figure it. I've had a lotta years to mull it over, and I know somebody planted that evidence, sure as I'm sittin' here. And you know where they got his fingerprints to match up to that soda can? From his Army records. Man serves his country and it comes back to bite him in the hind end." He spit again, harder this time.

"What makes you so sure?"

"Because Roosevelt was with *me* that night." He pointed to a wooden bench at the edge of his driveway. "We were standing right there, cleanin' fish. All night. But since nobody else saw us, they didn't believe our alibi. It was our word against the police, and you can guess who won."

"I'm also gonna guess that the lead investigator was Jenna's father."

"Yup. Ray Czarnecki. Dirtiest cop to ever wear a badge. I *know* in my heart of hearts that he planted that soda can, and boy, you shoulda heard him sell it to that judge and jury. Didn't make no matter that the can didn't have any liquid in it and even had a tiny bit of rust. You tell me, how's a soda can that was inside a store get rust on it? But they didn't want to hear that, no. They wanted someone to pay for that pretty girl's murder." Lyman hung his head and shook it from side to side, the pain of years of anguish welling up inside him. "That soda can coulda had the fingerprints of anyone who used to hang out at the country store. Coulda been me. For some reason only God can explain, they snatched the one with Roosevelt's fingerprints. My brother was a good man, Mac. A God fearin' man. Never been in trouble a day in his life. He didn't last five years in prison." Lyman choked back a hard rain of tears. "I tried to get him out, but I finally ran outta money to pay for lawyers."

It was a lot to absorb. Even though I'd only heard one side of the story, I fully believed Lyman's version of events. "I'm guessing that's why you don't trust the police?" He nodded. "That's a long time to hold a grudge."

"I can hold a grudge like rich people hold blue chip stock."

"But what about forgiveness?"

"How am I supposed to forgive somethin' like that? Ray Czarnecki put an innocent man in prison, and he *knew* it. And it turned out to be a death sentence. No, Mac, there are just some things in this world you can't forgive. That's why they invented the word 'unforgivable.' Look it up." I couldn't disagree. We sat in silence. I had no words. Lyman finally spoke. "So what are you gonna do with your theory about the timer?"

"I guess the next step is to go to the police and see if they'll reopen the investigation."

"You're on your own with that one."

"Yeah. Can't say that I blame you."

We both stood up. Protocol told me to shake Lyman's hand, but instinct told me to embrace him. I held onto him, feeling his pain. "Go get him," whispered Lyman into my ear. "Win one for the little guy." I nodded, my head still buried in his shoulder. Without another word, I walked away and retreated to my car.

My morning with Lyman had reinvigorated my pursuit for justice, but as intoxicating as it was to be latching onto the possible demise of Duncan Danforth, something in the back of my mind pulled me back. *Slow down* whispered my internal voice. *Slow down.* I had twice followed my raw instincts into the abyss of miscalculation, and I could ill afford another misstep. The sharpened steel of my excitement needed to be tempered with prudence. I had ruined so

many lives, including my own, through my eager ambition and rush
to judgment, and I couldn't allow my fermenting eagerness to bubble
over into yet another disaster. I needed more evidence before I
could go to the police. *Slow down.*

Jenna was gone by the time I got back to her cottage. It was a perfect
day for a long run, so I laced up and headed back out the door. I
figured a good ten miler would be enough to clear my swirling head.

I turned north off of Whiting and had only gone about two hundred
yards down Sandpiper before I sensed I was being followed. A man on
a bicycle wearing a helmet and wraparound sunglasses was keeping a
safe and steady distance behind me. Caught somewhere between
precaution and paranoia, I tried to convince myself I was imagining
things. People ride bikes up and down the road all the time. . . why
would I think he was following me? After the embarrassing "cat on the
patio" incident, I didn't want to overreact. Nonetheless, I sped up my
pace as I passed by the Sandbridge Community Chapel. The cyclist did
too, keeping the same relative distance between us. I slowed down, and
he followed suit. I was starting to sense danger, the same kind you feel
when you're alone in a dark parking garage late at night and you suddenly
hear footsteps behind you. I quickened my gait again, ramping up to a
5:30-mile pace. He stayed with me like a shadow. I cut over on Rock
Lane to Sandpiper, still at a blazing tempo. A quick glance over my
shoulder showed me the mystery man on the bike had followed me
and was now up off his seat, pedaling harder to keep up. I ran one
block south on Sandpiper, past Bonita, and he continued to chase.
Knowing I couldn't sustain this pace much longer, I took one final
glance behind me and then cut over on the public access and headed
for the beach. I knew he couldn't pedal through the thick sand and this
would be my opportunity to outrun him.

I powered through fifty yards of soft sand towards the water,
my thighs starting to burn like a downhill skier. I made it to the
hard-packed sand on the edge of the water and turned back south
with the wind at my back, trying to put as much distance as I could
between my increasingly fatigued body and my pursuer. As I looked
over my shoulder, I could see the man now carrying his bike through
the heavy sand and trying to get to the harder sand on the water's

edge where he could remount. I'd put three hundred yards between us, but he was back in the saddle and gaining fast. I made an abrupt right turn and bolted back toward the row of houses, again suffering through the lactic acid building up in my legs as I waded through the deep sand near the dunes.

I turned around and saw the man on the bike slow down and stop. Either he just didn't have the heart to portage his bicycle through the sand again, or he realized that this exercise of cat and mouse could go on for some time with no endgame.

My first instinct was to summon all my cardiovascular strength and race back to the safety of Jenna's house, so I took off down the pavement, checking over my shoulder several times to make sure I wasn't being followed. Feeling as though I was out of immediate danger, I knew I had to stop for just a moment to catch my breath and empty my shoes that had become loaded with annoying grains of sand. I pulled over and stood in the driveway of a vacant rental house while I regrouped. As I slipped out of my shoe and dumped out a handful of beach, it dawned on me that Jenna's cottage wasn't really a safe haven. The man on the bike had been following me from virtually the time I started out, so obviously he knew where I was staying. I hadn't had a nanosecond to consider my next move before I looked up and felt adrenaline seize my body. The man on the bike was suddenly five feet away, so close I could see my reflection in his sunglasses. With only one shoe on, I knew I couldn't outrun him. I backed up a few feet and grabbed the only hard object I could find to defend myself; a bleached white conch shell. I held it in a throwing position, like a shortstop chasing a runner back to second base. Jenna's bike helmet now seemed downright lethal in comparison to my latest weapon of choice. "What do you want!" I yelled at the man as he dismounted.

"Dude! Easy!" he called out like I was a barking dog, keeping his distance and holding up his palms to indicate he didn't want trouble. I immediately recognized the voice. When he pulled off his helmet, his tousled blond hair tumbled out. It was Trey from the Baja.

"What are you *doing*?" I yelled at him, lowering my conch shell and clearing away the burning droplets of sweat rolling off my forehead into my eyes. "I could have killed you!"

Trey pulled off his sunglasses as he looked at the conch shell and derisively cocked his head. "I don't think so."

"What do you want?" I asked, finally calming down.

"I heard you were looking for information about Victoria Boyd-Danforth. I might be able to help you. Why were you runnin' away?"

"I've had a tough coupla days. Sorry." I put my shoe back on and removed the other one, pouring out a few ounces of hitchhiking sand. "I guess I could ask you, why were you chasing me? Why didn't you just knock on the door?"

"Because I didn't know if Jenna was home, and what I'm about to tell you, I don't want anyone else to hear. And if you say I said anything, I'll deny it."

"You have my word. Sounds pretty serious."

"I'll let you be the judge."

"I'm listenin'."

We leaned against the retaining wall bordering the driveway as Trey launched in to his story, occasionally glancing around to make sure there was nobody eavesdropping. "I work days as a maintenance guy for one of the big realty companies here, mostly repairing air conditioning units. People check into their rentals and immediately crank up the AC, even though there's a little sign next to every single thermostat warnin' 'em not to. See, what happens, because of the high humidity here in the summer, that sudden stress on the air conditioning unit makes the compressor freeze up. It's a major problem, and keeps me really busy." I was starting to think Trey was approaching the threshold of "too much information", and perhaps had already crossed it, when he reined it back in. "Now then, you're probably askin' yourself, what's *that* got to do with the fire at Victoria Boyd-Danforth's?" Indeed I was. Trey looked around again, and started speaking in a hushed tone. "I was workin' a job late one afternoon at the house across the street from the Danforth place. I'm guessin' she saw my truck parked outside, so she came out and begged me to fix her AC. At first I told her I couldn't do it, but she said she was burnin' up and needed it repaired right away. So I finished up the job I was on, then went over to her place and started workin' on her unit."

"So why are you telling me this?" I asked, not yet putting the pieces together.

"Because while I'm there, this guy suddenly comes walkin' through the backyard, and I'm thinking that it's really strange that there's some dude walkin' through the backyard, and he's all spiffed up, like he's goin' to a fancy ball or somethin'. It was totally weird, ya know? Then I realized it was Duncan Danforth! I'd never seen him before in person, but I've seen lots of pictures, so I knew for sure it was him."

"Go on."

"Danforth's carrying a big shopping bag, looked kinda heavy, and he's movin' real quick, like he's nervous about somethin'."

"Did he see you?"

"I was kneelin' down behind the AC unit, and my truck was still parked across the street, so I don't think so."

"What happened next?"

"So, he goes in the back door of the house and pretty soon they're in the middle of a knock-down, drag-out fight. I can't hear exactly what they're saying, but I can tell that he is some kinda *ticked off*. The only thing I can make out is him yellin' at her 'sign it, sign it!' and she's yellin' back, 'no, no!' This goes on for about five minutes, then suddenly it's quiet. No sound. Then he leaves. He slams the door, steamin' mad. I notice he's not carryin' the shopping bag anymore. Well, I kinda blew it off, you know, husband and wife thing, but then the next day I find out her house burned down." He leaned closer, his eyes narrowing. "And here's what I can't figure out. . . the newspaper said the fire was started by a faulty space heater, right?"

"That's right."

"So why was a woman who was frantic to get her air conditioner fixed usin' a space heater? You ever wonder about that?"

"In fact, I have."

"Somethin' in the back of my head keeps naggin' at me if somehow it wasn't all related to Danforth comin' to visit her. And why did the dude *walk* to his own house? Why didn't he drive there? Who knows. But when I heard you were lookin' into it, I figured I owed it to her to at least mention it. Get it off my conscience. Maybe it's somethin', maybe it's not."

I nodded. I already *knew* it was something. Trey had provided me with one key fact: it placed Danforth at the scene on a day when he told authorities he was out of town. The neighbors hadn't seen his car because he'd parked some distance away and walked there to avoid detection. It certainly verified Lyman's theory that nobody on the entire island would be using a space heater on a night when the temperature was eighty-three degrees, especially someone suffering from hot flashes. And I could take a pretty good guess as to what he'd been carrying in the shopping bag. "Why didn't you tell this to the police?" I asked Trey.

"Because Victoria paid me off the books to fix her air conditioner. Cash. No work order, no record. If my boss found out, I'd get fired, and I need the job because bartending at the Baja doesn't exactly pay all the bills. So I didn't say anything then, and I can't say anything now."

"Well, you did the right thing coming to me." I extended my hand and shook his with reassurance. "I'm curious, Trey. . . I've always had the feeling that you didn't really like me. Maybe something to do with Jenna. So why are you willing to help me?"

"Jenna told me you're crazy in love with another woman. No threat. Simple as that."

"And you're in love with Jenna?"

"I don't know. I really like her. I guess I'd *like* to be crazy in love with her."

"No you don't."

"Why do you say that?"

I laughed the bitter laugh of a cynic. "Because when you're in love, you walk around all day with an anvil in your chest because all you can think about is *her*. You sleep with the phone clutched in your sweaty hand, hoping it'll ring. You start to worry if her texts don't have enough exclamation points or smiles. You fall apart whenever you first come together, because every time you see her it's like you discovered a new color. And then you fall apart again when you go your separate ways, and all you can think about is how much you miss her and how much you can't wait to see her again and look into those aquamarine eyes and kiss those lips. And every song on the radio is about *you*. It's awful."

"I don't know," said Trey, squinting to think better. "That actually sounds pretty good to me."

I smiled and nodded the nod of a romantic. "Yeah. It is."

"I gotta roll. Maybe see ya at the Baja later. I'll keep a cold Guinness ready for you."

"Thanks. And thanks for the tip."

Trey got back on his bicycle and rode away. Our conversation confirmed everything Lyman and I had wondered about. It seemed to indicate motive and it certainly placed Danforth at the scene. *Slow down* came that voice of warning again. But it was getting more difficult.

# Chapter Twenty-eight

I was stepping out of the shower that night when I heard Jenna returning to the cottage. At least I hoped it was Jenna. Just the sound of her key pushing into the lock made me jump like a skittish young watchdog.

"Hi, Honey, I'm home!" she called out in a singsong voice. "What's for dinner?"

I quickly scrambled into my jeans and t-shirt behind closed doors before stepping out to greet her. "I was hoping *you'd* made something."

"The only thing I know how to make for dinner is reservations. Not really the domestic type." She opened the freezer and pulled out a frosted flat box. "Frozen pizza sound good?"

"Fine," I said, smoothing back my wet hair.

"You get in a run?" she asked.

"Tried to. Got interrupted."

"By what?"

"Trey."

"Trey? Bartender Trey?"

"Yep. And he had a lot to say. About a lot of things."

In one fluid motion, Jenna slid the frozen pizza out of the box and tossed it into the cold oven, shut the door, and turned on the heat. She'd clearly executed this maneuver hundreds of times before.

"We got exactly eighteen minutes before dinner is served. Start talking."

A half-hour later Jenna and I were halfway through a pizza and a liter of diet soda that passed for what most people call dinner. I wiped my mouth with a napkin and summarized our conversation. "So, I think I know *why* Danforth killed Victoria, I think I know *how* he did it, and after talking to Trey today, I think I know *when* he set the timer. But I'm just not sure it's enough to prove it. If I take this to the police and it's not enough to arrest him and his band of merry henchmen, I'm in serious trouble. He'll find out about it, and I'm a dead man. It's gotta be airtight."

Jenna nodded in agreement and wiped the orangey ooze of pepperoni grease off her chin with the back of her hand, eschewing the paper napkins right in front of her. "So let me see if I got this. . . you think Danforth puts a space heater in Victoria's bedroom, sets a timer to make it go off in the middle of the night, and it catches the curtains on fire. And Trey puts Danforth at the scene at about five-thirty the night of the fire, which gives him enough time to set the timer, then jump in the car and drive to Richmond in plenty of time to arrive at his big charity ball. He even spends the night there, providing the perfect alibi. Meanwhile, his house burns down, kills his wife in the process, and the land in the conservancy immediately becomes all his, not to mention a few million in insurance money. Am I right so far?"

"Exactly."

"Then, he finds a stooge, who we'll call 'Mac' just to give him a name, who gets the entire island worked into a frenzy that there's some sort of deadly jellyfish lurking off the coast, and property values on Sandbridge plummet. Danforth swoops in with this sizable war chest of cash he now has, buys up all the distressed real estate at bargain basement prices, then after the jellyfish thing is declared a hoax, he flips the properties and makes a fortune. Does that about sum it up?"

"I suppose," I groused. "I could do without the 'stooge' part, but yeah, that's basically the storyline."

"Gee, that doesn't sound farfetched at all," said Jenna, now oozing more sarcasm than pizza grease. "Doesn't sound the least bit like a story that a bitter newspaper reporter cooked up to try to get redemption and revenge." She cocked her head to one side and widened her eyes as if to say *ya know what I mean?*

I knew exactly. It *did* sound farfetched. I'd sat in more than one courtroom where prosecutors and police had strung together a series of seemingly logical facts to reach a dubious conclusion as to the guilt of a defendant. Add into the mix my possible motives for wanting to bring down Danforth, and it all seemed a little suspicious. *Fishy* might be the most appropriate adjective. I leaned back in my chair and rested both hands on the top of my addled head. "I know. It sounds crazy. As much as I believe it's all true, it sounds insane."

"Do you *really* believe it, Mac, or do you just *want* to believe it so badly that you can't see any other scenario?"

"I don't know anymore. A big part of me is saying it's time to move on. Leave the island and this whole mess behind. I've done enough damage."

"It doesn't seem like your nature to just let things go."

"No, I suppose not. It's a family curse. MacClellans have a history of putting their noses in places they don't belong."

"The world needs people like you, Mac. Good people who pursue truth. Otherwise, evil wins."

I nodded ruefully, wondering where all that pursuit of truth had gotten me. It seemed like a good time to broach a delicate subject. "I talked to Lyman today about what made him so mad on the pier."

"Yeah, what was *that* all about?" she said, stuffing a generous portion of pizza into her mouth.

"It has something to do with your father."

Jenna momentarily stopped chewing, then finished off what remained in her mouth and washed it down with water. "Oh yeah? What about him?"

"Lyman told me a story about his brother, Roosevelt Gregg. Sent to prison for murder."

"Sorry. Not ringing a bell."

"Lyman says his brother was innocent."

Jenna laughed the laugh of a cynic. "Yeah, who behind bars *isn't* innocent?"

"Lyman says he was framed."

I had Jenna's complete attention now. The wry smile vanished. "Framed, huh? By whom?"

I swallowed hard and drummed my fingers on the table, unsure if I should keep going. "By the police. More specifically, your father."

I was expecting a reply somewhere between flat denial and rabid anger, but I got neither. All I got in response to my bold assertion was silence. Jenna lowered her head and stared at the empty plate beneath her. A full sixty seconds and three loud exhalations passed before she looked up and spoke. "I suppose there's only one way to find out." She stood up, grabbed her keys and jacket, and headed for the front door.

Thirty minutes after I'd raised the specter of her father's involvement in the conviction of Roosevelt Gregg, I found myself standing in the den of the accused: retired police Lieutenant Raymond Czarnecki. The wood-paneled room was haphazardly decorated with souvenirs of a long police career. Shoulder patches, tarnished old badges, and medals displayed in shadow boxes. Thin black frames held glossy black and white photos, certificates of meritorious actions, and newspaper headlines of major cases he'd worked. Conspicuously, there were no pictures of Jenna anywhere in the room. The balding old man sitting in front of me in a motorized wheelchair, sucking air from an oxygen tank, was only a fraction of the former cop whose pictures dotted the walls. A man who had no doubt barked orders at subordinates and shouted through bullhorns at fugitives, Ray Czarnecki was now unable to talk after suffering the ravages of a stroke and a lifetime of unfiltered cigarettes.

Abrupt as ever, Jenna cut directly to the chase. "Daddy, this is my friend, Mac. He's a newspaper reporter. He wants to ask you about an old case you worked." I'd interviewed retired police officers before. When you mentioned the words *old case* it usually brought a faint smile and a fresh posture of interest as they naturally assumed you wanted them to rehash one of their investigative successes. However, when Ray Czarnecki heard those words, without even having any idea what case we were asking about, his neck immediately stiffened and he recoiled to a slightly more defensive position. Jenna sat on the arm of a recliner and leaned closer to her father, clasping her hands between her knees. "Do you remember a case you worked involving a man named Roosevelt Gregg? It was about twenty years ago. He shot a clerk at a convenience store." She glanced over at me for reassurance that she was getting her facts right. I nodded. We both looked back at her father. "They matched some prints from a soda can. Ring a bell?" Ray hesitated for a fraction of a second, then slowly shook his head back and forth. *No.* He drew harder on his oxygen and his right hand trembled as he grabbed tighter to the arm of his wheelchair in a futile effort to stop the involuntary twitching. He was still shaking his head, but I could see the pungent muck of ugly history being dredged up. Tears were welling up in his grizzled face. Not so much tears of sadness, but of fear and remorse and even terror over some dark secret being revealed. There was no doubt that Ray Czarnecki remembered Roosevelt Gregg. I looked over at Jenna, her eyes still fixed on the frail remnants of the tough lawman in the glossy photos on the wall, and I wondered if she would accept *no* for an answer. I could sense that she was trapped midway in some indeterminate state of wanting to confront her father about some past misdeed, and taking pity on an old man who was clearly living out his final days. She nodded and stood up. "Well, I guess that's that, then. Take care of yourself, Daddy." She kissed him on the forehead and briskly walked out. My eyes locked on to Ray's. I wanted him to know *I knew.*

As we drove back to Jenna's cottage. I chose my words carefully. "What do you think happened back there?"

"What do you mean?"

"He seemed to get pretty emotional when we brought up the name of Roosevelt Gregg."

"Yeah, he sure did."

"Any idea why?"

"Who knows. His memory's a little fuzzy these days. Maybe the thought of the girl who got killed that night upset him. Or maybe it's just the fact that he's stuck in a wheelchair and not contributing to society anymore. Coulda been anything."

I took a deep breath, still trying to tread delicately. "Or maybe it could be that he—"

"That he framed him?" interrupted Jenna. "Is that what you want to me to say? That my father was a dirty cop who framed an innocent man and sent him to prison?"

"No, it's just that—"

"That *what*, Mac?"

"Well, you saw his reaction! Did that not seem like more than just a guy who misses the thrill of the chase?"

Jenna slammed on the brakes. "Get out!"

"What?"

"I said get out! Get outta my car!" I hesitated, not moving. "Out!" she screamed, reaching across me and jerking open the door handle. "Go!"

"Okay, okay. I'm sorry! Calm down!" I got out and closed the door. She sped off, leaving me and my indelicate approach standing on the shoulder of the road. I zipped up my jacket to ward off the slight chill of the night air and considered my exceedingly limited travel options. Since I'd left the house without my wallet, there was pretty much only one way home; hoofing it. I broke into an easy trot. I was watching Jenna's taillights get further away when they suddenly brightened with the application of her brakes. Her white reverse lights came on, and now the car was backing up nearly as fast as it had left. I moved into the grass, not sure if she was going to offer me a ride or run me over. She stopped next to me and rolled down the window, still staring straight ahead. "Get in!" she ordered with a slight bob of her head. "Get in before I change my mind."

We drove in silence for several minutes before Jenna finally spoke. "When we were driving over here tonight, I fully expected Daddy to say he'd never heard of Roosevelt Gregg and that'd be the end of it. There was no doubt in my mind that your friend Lyman was wrong."

"What about now? Doubts?"

"Based on his reaction, I'd have to say yes. Plenty. But as I sat there and looked at him, I just didn't think I could go down that road." Jenna looked over at me, fighting back rare tears. "That's my *father*, Mac. He was a good cop. A *great* cop. He was relentless. He solved a lotta cases that nobody else could crack. Did you see his den? He's the most decorated officer in department history! Let me tell ya, he was worshipped in that station, by everybody, including me. So do you really think that at this stage of the game I could broach the subject that he'd framed a guy? No way."

"I understand. But if you were so sure he hadn't done anything wrong in the Roosevelt Gregg case, then why did we even go over there?"

Jenna rolled her eyes upward, not certain how much to reveal. "Because."

"Because? Because what?"

"Because I wanted him to meet you. I'd been looking for an excuse to take you over there and you provided me one. It kinda blew up in my face, but that was the plan anyway."

"Why in the world did you want your father to meet me?"

"Because I wanted him to see how well I was doing." She paused to gather her thoughts, bracing her elbow next to the window and resting her head against two fingers. "When I screwed up that domestic call, it hit my father really hard. He wasn't just disappointed or embarrassed. . . he was ashamed. He'd cashed in a lotta chips to get me in that job, and when I did that, it killed him. And it about killed me. That's when I got so antisocial. Started drinking, quit dating, quit taking care of myself. . . the whole nine yards. I think my father blamed himself for that."

"For being so hard on you?"

"Yeah. So tonight, I thought if he could see me sober, see me healthy, see me with a nice lookin' guy. . ."

"He'd feel better," I said.

"Yep. But look how it turned out. Now there's a good chance that I have a reason to be ashamed of *him*. Way to go, Jenna."

"I'm sorry," I said in a hushed tone. "I shouldn't have brought it up."

"What's done is done. Not your fault."

Neither of us said another word until we had pulled up in front of her cottage and she was unlocking the front door. The moment she stepped inside I could see alarm bells going off in her head. "*Whoa!*" she whispered, pushing me back with her hand. She crept inside the darkened room and I followed two steps behind. She stopped and turned her head, trying to listen for anything beyond ambient noise. The only light in the room was coming from her computer screen, and that was where Jenna's attention was focused. She lowered herself with bent knees and reached under the couch, pulling out a metal softball bat. She yanked the chain on the table lamp and brought light into the room.

"What's wrong?" I whispered.

Jenna moved stealthily toward the computer like a trained police officer. Bat held high, she checked in the bedroom and bathroom for any sign of an intruder. She rattled the door to the back patio. Locked. She lowered the bat and walked over to her computer. "Hmmm. That's strange," said Jenna in a normal voice.

"What is?"

"When we walked in, my home page was up on the computer screen."

"Why is that strange?"

"Because I have it set to go to my screensaver after it's been asleep for five minutes."

"You think somebody was in here?"

"Probably not. But with everything going on lately, maybe I'm a little jumpy too. Not to worry. Probably just a ghost in the machine." Just as she spoke, the computer switched back over to her screensaver. It was a girl on a surfboard bouncing off the sides of the monitor. "Well, if somebody *was* in here, we now know they've been gone for five minutes." Jenna poked her head in the refrigerator, scanning the bare shelves. "I sure picked a bad time to give up drinking."

I laughed out loud. It was the first lighthearted moment we'd had in hours. "Well fortunately *my* stomach is still taking reservations for alcohol, and I'm pretty sure there's one more beer in there with my name on it. Would you mind?"

"I think you've earned it," called back Jenna from the kitchen.

I walked over to the hall closet to hang up my jacket. "And if you can scare up some peanuts, I would really—" The man came crashing out of the closet before I had any sense of what was happening. Wearing black from head to toe, including a ski mask to cover his face, he bowled me over and sent us both flying to the floor, the back of my head smashing against the bare hardwood. He jumped up and charged towards the front door. I should have let him go, but raw instinct fueled my fear and made me extend my arm to catch the front of his right ankle, tripping him into a side table. He scrambled to his feet and grabbed a heavy brass candlestick that had fallen off the table. I was dazed from the blow to the head and unable to move out of harm's way as he raised the candlestick in his gloved hand with the intent of cracking my skull. He never got the chance. The awful *thudding* I heard was the sound of a softball bat connecting with the intruder's lower torso. He staggered from the blow, retching from the pain and falling against the wall like a wounded animal. He tried to lift the candlestick in anger against his assailant but the searing agony of cracked ribs bit into him and he clutched his abdomen. Jenna took another swing with controlled rage, nicking the man on the tip of his elbow. He howled in suffering as he threw the candlestick at her in backhanded fashion and used the moment of separation to flee. He ran out the front door still grasping his ribs in horrible anguish.

Jenna followed him to the door, but no further. She shut the door and locked it, then tossed the bat onto the couch and came to my aid. With her help, I stood up and tried to shake off the clanging cymbals in my brain. I wasn't bleeding and wasn't concussed, but the knot on my head was growing. She felt it and we both winced.

"I'll get some ice for that."

An hour later I was outside of Jenna's cottage, leaning against the hood of my car and holding a plastic grocery bag full of ice against the back of my throbbing head. Police officers had taken our statements and were now inside collecting evidence and dusting for fingerprints. I had already explained to them that the intruder was wearing gloves and therefore the chances of any latent prints being left behind were highly unlikely. Nonetheless, I admired their diligence and wondered what might have been the outcome for Roosevelt Gregg had the crime scene in *his* case been examined so thoroughly decades ago. The Crime Scene Unit finally packed up and headed back to their van. The customary exit language of *we'll be in touch if we hear anything* was tossed out as they rolled out of the driveway and drove into the night. As I watched them leave, and the events of the night soaked into my soul, a moment of great clarity washed over me.

Jenna came over and rubbed the back of my shoulder blade. "How ya feelin'?"

"For the record, I prefer cats."

I walked inside the cottage and tossed the ice into the sink, then back over to the couch. I started stuffing all my scattered belongings into my suitcase and duffel bag.

"What are you doing?" asked Jenna with a twinge of alarm.

"I'm takin' off. I'm done."

"What do you mean?"

"I mean I'm leaving."

"I gathered that much. Why?"

"We both know Danforth was behind what happened tonight, which means he knows I'm here, and if he came at me once, he'll come at me again. I'm taking what I know, or at least what I think I know, and telling the police. Let them handle it. This has gotten *way* above my pay grade. Yeah, I wanted to do this on my own, yeah, I wanted to be the big hero. . . but it's not worth it. It's just not worth it. And now I've put *you* in danger. I'm nothin' but trouble, so I'm leaving before it gets any worse for you."

"I think I proved that I can handle myself." I couldn't disagree, but I kept packing. Jenna moved closer and grabbed my arm. "Listen to me, Mac. Listen to me! If you go to the police now, you know Danforth and his lawyers will crush you before you know what hit you. They'll make you look like a lunatic with all your nonsense about jellyfish and space heaters, and when the smoke clears, Danforth walks away like nothing happened. Meanwhile, your reputation is ruined, and you'll have legal bills the rest of your life. And *that's* if you're lucky."

I pulled my arm out of her grasp. "Reputation? *What* reputation? As the biggest fool to ever have a byline? If I'm lucky, Danforth shoots me later tonight and puts us both out of our misery."

"So you're just quitting? Just like that?"

My anger flashed and my voice got louder as I packed with more vehemence. "What do you mean, *just like that*? I've followed every thread of this thing as far as I can, and it's brought me nothing but trouble! Let's face it. . . Danforth wins! Munce wins! Evil wins! I lose. I learned when I was fourteen years old that life isn't fair and this is just further proof of what I already know." I calmed down a fraction. "It's just getting too dangerous. You coulda been killed tonight, Jenna! It's time to give up and let the authorities take over. I'm sorry. I'm done." I checked around one last time to make sure I'd packed everything I'd brought into the house. I zipped up my duffel bag and tossed it over my shoulder. I lifted up my tired old tweed suitcase and headed for the front door. "Thanks for lettin' me crash here. I'll let you know where I end up." I opened the door, lifted my luggage, and pushed one foot across the threshold to the outside world.

"What if we can connect Danforth *directly* to the space heater?" blurted Jenna from behind me. "Would that be enough of a smoking gun?"

I stopped in my tracks and slowly turned around, trying to absorb this blast of new information. "How would we do that?"

Jenna moved closer, her voice rising with excitement as she brainstormed a new plan. "I don't know. . . somehow we figure out where he bought it. Get a credit card statement, something like that."

I dropped my luggage on the floor and shook my head. "A guy that smart wouldn't use a credit card. He'd pay cash. Or get one of his minions to buy it for him."

Jenna shook her head back at me. "I don't think so. If he was gonna involve them in murdering his wife, he woulda sent *them* over to Victoria's house and kept his own hands clean. No, something tells me he wanted to do this himself to exact a little revenge for her not signing that land over to him. It was a pretty clever way to kill someone, and a guy like Danforth would find tremendous satisfaction in that."

"Good point. And based on what Trey saw, I'm guessing he bought the heater fairly recently. I gotta believe that's what Danforth was carrying in the shopping bag. So. . ."

"So now all we have to do is figure out *where* he bought it!" declared Jenna, drumming her palms loudly against her thighs. It was not until that moment that it dawned on me that this quest to bring down Danforth, this Odyssean journey for justice, was just as crucial to Jenna's sense of redemption as it was to mine. I had only been focused on what it might mean to me in the eyes of Grace Chastain, but suddenly I realized it would mean as much in the eyes of Ray Czarnecki. This was her opportunity to prove that she was as capable a detective as anyone on the force. Albeit in different ways, we had both failed the people we loved and this was our chance to recapture that. I don't know why that had not occurred to me before, perhaps only explained by the fact that I spent so much time trying to push Jenna away. She walked slowly towards me, pulled my bags back inside, and kicked the door closed behind me. "Maybe we can start on that problem first thing in the morning," she said in a soothing tone. "Right now it's time for you to put that aching head to bed."

I nodded, surrendering to her sound logic. I began making up the couch for a night's rest. Jenna stopped me.

"Would you mind sleeping in my room tonight?" she asked, biting her lower lip.

"Why?"

"Protection."

"Yours, or mine?"

She chuckled, then revealed to me the most vulnerable expression I'd ever seen on her face. "I'd feel safer. Right now, big tough Jenna is a little scared. Of a lot of things."

"Okay, but I'll sleep on the floor."

"Close enough."

On a makeshift bed of pillows and blankets, I stretched out on the hardwood floor next to Jenna's bed and stared at the ceiling. My headache had finally subsided. "You know he likes you, don't you?" I said softly into the night.

"What?"

"Trey. He likes you."

"He *likes* me? What is this, seventh grade?"

"You know what I mean."

"I think you've been hit in the head, that's what I think."

"He cares about you, Jenna. You should think about letting him get past your walls. He's a nice guy."

There was a long pause. "I know he is. Which is why he can do better. I'm damaged goods."

"You just need someone to love you. Maybe he's the one."

"Go to sleep, MacClellan. You're delirious."

As Jenna dove off the cliff into gentle slumber, I was thinking about Grace and how we used to lie on the floor and talk in the dark when we couldn't even see each other. We'd talk about life, love, family, faith, any topic we chose, all in a gentle back and forth flow of sharing and listening. On our travels we'd turn off the lights at night and recount the events of the day, piecing together all the places and faces we'd encountered so they'd linger in our memories far beyond the fleeting moments of first discovery. Grace was the perfect traveling companion, finding joy around every corner with an innate curiosity that begged her to explore and admire the world's wonders. She was also an expert at navigating, able to decipher even the crudest of maps and save me from getting hopelessly lost on all the obscure paths I felt certain would eventually lead to something worth seeing. I resisted the urge to buy a GPS system for my car or use an app on my phone just so we wouldn't lose that teamwork. We weren't just a couple—we were partners, in all matters. I choked back a sardonic laugh as I realized that I was as lost as I'd ever been, and my navigator wasn't there to steer me back on course. And then it hit me. I shot bolt upright.

"Jenna! Wake up!"

"What?" she yelled out as she sat up in a mild panic, clutching the baseball bat she'd taken to bed with her. "What is it?"

"If you had a recognizable face in a small town and you needed to buy something you weren't supposed to, like for example a space heater. . . how would you go about it?"

Jenna closed her eyes and pinched the bridge of her nose as she tried to clear her mind. "I don't know. . . I'd guess I'd get it off the internet."

"But what if you didn't want any record of it?"

"I don't know. Can't you just tell me?"

"You go to another town to buy it, someplace where nobody knows you. And how do you know how to get there? You use a GPS!"

# Chapter Twenty-nine

Neither of us had gotten much sleep the night before as we formulated a new plan to go after Danforth. Bunking on the floor hadn't helped either. We were both trying to pry open bleary eyes with coffee as we drove my car into Virginia Beach. The first step of our operation should have been the easiest, but we had no earthly idea how hard it was to find a working payphone. Whereas they used to sprout up like scrub pines, the payphone has become merely a nostalgic reminder of our technological past. To find one fully operational in a land where they're constantly exposed to salt air proved nearly too much to ask, but we finally found one at a 7-11 on General Booth Boulevard. I found it ironic that we were going to use this dinosaur of electronic communication to launch a plan that relied heavily on modern invention, but the archaic payphone circumvented one common technology we needed to avoid: caller I-D.

I leaned close to her as Jenna slipped some quarters into the coin slot and dialed. It was answered immediately.

"Hello?" replied the unmistakable voice of Duncan Danforth through the handset. He sounded curt, annoyed that anyone dare to call him.

Jenna delivered her rehearsed lines in a manner worthy of any thespian. "Mr. Danforth? It's Hayley Wozniak."

"Who?"

"Hayley Wozniak. I'm the girl you hired to pretend I was a receptionist at the doctor's office. Ya know, Dr. Hartog."

"I'm afraid you're mistaken, young lady. I don't know what you're talking about. Good day."

"Mr. Danforth, the police are asking me a lot of questions!" Jenna injected panic in her voice.

There was a long pause on the other end. I could picture a man in a very expensive suit starting to squirm. "How did you get this number?"

We'd anticipated that question during our rehearsal and didn't have a plausible answer, so we chose to ignore it. "They're threatening to put me in jail if I don't tell them what they want to know! I don't know what to do! Can they do that?" Jenna mustered up what sounded like real tears. I was impressed by the authenticity she brought to her acting.

"Calm down, calm down!" said Danforth. "Nobody's sending anybody to jail."

"I'm scared, Mr. Danforth. A detective told me he's coming by my apartment this afternoon. I don't know what to do. I really need to talk to you." Jenna sobbed into the handset, an actress playing an actress.

There was another long pause as Danforth formulated a plan to iron out this latest wrinkle. "This is not something we can discuss over the phone. Is there someplace I can meet you?"

Jenna and I exchanged a knowing glance. He'd taken the bait. "I work as a waitress at a place called Rudee's on the Inlet. Do you know it?"

"Yes. What time?"

"Is noon okay?"

"Done. I'll see you then. How will I know you?"

"I'm about five feet four, glasses, and I'll be wearing a red visor and a yellow jacket."

"I will see you at noon. In the meantime, you don't say anything to anybody. Is that understood?"

"Yes. Please help me, Mr. Danforth!" Jenna started to cry again. It was close to being over the top.

"Noon. Don't be late." Danforth ended the call, no doubt with a hard mash of his index finger.

Jenna returned the handset to its resting place. "He bought it!" she squealed.

"Sure sounded that way. But you never know with a guy that smart. He may be playin' *us.*"

"I don't think so. He sounded a lot like a man who was watching his evil empire unravel at the hands of a frightened college coed. So what now?" asked Jenna.

"Go inside and get some doughnuts," I declared boldly.

"Why?"

"Because, Detective Czarnecki. . . *we* are going on a stakeout."

Neither of our health conscious bodies would allow us to actually buy doughnuts, so we settled for some blueberry muffins and let them crumble into our mouths as we drove over the bridge and turned left on Winston Salem Avenue into Rudee Inlet. We sat in the parking lot of the restaurant and waited.

"I'm trying to decide," said Jenna, drumming her fingers on the armrest.

"What's to decide?"

"When it comes time to distract the valet, do I go with sexy or clumsy?"

"I'd go with whatever you're sure is gonna work. We only get one crack at this."

Jenna's face turned pouty. "So you're saying I shouldn't try sexy, is that it?" I honestly couldn't tell if she was kidding.

"I didn't say that."

"You inferred it."

"I neither said anything, nor inferred anything. Can we please focus?"

"You know, a lot of men find me very attractive."

"Let's not go there right now."

Mercifully Danforth's distinctive Jaguar wheeled into the parking lot, his tires squealing as he made a quick turn down towards the valet stand.

"Okay, Jenna, there's our boy," I said, feeling my adrenaline surge.

She nodded, slipped on a pair of large sunglasses, a floppy sun hat, and took a deep breath. "It's showtime."

Jenna quietly stepped out of the car and hoisted a canvas tote bag over her shoulder as she headed towards the valet stand. I kept my eyes on Danforth as he exited his car and handed a gratuity to the valet. He pointed to the short row of parking spaces where the nicer cars are given preferential parking treatment, and the valet nodded in understanding. Danforth walked closer to the restaurant and stood by the railing near some glider chairs next to the water, no doubt scanning the area for a young woman wearing a yellow coat and red visor.

I quietly got out of the car and followed a safe distance behind, splitting my attention between Jenna, the valet, and a nervous Danforth pacing the wooden walkway down by the water. Jenna's usual bouncy walk, tomboyish at times, suddenly transformed into something you'd see on the runway of a Paris fashion show. Her posture straightened and her hips swiveled back and forth like a 1940's movie star. It was only now that I realized she was wearing high heels which accentuated her tanned and athletic calf muscles. I watched the valet carefully as he parked the Jaguar, then placed Danforth's keys on a hook on the very top row of a pegboard. Jenna brushed past him, her sultry sashay clearly catching his eye. She walked another fifteen feet closer to the restaurant, turned slightly to make sure I was in position, then grabbed her heel in pain. "Ow!" she yelped loud enough for the valet to hear. Perfectly on cue, the young man abandoned the peg board and rushed over to her aid.

"You okay, Miss?" he asked, jumping at the opportunity to make contact with her.

"I feel like something stabbed me on the bottom of my foot! Do you see anything?"

While the valet-turned-paramedic attended to Jenna, I swooped in and grabbed Danforth's keys off the pegboard. I had them in my pocket and was walking away in less than five seconds. I eased over towards Danforth's Jaguar and waited for my next cue. By now Jenna had disengaged with the valet and disappeared into the restaurant. Danforth continued to pace along the water, checking his watch with growing nervousness. Less than a minute later, Jenna exited from the door on the far end of the restaurant. Her sunglasses and floppy hat were now gone, replaced by a lemon yellow jacket, eyeglasses, and a red sun visor. She stood on the veranda all alone, and finally her blatant conspicuousness caught Danforth's eye. He sent a half-wave in her direction, hoping to catch her attention, but she ignored him and walked down a short staircase to the pier where the fishing charter boats are moored. Danforth walked quickly in her direction. She would make certain he'd never catch up to her.

I unlocked Danforth's car and slid inside, making sure I wasn't noticed. I put the key in the ignition and brought the electronics to life, most importantly his onboard GPS navigation system. As quickly as my nervous fingers would allow, I called up RECENT SELECTIONS on the GPS and scanned the "history" of Danforth's searches. It immediately displayed the last fifty places for which he'd requested directions. It only took an instant to pinpoint one that leapt off the screen: a hardware store, visited on September 14, the day before the fire at the home of Victoria Boyd-Danforth. My hand was shaking almost uncontrollably as I snapped a photo of the screen with my phone.

I shut off the car, crept out, and gently closed the door. As I moved as unobtrusively as possible back to the valet stand, I saw Danforth at the far end of the pier, looking mildly frantic in his futile search for the mysterious Hayley Wozniak.

By this time, Jenna had gone back inside the restaurant, stuffed the yellow jacket and red visor into her canvas tote bag, and once again donned her sunglasses and floppy hat. She came out the front entrance and we met back at the car. We quickly drove away, catching a final glimpse in my rear-view mirror of Danforth still stalking the waterfront. It probably wouldn't take him much longer to figure out he'd been stood up.

"Did you get it?" asked Jenna with brimming excitement.

"Oh, I got it all right." I showed her the photo on my phone. "It's over in Chesapeake."

"Oh yeah!" she squealed, punching me in the shoulder.

"And I gotta admit. . . you certainly pulled off sexy."

"Why thank you. Glad you finally noticed."

Less than thirty minutes later we arrived at a hardware store on South Battlefield Boulevard in Chesapeake that matched the address on Danforth's GPS. As I reached for the door handle, I suddenly stopped. "I just realized something. How are we gonna get access to their surveillance video?"

"Don't worry," replied Jenna with cool confidence. "Got ya covered."

"How?"

"Just FML."

"FML?" I asked. "What's that mean? Actually, I'm not sure I wanna know."

"FML. . . Follow my lead. It's something my old partner and I used to say to each other when we were in a situation where we had to improvise a little."

"And by 'improvise,' you mean lie?"

"Think of it as 'acting.' Don't tell me you've never done it to get a story."

"No comment."

"Come on, I got this. We're going in. FML."

I shrugged my shoulders as if to say *whatever* and followed Jenna inside.

The same woman who had channeled her best Rita Hayworth in the parking lot at Rudee Inlet had suddenly turned into Humphrey Bogart. Jenna flashed a police badge as she strode up to the cashier like she owned the place. "I'm detective Jenna Holden with the fraud unit. I need to see the manager." Her chutzpah was not only impressive, it was a little frightening. And the instant they saw that badge, they bought it, no questions asked.

"I'm the manager," came the voice of a middle-aged man emerging from an aisle of chain saws and hedge trimmers. He was slightly overweight with balding hair, wearing a short sleeve dress shirt with a tie that stopped about five inches above his belt buckle. "What can I do for you, officer?"

Jenna leaned over. "Mind if we talk privately in your office?" she asked him in a hushed tone. It was a brilliant maneuver. It drew the store manager into the investigation and made him feel like he was a part of the crime solving team. She'd clearly employed this technique before.

"Absolutely. Right this way."

A minute later we were in the back office of the hardware store, alone with the manager. Jenna pressed our case. "We're looking for a guy who's been passing some counterfeit bills in the area. We have reason to believe he may have done it here. We'd like to take a quick look at your video to see if we might spot him. Is that okay?"

"Of course. Whatever you need."

The store manager opened the doors on a cabinet to reveal a fairly sophisticated video surveillance system.

"How far back does your system go?" asked Jenna.

"As far back as you need," answered the manager proudly. "Everything we record is stored in the 'cloud' now, so I can go back years if I want to. Pretty slick, huh?"

Jenna nodded. "If every merchant were as diligent about security as you are, sir, it would certainly make our lives down at the police department a lot easier." The manager beamed over being such a worthy corporate citizen. I still hadn't spoken a word.

"We're interested in the date September 14th of last year. Not sure what time of day."

"No problem." The manager sat down at a keyboard and with a few swift keystrokes called up the date we wanted. "There you go. That's from 0800 when we opened the doors. I can take you all the way through to closing time, which is 1900 hours." I got the sense that the manager was secretly hoping that his usage of military time would further ingratiate him to his audience of law enforcement, and further cement his position as a part of the "team." Jenna was immediately able to intuit his intentions and nodded her approval. I'd never seen her like this and I marveled at her confidence and skill.

We fast-forwarded through several hours of customers completing transactions at the counter and finally saw what we wanted: Duncan Danforth stepping up to the cashier, looking somewhat out of place in a hardware store in his tailored suit and distinctive cufflinks.

"Freeze it!" ordered Jenna. "That's our man!" The manager eagerly complied with the directive. Jenna leaned over to get a closer look, pointing to the screen and patting the man on the back for a job well done. "That's him."

"Really? We caught him?"

"We sure did," I replied, suddenly trying to now feel as much a part of the "team" as the other two. "We got him."

Even though we'd expected to see it, the frozen image on the screen was nonetheless riveting. Duncan Danforth, buying a space heater *and* an electronic timer, with murder in his heart. It was visual proof of everything we'd surmised up to this point, similar to deducing the answers to the secret cards in a game of *Clue*. I finally felt confident that we had enough proof to go to the authorities and there was nothing the Danforth machine could possibly do to stop us. More than that, it was the awakening from my nightmare of the last two years. The debacle at the *Herald*, the disaster with the phantom Irukandji, and all the human carnage in between, was about to be buried. I could finally see a future.

"Is there any way we can get a copy of that?"asked Jenna, once again taking charge.

"Sure, officer. I can burn you a DVD. Take me two minutes. Hang on."

Minutes later we'd said our goodbyes and were back in the car, disc in hand.

"That was *so* much fun!" chirped Jenna.

"Make you feel like a cop again?"

"Yeah. It did. Felt good."

Jenna sat in the passenger seat with an unerasable smile. It was clearly more than just the giddiness of the moment for having pulled off a minor caper. Her face bore the indelible look of a young woman who was on the verge of reclaiming her lost soul. I was grateful to be a witness to the transformation.

"By the way, where'd you get that police badge? I thought you had to turn in your badge and gun."

"Don't ask." The smile on her face got a little bigger.

# Chapter Thirty

We picked up a large pizza at Lago Mar and drove back to Jenna's cottage. We intended to map out a plan of action as to exactly how we would go about presenting our findings to the authorities, and most importantly who we would approach. Though I didn't verbalize it to Jenna, Lyman's story about his brother Roosevelt had stuck in the back of my mind as a cautionary tale about the possibility of unscrupulous police officers. Who knows how far Danforth's influence reached, and it would only take one local cop in his pocket to put us both in serious danger. I'd finally convinced Jenna that the FBI was our best alternative. We'd take tonight to put together a summary of our evidence and take it to them first thing in the morning. Our plan was about to change.

The instant we walked into the darkened cottage we knew there was trouble. The smell of lingering cigar smoke hung heavily in the air, the initial sign that we were not alone. The lamp flicked on and revealed Duncan Danforth sitting in Jenna's chair, legs crossed, and calmly puffing on a hand-rolled Cuban. "I hope you brought enough food for everyone."

Jenna and I tried to turn and bolt back out of the front door, but our progress was immediately stopped by the gun we saw pointed in our face. Maggie Doolan was standing in the doorway, holding the weapon with a steady hand, and looking as though she might enjoy using it. "Get in there," she motioned. We obeyed, slowly retreating back inside the cottage.

Jenna raised her hands in surrender, and I would have done the same, but I was still holding the large pizza box. "I'm just gonna set this down," I said to Maggie. "Just take it easy." I slowly set the pizza on the corner of the end table, but intentionally left more than half of it hanging over the edge so that it would fall off and onto the floor. "Sorry!" I told the room, kneeling down to clean it up. I surreptitiously reached for the softball bat Jenna kept hidden underneath the couch, but it wasn't there.

"Sorry, mate, beat ya to the punch." I looked up and saw Kenneth Batterbee lording over me with bat in hand. "Go ahead. . . do something stupid. I'd love to return the favor." He patted his ribs, clearly indicating that he was the masked intruder from the night before.

"Enough with the pleasantries!" barked Danforth. "Sit down!" With both a gun and a bat aimed in our direction, Jenna and I readily complied, sitting next to each other on the couch. Batterbee handcuffed our arms behind us with zip ties while Doolan kept her gun trained on us. Jenna seemed fairly calm on the exterior and I tried to appear the same, although I was feeling a panic start to seize over me. I'd been in dangerous situations before, but nothing I didn't think I could overcome. This was different. I had fear gripping me as never before. I could see the rage boiling in Danforth's eyes and I knew that if he'd already committed two murders, then what were two more to cover up his sins? I thought back to the night before when I was packing up and trying to get out of Jenna's apartment and leave all this behind. I should have never let her talk me out of it. Now she was caught up in something bigger than both of us and we were going to pay a heavy price for having pushed forward. As my attention darted back and forth between Danforth's menacing eyes and the weaponry being wielded by his confederates, all my fears were distilled into one singular thought: how much I had left undone. Danforth pulled Batterbee into Jenna's bedroom but didn't completely shut the door. Danforth was doing almost all of the talking, as if giving instructions. Maggie Doolan sat on the edge of the coffee table and kept the gun pointed directly at my chest, looking unafraid to actually pull the trigger. For the most part I could only hear murmuring in the back room and couldn't decipher the full text of the conversation, but I did manage to hear a few words; *boat, marina,* and *bodies.* My adrenaline surged as I thought this might be my only chance to escape. If I could distract Doolan, get her to lower the gun for even an instant, I could spring up off the couch and bullrush her and even with my hands tied behind my back, somehow gain control of the gun. I had to think this through, which I was finding to be nearly impossible under the oppressive cloud of fear weighing on me. I tried to catch Jenna's attention with my eyes but she was fixated on the gun held steady in Doolan's hand. With two of us on the offensive, perhaps our chances were better, but even if we could overpower Doolan and disarm her, how would we hold a gun with our arms behind us? And it would only be a matter of seconds before Danforth and Batterbee came charging back in, and how would they react? But if we were going to die anyway, what would it matter? On the other hand, maybe this wasn't my best window of opportunity to escape. It might be a fatal attempt. Or this could be my last chance. I couldn't think straight, paralyzed in swirling thought. For some reason the irony struck me that one week ago I felt as though I had nothing to live for, and now all I wanted to do was somehow survive this and start a new life. My senses told me that the time of reckoning was upon me and it was literally do or die. My plan was to appeal to her softer side, hoping that she had one.

I eased my way a little closer to the edge of the couch to make it easier to lunge at Doolan. I braced the balls of my feet against the floor and prepared to explode forward, like a sprinter waiting in the blocks for the sound of the starting gun. "It's kinda funny, don't you think?" I asked her, forcing a soft smile.

"How's that?" she replied, tightening her grip on the pistol.

"The first time we met, I actually tried to help you. I gave you money. A perfect stranger, and I tried to give you a hand. Remember?"

"I remember. Why is that funny?"

"Well, maybe not *funny*. . . more like ironic. Look at us now. You're ready to kill me."

"All that means is that you're a chump. You got played."

"Maybe *you're* the one getting played."

"What do you mean by that?"

"Maybe those two are back there plotting how to get rid of *you*. That's one less person to pay off, one less person who can talk."

"Shut up!" snapped Doolan, raising the gun in her outstretched arm and pointing it straight at my face.

This was good. An agitated captor is more likely to make a mistake. "Think about it, Maggie. Why would they be back there whispering without you? I'd find that highly suspicious if I were you." I inched up closer, ready to pounce.

"I said *shut your mouth!*" she yelled.

My heart was pounding out of my chest and I was breathing with excessive force as I tried to maintain a semblance of outward calm. I just needed her to lower the gun a few more inches and give me a chance to overpower her. I waited too long. Danforth and Batterbee pushed open the bedroom door and hastened into the living room. My window had closed. Batterbee had the softball bat gripped tightly in his hand. "Is there a problem here?" asked Batterbee.

"No," replied Doolan coolly. "No problem here. Any problems back there?" Just from the way she asked the question, I could tell that the seed of doubt I'd planted moments before had taken root in Doolan's mind.

"Everything's set," interjected Danforth. "Nothing to worry about." Danforth turned to Jenna and me and ruefully shook his head. "It's a shame you two had to meddle in my affairs. This could have all been so neat and tidy, and we all could have gone about our lives. Now, I'm afraid, yours are about to end. Shame."

"So you'll have the blood of four murders on your hands?" said Jenna, the first time she'd spoken in quite some time. "For *what?* Money?"

Danforth chuckled with wry amusement. "Not just money, my dear. Something much better, much more—intoxicating."

"What might that be?" I asked with as much contempt as I could summon.

Danforth walked closer and leaned in for emphasis. I could see the full expression of insanity saturating his eyes as he grinned with delight. "Power. Control. The ability to tell people what to do and when to do it, completely on my terms. It's a *lovely* feeling. You should try it sometime. It's like being king."

"Or dictator," I shot back. Danforth's face soured. His fingers twitched and I could tell he wanted nothing more than to attack me with savage fury. My sudden courage was fueled by the realization that I was most certainly going to die tonight, so if I could provoke Danforth enough to commit murder right here, the chances he'd be caught later on were exponentially greater. "Go on, King Duncan. Hit me. Better yet, take her gun and kill me, right here, right now. Come on. You know you want to. Or are you afraid to? Afraid to get actual blood on your hands? It's a lot easier to set a timer on a space heater and be a hundred miles away, isn't it? So much better to have your minions do your dirty work for you. You don't have the stomach for it, do you, King Duncan?" Danforth was trembling with deep-seated anger. I'd clearly struck a nerve embedded in his core. His gaze was suddenly distant, back to another time and place. His face carried the pain from the kind of primal, turbulent emotion that seemed to dredge up some unspeakable childhood trauma.

"*Enough!*" he screamed, slapping me across the face. He stood up and walked to the edge of the room, turning his back on all of us. The sideways glance between Batterbee and Doolan clearly indicated that even they had never seen the mask pulled so completely off the face of the madman. After several moments to collect himself, Danforth turned back and marched toward the door without making eye contact with anyone in the room. "I'll be at home. We'll meet tomorrow at the usual place when it's done. You'll get your money then." He stared directly at me with those cold, insane eyes. "I only regret that I can't do it myself." Danforth turned quickly on his heels and walked out, slamming the front door as an exclamation point to the encounter. Seconds later we heard his Jaguar roar away.

Batterbee and Doolan continued to look at each other, not sure what to make of what just transpired. Batterbee finally moved into action. He took the gun from Doolan and wisely pulled the coffee table a much safer distance from the couch and sat on it, holding us at bay. He checked his watch.

"We on a schedule?" I asked.

"Shut your mouth, wise guy." He waved the gun at me. "*I'm* not afraid to use this."

"Sorry. I just wanted to stay in the loop."

Doolan sat across the room and lit up a cigarette. Her hands were visibly shaking, undoubtedly from the knowledge that sometime that night she was going to be intimately involved in two homicides.

"Hey!" yelled Jenna instinctively. "You can't smoke in here!"

Doolan paused for a split-second over the admonishment, then snorted a laugh when she realized the order had come from someone who had her hands tied behind her back and a loaded gun pointed at her. Doolan took a long drag on her cigarette and blew the plume of smoke defiantly in Jenna's direction.

Batterbee nervously stood up and walked to the window, drawing back the curtains and having a quick look outside. The fact that he only looked skyward indicated to me that his sole concern was how much daylight was left and not who might be watching us. Whatever they had planned for Jenna and me, I now believed it would come after nightfall. That gave me less than an hour to come up with a plan to escape.

Batterbee sat back down on the coffee table and again checked his watch. It was so quiet you could hear it tick. Doolan puffed on her cigarette and stared at the floor, perhaps wondering how her life's journey had turned down such a dark fork. We all sat in gloomy silence, awaiting the next step with a crushing sense of dread. As the minutes passed, I recalled the words of Melvin the chess player: *Never accept one's fate as pure destiny. It is only the fool who doesn't anticipate what his opponent will do. Not just his next move, but the next six or seven.* I tried to think like Danforth and anticipate what he had planned for Jenna and me. The snippets of the conversation between Danforth and Batterbee rolled around in my brain. . . *boat, marina, bodies.* Why not just kill us here? Too much noise and too much forensic evidence, for starters. If I'd learned one thing in my newspaper days, most killers get caught because they don't cover their tracks, especially when it comes to disposing of the victim's body. More importantly, in the crazed mind of Duncan Danforth, gunning us down in a cottage didn't carry with it enough drama. Simply shooting someone in cold blood was not clever enough to meet the standards of an 'evil genius.' Danforth wanted a final solution that was more elegant, more befitting of the machinations of his twisted mind. *Boat. Marina. Bodies.* I theorized that the plan was to take us out into the ocean, put a bullet in us, and dump us overboard. No one would hear the shots, and when the sharks were done with us, no one would find the bodies. Figuring that he'd killed Morton Boyd on a boat at sea, it seemed to fit with Danforth's manner of eliminating people who got in his way.

I glanced over at Jenna as she stared deep into the hardwood of the floor, her chiseled jaw locked in place. I couldn't read her. I couldn't tell if she were resigned to her fate, or, like me, if she were contemplating some heroic action. Unlike me, she did not seem to be cloaked in a fog of fear. She appeared stoic, like a prisoner of war bravely awaiting the firing squad. In this absurd theatre, it would have made considerable more sense for Jenna to be the one smoking a cigarette. The fact that she had the willpower to quit smoking and drinking was an indication of how far she'd come in the months I'd known her, and her svelte physique reflected the change. Her skin was radiant and smooth, her muscles lean and toned, and she'd regained the sparkle in her eyes. She was no longer the wheezing alcoholic I'd met that first night at the Baja. I permitted myself to take a modicum of credit for the transformation. I felt that in some small way, I had helped Jenna to clear out her head, liver, and lungs. Ironically, she was far more whole than I was at this point. Perhaps that was what she was thinking. She'd pulled herself out of the depths of despair and carved out a brighter day ahead, and was now realizing that new day would never dawn. The lower the sun fell over the Back Bay, the closer we both came to our deaths.

As if by divine intervention, a bolt of brilliant clarity shot through my brain. It suddenly became clear, as if I were seeing Melvin's chessboard like a Grandmaster. The words *boat, marina,* and *bodies* were replaced in my head by three new ones: *bay, light,* and *lungs.* It was my only move.

I waited patiently for Batterbee to take his eyes off me. He glanced back at the window to check the fading light, and in that instant, I gently kicked Jenna's ankle. She broke out of the mild trance she'd been in and cocked her head sideways. She raised her eyebrows as if to say *what are you thinking?* I turned back and looked Batterbee squarely in the eye.

"FML," I said loudly.

"What?" he replied tersely.

"I said FML. Don't you know what that means?"

"No," said Batterbee with growing annoyance. "Stop talking."

I glanced over at Jenna to see if my cryptic message had been received. She nodded almost imperceptibly, signaling that she understood. *Follow my lead.* "I forgot," I said to Batterbee, disobeying his orders. "You're not actually the brains of this outfit, are you? My mistake."

He pointed the gun at my face. "You need to stow it, mate. Right now."

"What are you gonna do, shoot me right here? I don't think so. That's not part of the plan, is it? Let me guess. . . Danforth ordered you to wait until it gets dark, take us a few miles out to sea in a boat, shoot us, and dump us over the side. And the only way you can get out to deep water is by taking a boat out of the marina. Is that about right? I sure *hope* that's the plan."

Batterbee lunged forward and backhanded me across the face, drawing blood from the corner of my mouth. "That's enough!" Batterbee waved the gun at the couch. "This is as much your fault as anyone's, ya know. I tried to scare you off this island and you didn't take the bait, so blame yourself. That's why you're in this mess. Now then, you got another hour to live. Make it a quiet one." He sat back down, the gun now resting on his knee, but his finger still on the trigger.

I kept talking, figuring I had nothing to lose at this point besides more blood. "You know he's settin' you both up, don't you? I'm guessing the arrangement with Danforth is that you don't get paid until after the job's done, am I right? And it's kinda hard to collect your cash when you're behind bars, isn't it?" Batterbee narrowed his eyes and looked at me askance.

Doolan got out of her chair and walked up behind him. "What's your point?" she asked.

Jenna chimed in. "What he's trying to tell you is that if you kill us, you're going to get caught."

"How so?" asked Doolan. I could tell that our story had more than piqued her interest.

"The closest marina for ocean access is Owl's Creek," I said. "The place is crawling with people all hours of the day and night."

Jenna continued to weave our improvisational tale. "And not just lots of people hanging around the marina. There are surveillance cameras everywhere, so surely you'll be spotted pushing around two people in handcuffs."

I dovetailed the narrative. "Plus, once you hit the water, you run the risk of running into the Coast Guard out there, or maybe even a few Navy Seals out of Dam Neck. On top of that, the tide's coming in tonight. If you dump us in the ocean, our bodies wash in with the tide and some unlucky shell seeker finds us in the morning. That puts the cops hot on your trail. Don't you see? Danforth *knows* all that! He *wants* you to get caught! It wouldn't surprise me if he's the one who tips off the police."

Batterbee started to pace nervously back and forth, trying to shake out the seeds of doubt we'd planted in his head. "No, no, you're wrong. Danforth has been square with us this whole time. He wouldn't turn on us now."

"Let me guess," I continued. "All this time, Danforth has made it crystal clear that there's to be absolutely no direct contact with him. No cell phone records, no meetings in public, no financial transactions, nothing that could ever connect the two of you with him, am I right?" The glance that they exchanged told me I was spot on. "So if you two get picked up by the cops, there's nothing to trace it back to Danforth. You could holler all day that he was the mastermind and it'd never stick."

"And this way," said Jenna, "Danforth never has to worry about the two of you blackmailing him in the future. All four of us in this room are going down, and Danforth walks away to a life of luxury."

Batterbee was getting more agitated. "No, no, you're just tryin' to confuse us to save your own necks."

I looked directly at Doolan, who seemed to be thinking more clearly than her partner. "Think about it, Maggie. You know how smart Duncan Danforth is. If he *really* wanted you to get away with murder, he would have ordered you to slip us out into the Back Bay in a jon boat with a quiet little trolling motor. You two ever actually *been* on the Back Bay?"

They both shook their heads. "No," said Batterbee.

"There's not a soul around. Nobody would ever know you're there, especially as dark as it gets back there at night. You can't even see the crab pots without a good flashlight. You could dump us in that still water with some cinderblocks tied to our legs and we sink to the bottom and rot. You wouldn't even have to fire a shot. If the fish don't eat us, the water moccasins will." I turned to Jenna and stared directly at her, trying to penetrate her mind with my eyes. "And if we have a northeast wind, it'd be duck season before anyone finds us. *Duck season*." I held my forceful gaze for another few seconds, then turned back to my captors. "If Duncan Danforth *really* wanted you to get away with murder, *that's* what he would have told you to do."

Jenna kicked me. "Hey, genius, you want to quit tellin' 'em the best way to kill us?"

"I'm just trying to show them that there's a better solution. One we can all live with."

"And what might that be?" asked Doolan.

"You're both in this for the money, right? You keep your meeting with Danforth and tell him you did the job. He pays you off, then you let us go, and you both skip town and disappear. Then I go to the cops with the evidence I have on Danforth and he's arrested. He'll never be able to come after you. You're both free and clear, and we're still alive. What do you think?"

Doolan and Batterbee took a long look at each other as they let my plan take root. I could tell they were considering it.

Batterbee turned back to me. "How do we know you don't turn us in too?"

"Hey, if you're gonna spare my life, I think that's the *least* I can do, right? All I want is to survive this night, and nail Duncan Danforth. You can go live in peace with his money and I promise you'll never hear from me again."

Batterbee stood up and motioned Doolan to the far corner of the living room, careful to keep the gun trained on me. They conferred for several minutes in whispers. My eyes met Jenna's, both wondering if anything we'd said might have changed the outcome of the night. Batterbee and Doolan both nodded to each other in agreement over whatever they'd been discussing, then he walked back over to us and waved the gun. "Get up." He motioned his head toward the door.

"Where are we going?"

"There's been a change of plans, mate."

# Chapter Thirty-one

With his gun planted firmly in my back, Batterbee pushed us out the door of Jenna's cottage and into the backseat of a black SUV. He tossed the keys to Doolan. She got behind the wheel while he slid into the passenger's seat, the gun barrel never leaving us.

Night had completely fallen as Doolan turned left, heading for the south end of the island.

"Where are you taking us?" asked Jenna.

Batterbee smiled. "Back Bay. Like you said, nice and quiet. Nobody will hear you scream."

"Hey, I thought we had a deal!" I yelled.

"What do you take me for? You know as well as I do that you're gonna put the cops on us the minute we let you go."

"I won't, I swear!"

"Doesn't matter. There are so many other people who can connect us to Danforth and would gladly cut a deal to save themselves. We might get away for awhile, but we'd be lookin' over our shoulders the rest of our lives. Sorry, mate, but this is the only way. And thanks for makin' our job easier. We hadn't considered all the problems we might run into at the marina."

"I told you!" yelled Jenna, kicking me again, harder this time. "Thanks to you, they're gonna get away with murder!" She looked panicked as we continued to head south on Sandpiper Road. We could see someone on a bicycle approaching in the opposite lane. The rider held up his hand to shield his eyes from our headlights. *"Help!"* screamed Jenna through the glass of the car window. *"Help us!"* Batterbee reached over the seat and slapped Jenna across the face. It made my blood boil, but there was absolutely nothing I could do about it.

A few minutes later we'd pulled into the empty parking lot at Back Bay Outfitters, which rented kayaks, boats, and jet skis to tourists. Doolan parked behind the lone building on the property, hiding the vehicle from view. It was so dark that even from fifty yards away, I could barely make out the waters of the Back Bay. Batterbee handed Doolan the gun and she gave him the car keys in return. He got out and popped open the tailgate. Seconds later he climbed into the backseat of the SUV with a roll of silver duct tape and slapped a piece across our mouths, ending all chances that we might yell for help.

Batterbee walked back to the rear of the SUV and removed a large pair of bolt cutters, standard issue for most petty thieves, then took off on foot towards the water. Jenna and I sat in taped silence in the back seat, unable to attempt any more dialogue with Doolan. Batterbee returned in less than five minutes, tossed the bolt cutters back into the rear of the SUV and quietly latched the lid.

Moments later Jenna and I were out of the vehicle and marching at gunpoint towards the water's edge. The wind was out of the northeast. I could hear the music and laughter pouring out of the Baja just down the road. My eyes met Jenna's as she heard it too, and I wondered if she was regretting that I'd ever walked in the place and made her acquaintance.

When we reached the water there was a jon boat waiting for us, which Batterbee had obviously just stolen from Back Bay Outfitters. The boat was loaded down with four weight belts for scuba divers, each pouch of the belt loaded with lead. As the four of us stepped in, the sides of the jon boat sank deep into the water from all the weight, making it less than steady. Batterbee snapped two of the heavy diving belts around each of our waists. Anchors of death that would pull us straight to the bottom of the bay.

Jenna and I were next to each other in the middle seat, with Batterbee taking a kneeling position on the front seat next to the bow. Doolan was seated in the stern with her hand on the tiller of the 3.5-horsepower Evinrude engine. As we quietly moved away from shore she turned left and opened the throttle a little more, heading south towards Skidd's Bay. Without a trace of the moon or artificial light pollution, it couldn't have been darker.

"How much further we going?" Doolan called out.

"Just a few more minutes, I think," replied Batterbee. He briefly took his eyes off of us and looked forward across the liquid blackness. "We need to get into deep water."

The moment I heard that, I locked my eyes onto Jenna's with strong intent. I could tell that she understood I was trying to send her a message, but she softly shook her head in puzzlement, indicating she wasn't quite following. I started breathing deeply and purposefully through my nose, filling my lungs with rich oxygen with each draw of night air. I kept doing this, imploring Jenna with my eyes to follow my lead. FML. I motioned to the water with a slight bob of my head and sucked in another deep breath, the same way runners or swimmers do just before the starting gun. The brilliant light bulb of comprehension suddenly appeared across her face and the swirling fear in her eyes was replaced with a new sense of purpose. She nodded and started to hyperventilate in the same fashion, sucking in huge gulps of air through her nose to fully inflate her swimmer's lungs.

Batterbee turned back and kept his eyes locked on me as I peered through the darkness out over the front of the jon boat, squinting in a futile attempt to improve my night vision. I forced myself to appear as calm as possible but my insides were upside down. As we moved further south toward False Cape, the time had come to force the issue.

"*Mmmmm!*" I suddenly murmured as loudly as I could through the duct tape covering my mouth, widening my eyes in fear and motioning my head forward as if to indicate there was some approaching danger off the bow, perhaps a duck blind or a crab pot.

Batterbee instinctively whipped his head toward the bow at my warning to see what impending danger might be lurking straight ahead. In that precious instant when he took his eyes off of us, Jenna and I drew one last breath and bailed out, splashing overboard into the water. The lead weights of the diving belts dragged me immediately towards the bottom. With my hands still tied behind my back and the extra fifty pounds of weight, I couldn't swim away.

I just sank into a liquid black hole and stayed there, waiting for events on the surface to unfold as I prayed they would. I couldn't see Jenna through the murk, but I could only hope she was doing the same.

I could hear unintelligible yelling above the surface as our captors realized their quarry had escaped. I heard the Evinrude outboard crank up to full power and the jon boat spun around, heading back for the ripples of our entry point. The engine cut off as the jon boat hovered directly overhead.

The next sound I heard was the crack of a pistol. Batterbee was shooting into the water and I could feel the bullets whizzing around me. I couldn't go any deeper, and was praying that if it's hard to hit a stationary target you can see on dry land with a handgun, then trying to hit an invisible target while standing in a moving boat would be exponentially harder.

"Save your bullets!" I heard Doolan yell. "They'll be drowned in no time!" She was right. By now we'd been underwater for close to a minute, and the battle to stay below the surface was quickly draining my oxygen. I prayed that Jenna's lungs were equal to the task.

Batterbee's next move was the one I'd been waiting for all night, like the chess player anticipating his opponent pushing a valuable piece into harm's way and lifting his finger to complete the move. He clicked on a flashlight and sprayed the beam all across the water, searching for his prey. It was the beacon of hope I'd been counting on. We'd now been underwater for a minute and a half. I could feel the burn in my lungs. I needed my plan to come to fruition right now. 1:45, 1:50, 1:55. My lungs were starving for air and I could only imagine what Jenna was going through, but I knew that coming up meant certain death. *Dig deep* I silently screamed to the part of my brain that controls mind over matter, the part that makes you keep running to the finish line despite the intense pain of oxygen debt. I could see Batterbee's searchlight flashing above the surface, and hoped it couldn't see me. Now two minutes underwater. I couldn't hang on much longer. 2:15, 2:16, 2:17. I knew my oxygen was nearly depleted as my blood begged for nourishment. I decided that if I came up first and forced Batterbee to use the rest of his bullets, Jenna might have a fighting chance. As my brain dulled to black from the lack of oxygen, the last image I locked onto was Grace. I hoped I would see her in heaven.

Suddenly I heard the whine of another boat approaching. Out of the shadows of an old duck blind in the middle of the Back Bay roared a Park Service patrol boat with one Ranger Rob Martinez at the helm of his Boston Whaler with a 200-horsepower Mercury Sport Jet engine thrusting him across the water. As he did every night, Martinez had been out looking for loggerhead turtle poachers, and Batterbee's gunshots and flashlight had drawn him straight to us. The jon boat was now bathed in the shimmering light storm of 800 lumens from a 100-watt halogen spotlight mounted to the bow of the patrol boat. I could hear Martinez barking orders over a megaphone as Maggie Doolan opened the throttle on the Evinrude and sped away as the Ranger gave chase. A few more shots cracked through the night air as the two boats roared off into the night.

I breached the surface and sucked in life-giving air through my nose into my aching lungs. I could actually stand up because the water was only four feet deep. By now the brackish water of the bay had dissolved enough of the adhesive on the duct tape to where I could push it away from my mouth with my tongue. "Jenna!" I yelled into the night. No answer. I imagined the worst, fearing that one of Batterbee's reckless shots had found its mark. "Jenna!" I screamed again into the silence, moving forward through the water but having no real idea as to where she might be. "Jenna!" With absolutely no warning, she popped up directly behind me, nearly causing my heart to stop. She was gasping for air, breathing in rapid-fire through her nose like a winded dog. I bent over and used my teeth to tear the duct tape off her mouth. She continued to gulp in breaths of air until she finally nodded that she was close to revival. She heaved in one large breath, then blurted out, "I stayed under longer than you!" We both fell into uncontrollable laughter, the kind that involuntarily pours out of your soul to keep you from crying.

Moments later we were slogging back to shore through the shallow waters of the bay, no easy task with our hands still zip tied behind our backs and two diving belts sagging around our midsections. The northeast wind chilled us, but it had been our savior. Beginning with the first duck hunting clubs that came here in the 1870s, everyone in Sandbridge knows that when the wind blows out of the northeast, it pulls water out of the Back Bay and makes it shallow. Four feet deep at the most. If it had been blowing out of the south/southwest, the bay would have been filled with water out of the Albemarle Sound and we would have been sunk. Literally. Everybody knows that. Everybody except Kenneth Batterbee and Maggie Doolan.

By now we could see a host of blue lights flashing on the shoreline. I knew the jon boat would be no match for the Ranger's Whaler and it was obvious that Martinez had radioed ahead for help and gotten ample backup. I felt badly that he had been out looking for poachers and had unwittingly interrupted a near double-homicide, and I made a mental note to apologize for involving him in my escape plan without his knowledge. Thank God for dedicated Park Rangers.

"I gotta tell ya, Mac, that was brilliant," said Jenna with a nodding head. "As soon as I heard you say 'duck season' I had a pretty good idea of what you were up to."

"I figured you'd catch on. You're pretty amazing, Jenna Czarnecki."

"Not bad yourself, Seth MacClellan." It was the first time Jenna had ever called me Seth. I didn't even realize she knew my real name. It was also the first time in a long time that I felt like myself again. When we finally dragged ourselves onto dry land, detectives were there to take our statements. As I stood on the water's edge, dripping wet and slightly chilled by that blessed northeast wind, I realized I had one more stop.

I pounded relentlessly on the front door of the oceanfront mansion with the side of my fist as loudly as I could. The tympanic sound echoed across the Italian marble floors of the foyer inside. Soon enough I heard the padding of approaching footsteps, no doubt motivated by the angry sentiment of *who is knocking on my door at two in the morning?*

The door swung open to reveal Duncan Danforth in his nightclothes with disheveled hair flowing over the deepening wrinkles of his forehead.

"What in the—"

I held my camera at arm's length and fired off the flash in Danforth's eyes, momentarily blinding him. When his pupils readjusted and he realized who was standing in front of him he went from sightless to speechless, as if an apparition had returned to haunt him. He inhaled and rounded his lips to speak but no words escaped.

"I'm sorry, Duncan, did I wake you?"

"What. . . what are *you* doing here?" queried Danforth, shaking his addled head and desperately trying to separate the fiction of dreams from the reality standing in front of him. "You. . . you're supposed to be dead!"

"I know. I'm as surprised as you are. But really, the better question is, what are *they* doing here?" Out of the shadows appeared three police officers, two uniformed, one in plain clothes, flanking me on either side. The detective stepped closer to Danforth and flashed a badge.

"Duncan Danforth, you're under arrest for murder," said the detective with the matter-of-fact tone of a veteran cop who'd done this before.

Danforth slicked back his hair, laughed nervously, and attempted to appear calm. "I assure you, there's been a mistake." He looked at me. "A very big mistake."

The detective shook his head. "No mistakes." He motioned to the uniformed officers to take Danforth into custody and they eagerly obliged. The ratcheting of police handcuffs echoed across the lavish floors of Danforth's mansion, in which he would never set foot again.

"Anything you'd like to say to the press, Mr. Danforth? I'm working on a deadline here."

I starting firing off as many photos as I could, ironically with the same trusty Canon camera Munce had issued me, as the three officers led Danforth to the back of a squad car. The reading of his Miranda rights floated across the salty night air. The rhythmic pulsing of the police lights warmed me with the calming satisfaction of redemption. All the events of the last year flipped through my brain like a slideshow. The firing from the *Herald*, the phantom Irukandji, and my near-fatal encounters with Duncan Danforth and Batterbee and Doolan, all behind me now. I finally felt as though I could move forward in a life that had been dragging anchor for much too long. The only matter that had not been reconciled was Grace. Despite the deep love I still harbored for her in my heart, perhaps now I finally had the strength to put her inside my box of cherished memories and move on.

It was after midnight before I would finally lie down on Jenna's couch, emotionally and physically spent. I reached inside my tweed suitcase and pulled out one of my favorite letters.

> My Darling Seth,
> I think of the many gifts you've given me, more than I deserve. I have opened one called "half-full," filled with joy, excitement and anticipation. There was a heart shaped box. . . inside that one I found trust and intimacy, both precious and rare. It was protected by a wrapping of laughter, warmth, and caring. In this same box I also found my own heart. . . a surprise for me. Little did I know that someone would care enough to find my heartbeat, and tenderly bring it back to full capacity. I look forward to the day when we sit next to each other as the sun sets, and the fireflies twinkle. Thank you for all my gifts.
>
> Always and Forever,
> Grace

I clutched her letter in my hand, closed my eyes, and slept better than I had in a year.

# Epilogue

# Chapter Thirty-two

Two days later, I would read in the morning edition of *The Bay Breeze* that Kenneth Batterbee and Maggie Doolan had been arrested in the Back Bay without any exchange of gunfire and that they had immediately implicated Duncan Danforth as the mastermind of their operation. I smiled when I saw that my old friend Hank "Scrim" Shaw got the byline. Banner headline, 72-point type, above the fold. Sixteen inches on the front page with a photo, another fifty inches on the jump page. My uncredited photo of Danforth being led away from his mansion in handcuffs was amateurish at best, but it fulfilled its journalistic mission of telling a thousand words. Scrim would have enough follow stories to last until retirement. Well done. I regretted not being there to cover the story myself, but when I turned on the noon news and saw that a local TV crew had scrambled into action to get video of Danforth being led into the magistrate's office in handcuffs, looking more frightened than angry, it made me proud to be a journalist.

Paul Munce had been arrested at the Norfolk airport, apparently trying to flee the country. Something devilish inside me couldn't wait to send him the newspaper clippings of his demise while he rotted in prison.

Best of all, everything happened before any of the Sandbridge homes had been sold. The "Sale Pending" signs came down, and vacationers starting booking rental houses again now that the hoax had been exposed. The island had taken a hit, but at least it was back open for business.

I had given the police the video of Danforth buying the space heater at the hardware store just in case investigators needed more evidence than what Batterbee and Doolan would provide. They informed me that I was eligible for a substantial Governor's reward for providing valuable information about the murders of Morton Boyd and Victoria Boyd-Danforth. It would take some time to process the paperwork, but they assured me it would be well worth my hanging around town to collect. I figured I would keep a third of the reward money for myself since I was currently jobless, and split the remainder with Jenna and Lyman. I couldn't wait to visit with the boys, and I drove directly to Little Island Pier as the sun was beginning to set.

My arrival at the pier that evening was like a conquering hero coming home from the war. I pushed through a gauntlet of vigorous handshakes and slaps on the back. Rubes even gave me a kiss on the cheek. My status as a minor celebrity had never been greater.

Topper raised his voice above the din. "You know, one time, when my Uncle Earl was with the Sheriff's department, there was this serial killer on the loose and he—" As if on premeditated cue, they all turned their backs and walked away.

As usual, Lyman was off by himself, working a flounder rig. He didn't take his gaze off the ocean as I sat down next to him. "Well, well, well," said Lyman with a wry smile. "Looks like you finally caught the big fish."

"Yeah. Hunting down sociopathic killers. JLF. Just like fishin'."

Lyman smiled and cast again. "You done good, Mac. You done a whole garden of good."

"Thanks, Lyman. We both know I couldn't have done it without you. Truth is, I wouldn't even be sitting here without you."

"You give me too much credit."

"And you never take enough."

"So what's next for you?"

"I don't really know. I guess I'll hang around the island for a little while, tie up some loose ends. Who knows, if I can find a job, I might wait around until Danforth goes to trial. Maybe whoever buys the *Breeze* will need a good reporter. Who knows. Haven't had much time to think it through."

"I figured I'd find y'all here," came a voice behind us.

We both turned around to see Jenna standing behind us. Our reactions to her presence were decidedly different. Lyman turned back to the water, a scowl now covering his face. Jenna moved closer and held out a large manila envelope. She forced it into Lyman's hand. "Here. This is for you."

Lyman warily examined both the envelope and the messenger. He slowly opened it and slid out the sheaf of papers inside. I could read the name "Roosevelt Gregg" handwritten in felt-tip pen.

Jenna pointed to the papers Lyman was holding in his trembling hands. "My father wanted you to have these. They're his original notes from your brother's case. It tells you what *really* happened, not the version that finally ended up in the District Attorney's hands." On the top of the yellowed notes and police documents was a handwritten letter, scrawled in the wandering cursive of a quivering hand. "He also wrote you a letter," continued Jenna. "I read it. I hope you don't mind. My father talks about 'the code,' the secret pact cops have that says you back your partner to the hilt, even when he makes a mistake. That's what my father did. He was old school. He covered up the mistakes that other detectives made in your brother's case. The community wanted a conviction and he made sure they got one, one way or another. It doesn't excuse him, but it helps to explain him. The fact that he saved his original notes all these years proves to me it's haunted him. Maybe *that's* why he was so hard on me all those years. Didn't want me to make the same awful mistake." Lyman nodded quietly as he pored over the contents. "I already made copies that I'll turn over to the District Attorney. I know it doesn't bring your brother back, but it'll clear his name, and maybe it brings you some peace. I hope so."

Lyman nodded, offering silent gratitude. Tears were welling up in his eyes as he finally turned and looked directly at Jenna for the first time. He spoke softly and sincerely. "You're a better cop than he ever was. You should be the one still wearing a badge."

"I don't know," replied Jenna. She reached in her pocket and pulled out a tarnished brass police badge, the same one I'd seen her flash at the hardware store. "I think I'll leave that to someone else." She took one last look at the badge, then with athletic motion, suddenly flung it deep into the ocean. "Let's hope my father doesn't miss it."

I stood up and patted Lyman on the shoulder. "I'll give you some time alone." He nodded again as he looked through the papers, unable to speak.

Jenna and I walked slowly down the weathered planks of the Little Island Pier. The sun had gone to bed over the Back Bay and a half-full moon had taken its place in the first chapter of nightfall.

"You got plans for dinner?"

"Only that I plan to eat something besides pizza," she replied. "Why?"

"I was thinking maybe we could. . . ya know. . . eat."

"Isn't that what most people do at dinner? Eat?"

"I meant together. At a restaurant. Like a date."

Jenna was clearly taken aback. She looked at me with caution, her eyes narrowing. "*Like* a date? Or an actual date?"

"A date. A real date."

"What. . . what's going on here?" she asked.

We stopped walking and leaned against the railing of the pier, both gazing out over the water. "I've been thinking about what you said a few weeks ago. That I've been in love with a ghost." I took a long pause, then turned my head to face her. "I think you're probably right. I think it's time for me to move on."

Jenna shook her head and stared at the swirling sea. "What are you saying? Are you leaving Sandbridge?"

"Actually, just the opposite." She finally turned to face me, trying to decipher my intent. "This has been a tough stretch for me, and you've been beside me every step of the way. I needed you, in lots of different ways, and you were always there for me. You were truly a gift when I needed it most. So I don't know where the path might lead us, but I'm willing to take the first step. With you."

Tears were welling up in Jenna's eyes, even as she broke into a smile. She didn't say a word, just nodding her head as she swallowed hard and stared back at me. Simultaneously, we wrapped our arms around each other, clinging for life. She sobbed into my shoulder, as a flood of joy and relief washed over us both. As we embraced on the pier, the same structure of pilings and planks where I'd nearly jumped to my death to escape my despair, I now felt all the anguish of the last two years flowing out of me and floating away in the soft breeze of the salty night air. My body relaxed, like a barren field soaking up water from a summer shower. At long last, I felt whole again, and I imagined she did too. Redemption. For both of us. I don't know how long we held our desperate embrace, but it was long enough for everyone else on the Little Island Pier to stop and take notice. We didn't care.

I had the sudden impulse to reach into my pocket and pull out the tiny heart-shaped shell that I'd picked up the very first day I'd met Grace on Folly Beach, and had carried with me every day since. I took one last look at its pristine color and perfect form, and then gently flicked it over the side of the pier, letting it tumble through the maritime mist to its birthplace.

I lifted Jenna off her feet and held her close to my soul, savoring the touch electric. I breathed in the rich air of the moonlit night, truly believing that whenever there is water beside you, and a moon above you, anything is possible. I felt the wind shift. It was time to go home.

Cameron Kent grew up in Alexandria, Virginia, and after graduating from Wake Forest University, he embarked on a career in television journalism that spanned nearly 40 years. He received 14 Emmy nominations for his work in broadcasting, and won an Emmy for his reporting on the Pentagon after 9/11.

Cameron is the author of three previous books: *Make Me Disappear, When the Ravens Die,*and *The Road to Devotion.*

He credits his parents for his love of writing, raising him in a home full of opportunities to learn about books, art, and music. He's also thankful for wonderful teachers along the way, including his high school English teacher, Julie Wilson, who introduced him to Hemingway and Steinbeck, and his college Journalism professor, Bynum Shaw, who encouraged him to pursue his writing dreams.

He currently resides in Winston-Salem, North Carolina.

CPSIA information can be obtained
at www.ICGtesting.com
Printed in the USA
BVOW08s2058131117
500314BV00001B/45/P